Coolamon

✓ Feb 2011

‖‖‖‖‖‖‖‖‖‖‖‖‖‖‖‖ P9-BYQ-460

MIDNIGHT

Josephine Cox was born in Blackburn, one of ten children. At the age of sixteen, Josephine met and married her husband Ken, and had two sons. When the boys started school, she decided to go to college and eventually gained a place at Cambridge University. She was unable to take this up as it would have meant living away from home, but she went into teaching – and started to write her first full-length novel. She won the 'Superwoman of Great Britain' Award, for which her family had secretly entered her, at the same time as her novel was accepted for publication.

Her strong, gritty stories are taken from the tapestry of life. Josephine says, 'I could never imagine a single day without writing. It's been that way since as far back as I can remember.'

Visit www.josephinecox.co.uk to read her exclusive serial, catch up with her online diary and to find out more information about Josephine.

Also by Josephine Cox

QUEENIE'S STORY
Her Father's Sins
Let Loose the Tigers

THE EMMA GRADY TRILOGY
Outcast
Alley Urchin
Vagabonds

Angels Cry Sometimes
Take This Woman
Whistledown Woman
Don't Cry Alone
Jessica's Girl
Nobody's Darling
Born to Serve
More than Riches
A Little Badness
Living a Lie
The Devil You Know
A Time for Us
Cradle of Thorns
Miss You Forever
Love Me or Leave Me
Tomorrow the World
The Gilded Cage
Somewhere, Someday
Rainbow Days
Looking Back
Let It Shine

The Woman Who Left
Jinnie

Bad Boy Jack
The Beachcomber
Lovers and Liars
Live the Dream

The Journey
Journey's End
The Loner
Songbird
Born Bad
Divorced and Deadly
Blood Brothers

B+

JOSEPHINE COX

~

Midnight

HarperCollins*Publishers*

HarperCollins*Publishers*

77–85 Fulham Palace Road,
Hammersmith, London W6 8JB

www.harpercollins.co.uk

Published by HarperCollins*Publishers* 2011
1

Copyright © Josephine Cox 2011

Josephine Cox asserts the moral right to
be identified as the author of this work

A catalogue record for this book
is available from the British Library

ISBN: 978-0-00-730147-8

This novel is entirely a work of fiction.
The names, characters and incidents portrayed in it are
the work of the author's imagination. Any resemblance to
actual persons, living or dead, events or localities is
entirely coincidental.

Set in New Baskerville by Palimpsest Book Production Limited,
Falkirk, Stirlingshire

Printed and bound in Australia by
Griffin Press

All rights reserved. No part of this publication may be
reproduced, stored in a retrieval system, or transmitted,
in any form or by any means, electronic, mechanical,
photocopying, recording or otherwise, without the prior
permission of the publishers.

This is for my Ken, as always

This book is very special to me. During the writing of MIDNIGHT, my darling sister took ill, and never recovered. It was one of the most traumatic times of my life, because a sister is extra-special, a gift to be treasured. And I treasured her far more than I can ever describe. Winifred was my best friend, my confidante and soulmate. We did girlie things and talked naughty as only two women can. We cried together, laughed together, and shared every intimate moment from when we were children.

She was there when I was born, and she will be with me forever, though sadly not in person. My first memory of her was when she was pushing me in my pram and it tipped over. I remember screaming for my 'Mammy' and I recall Winifred picking me up in her little chubby arms and rocking me quiet. My Mother never knew where I got the scratches and bumps.

Growing up, we were mostly inseparable. We played tricks and were wonderfully naughty. We laughed and cried and fought anyone who hurt the other. Our Winnie was kind and fierce and gentle and harsh. She did not suffer fools gladly, and she said what she meant. We all loved her without condition; her brothers and sisters; her many lovely children; and the men she gave her heart to; especially dear Mick. We will all miss her. She was a one-off. The like of which we will never see again.

My sincere condolences to all of you who have lost a loved one. Keep the memories close. They will comfort you when you're low. And for those of you who have fallen out with family, please make up if you possibly can. The family is the most precious gift you could have. Cherish it. Because you never know when it might be snatched away.

CHAPTER ONE

Disturbed from her sleep, Molly shifted across the bed to him. 'Wake up, Jack. I'm here. You're safe now.' Wrapping her arms about him, she kept him close.

Lost in the darkness, Jack heard her faraway call. Beneath his body the earth was soft and pliable. He was not alone, though. Something else was here. Something shocking.

He heard Molly calling, and he knew instinctively she was his only way back. 'I've got you,' she promised. 'I won't let anything hurt you!'

With each crippling nightmare, Molly was there for him. 'I have you safe, Jack,' she murmured. 'I won't let you go.'

For as long as he could remember, Jack had fought his demons. They were always there, in his sleep, in his dreams. Always in the darkness. Hazy, shifting shadows, hiding in the moonlight. And all around him, a sense of evil and the eyes . . . cold, unmoving.

1

He could hardly breathe. *He needed to get away from here.*

He could hear Molly calling. He knew she would save him – but for how long? So many times he'd escaped, only to be drawn back, time and again, to this lonely midnight place.

The darkness and the images had haunted him forever; almost to the edge of madness.

From far away Molly's insistent voice quietened his heart, 'Wake up, Jack . . . wake up!'

Desperate to leave, he was instinctively compelled to stay.

Why had the visions plagued him all these years? Why would they not let him be?

'Ssh now.' Folding the corner of the bedsheet, Molly wiped away the beads of sweat that poured down his face. 'Listen to me. It's just a dream,' Softly she coaxed him, 'Open your eyes, Jack. Come away now.'

Most times she could waken him, but this time he resisted. Closing her fingers about his flailing fists, she spoke sternly: *'Jack! You need to open your eyes and look at me.'*

Suddenly, without warning, the fight went from him. His clenched fists fell heavily by his sides and Molly felt his whole body tremble and shiver. He woke up and turned to look at her, his eyes scarred and heavy with what he had seen, back there, in that place.

'Midnight,' he whispered brokenly. The remnants of horror lingered like a cloak over his mind. 'Where is it, Molly?' he murmured. 'What does it mean?' He gave an involuntary shiver. *'Why won't it let me be?'*

She searched for an answer. 'It isn't real,' she said finally. 'It was just a dream – a bad dream – and now it's over.'

When he slowly shook his head, she placed the palms of her hands either side of his face. 'Let it go, Jack. Don't think about it now.' Like many times before, she saw how deeply it affected him. Tenderly, she kissed him, once on each cheek, much as a mother might kiss her child. 'It's gone now,' she comforted him. 'Maybe it won't ever come back.'

'Maybe.' He leaned into her embrace. '. . . Maybe not.' He knew it *would* be back. Molly meant well, but she didn't know what it was like. How could she?

All his life the nightmare had haunted him, and not only when he slept. Sometimes in the daylight hours, something evil carried him back there. Something urgent. Something deep in his psyche.

As a boy he might be playing in the street with his pals, when the darkness would suddenly come over him and he would creep away to hide in some quiet corner. The other boys began to tease him. They said it was no good having Jack Redmond on your side, because halfway through the match he would suddenly run away to huddle in a dark corner. He never told them the truth. *He never told anyone.*

If he had, they might have thought he was 'off his rocker' and should be locked away – like that poor soul on Tamworth Street who had drowned her

3

newborn twins before killing herself. He heard the cruel talk, about how she should 'rot in Hell'. The thought of it filled him with a different horror.

Jack Redmond had never betrayed the awful secret he carried with him. He began to believe he must have done a bad thing. If not, then why was he afraid to close his eyes and sleep?

And what about the drawings he'd made at school? Those frightening images that appeared on the paper, almost as though something – or *someone* – else was making the pictures and not him.

The teachers were annoyed. They took the drawings away. They said he should pay attention and listen to what was asked of him, instead of allowing his imagination to run riot.

They never understood – but it wasn't their fault. How could they see what he saw, trapped in that lonely hellhole, so real and terrifying? Was it his warped imagination? Or was there really a place like that somewhere?

What a shocking thought . . . that it might actually exist outside of his nightmares. He shuddered. Surely that could never be.

Or could it?

As the years passed, the fragmented images remained, as did the feelings of helplessness. He had so many questions, and no answers. Jack wondered if he would ever know the truth, and more importantly – did he really want to?

All he had ever wanted was for it all to go away, and for him to be normal, like other people. Instead, the nightmares were growing stronger, more persistent. He wanted to know, but he was afraid.

Jack took a deep breath, thrusting the images from his mind. Outside, the early-morning sun in Leighton Buzzard was already spreading a brightness over the day. Soon, the alarm would go off and he would get up and go about his business. For now though, he felt halfway between that place and this. It was a strange, disturbing feeling.

He heard Molly speaking softly in his ear. 'Feeling better now?'

A quietness came over him as he gazed on that wide, pretty mouth and troubled brown eyes. Molly was everything to him. She was his woman, and she kept him sane.

He had always believed that he and Molly were meant to be. To have her as his wife, settle down and raise a family was his dearest wish. But he dared not make any plans for a future together. At least, not until he was rid of the demons that tormented him.

Drawing her close, he kissed her tenderly. 'Yes, I'm all right.' He needed her, but he did not deserve her. 'Thank you, Molly,' he murmured. 'I'm sorry.'

'Ssh.' Running her fingers through his unruly mop of brown hair, Molly thought him to be a fine figure of a man. He had such strength of character in his features, particularly his eyes, which could be very mischievous at times; yet even when he laughed, those eyes were brooding, as though hiding a secret – a cruel, unforgiving secret that haunted the mind.

'Molly?' Jack leaned forward, to bury his face in the

softness of her neck, 'I'm sorry.' He drew away, but kept his arm about her. 'None of this is fair on you.'

'No, it isn't!' Her quiet anger was fuelled by a pressing desire to get on with their lives. 'You're right. What's happening is not fair – on either of us.' It was time to say what she felt.

His silence made her feel guilty, but she continued: 'It's been going on for too long, and I'm afraid.'

'Afraid?' Jack thought it an odd thing for her to say. 'Of what, exactly?'

'The nightmares . . . the way they affect you. I'm afraid for you, Jack.'

She was also afraid for herself. Angry too. Why would he never listen to her?!

Jack remained quiet. He was used to her sudden bursts of anger, but this time he believed she was right to speak her mind.

'You need help,' she insisted, 'Surely you can see that?'

Shrugging her off, Jack replied, 'It was just a bad dream and now it's gone – maybe for ever.'

Molly grew impatient. 'You must see what's happening to us! The nightmares . . . the lack of sleep, and the fear of where it's all leading. We can't go on like this – it's eating into our lives. You have to see someone!'

Impatient, Jack moved away. 'I've heard it all before, Molly. I don't need to hear it again!'

'Oh, but you do.' Clambering up, she stood before him, deliberately blocking his way. 'I see what it does to you, Jack, and this time it was worse than ever, because this time I was beginning to think I would not be able to bring you back. I was frightened, Jack. I was really frightened!'

'You needn't have been.'

Her voice shaking, Molly gave him a warning, 'I can't put up with this, Jack. Can't you see? This *thing* is taking over! You can't sleep and when you do, you go to a place where there is no rest, no peace, and sometimes lately when I talk to you, you're not even listening. You're back there somewhere . . . lost in a place I can't go.'

'Oh, now you really *are* talking rubbish!'

But Jack knew she was right. Sometimes in the evening, when he sat down after a hard day at work, he felt himself drifting into the darkness. Up until now, he had not realised Molly was aware of it.

'Jack?'

'Yes?'

In a stern voice Molly told him what was on her mind. 'These nightmares . . . the lack of proper sleep – it's only a matter of time before it affects your work, and mine too.'

Jack was adamant. 'That won't happen!'

'But it *could*!' Molly was relentless. 'I mean, it's definitely beginning to affect our relationship.'

In that moment, a sobering thought came to her. 'Oh my God! Maybe it's not the nightmares or lack of sleep that's taking you from me!'

'What d'you mean?' Jack was shaken. 'Nothing is taking me from you!'

'Don't fob me off, Jack! Every time I raise the question of marriage, you're full of excuses. You need to save more money first, or you want to wait until I'm absolutely sure I want to spend the rest of my life with you. Well, I can tell you now, I'm beginning to think you want rid of me but you don't have the guts to tell me, so then you worry, and the worry plays on your mind and you have these bad dreams. That's the truth of it, isn't it?'

'*No!*' He was genuinely shocked. 'No, it isn't, and I can't believe you're even thinking that.'

'So what am I *supposed* to think? Tell me, Jack. I mean, we don't talk at any great length, do we? We don't even go out any more. We don't have friends back – and we haven't made love in weeks! Can you blame me for thinking you don't want me any more?'

Wrapping his capable hands about her small shoulders, he drew her closer, 'I love you as much as ever. You're a very special part of my life, and always will be.' He kissed her full and longingly on the mouth. 'You and me, we belong together,' he whispered. 'I knew it from the start.'

'Do you really mean that?'

'You know I do, Molly, and like I say . . . I'm really sorry for putting you through all that – the nightmares and lack of sleep. Making you think I didn't want you any more.'

Gently moving away from him, she sat on the edge of the bed. 'It's not just the nightmares,' she mumbled. 'It's the fact that you won't do anything about them.'

'There's no need. They'll probably go away in time.'

Deliberately ignoring his protest, Molly went on, 'The trouble is, you can't see what I can see.'

'What does that mean?'

'It means that when you're inside the nightmare, you make these weird little sounds, like you can't breathe, and you lash out violently, as though fending off some kind of attack – as if there's something that means to harm you. What is it, Jack? What fills you with such terror?'

Jack looked away. 'I don't know.'

'So, do you *want* to know?' Molly's anger bubbled to the surface. 'Do you *want* answers?'

He shrugged. 'I just want to be rid of the nightmares.'

'What if they're *not* nightmares?'

'What d'you mean?'

Molly searched for the right words. 'I'm not sure, but maybe you should get a medical. Maybe it's something to do with the brain?'

'*No medical.*'

Agitated, he got up and went to stand beside her. 'Listen to me. I know you're worried for me, and I'm sure the lack of sleep is beginning to affect you too. So I was thinking, maybe the answer is for us to sleep in separate rooms, at least for now?'

'I don't want to sleep in separate rooms,' Molly snapped angrily, 'unless I was right just now, and you really do want to be rid of me. What's the plan, Jack? Get me out of your bed then the next move is out the door. Is that it?'

Jack grew agitated. 'Look, all I'm saying is, we're both getting ratty, and it's my fault.'

'So get checked out.'

'OK then, yes – I will.'

'When?'

He gave a shrug, 'When I find the time.'

'In other words, never.'

When Molly began to push him further, he backed off. 'I'd best get ready for work. I don't want to be late again.'

'I'm not letting this drop,' she warned him. 'I mean it!'

'I can see that.'

'So tell me,' she demanded, 'why you won't get help. Explain it to me, because I don't understand.'

'Just leave it, Molly. Like I said . . . I'll deal with it.'

There was no feasible way of explaining to her. How could he describe to anyone else what he experienced when inside the nightmare? The answer was, he couldn't. There were no words for it. The whole terrible experience was like a part of him, like an arm or a leg. Sometimes, that haunting place really felt like an extension of himself. How could anyone ever understand?

Seeing him looking so lost, Molly's heart went out to him. 'I'm sorry, Jack. I didn't mean to be angry,' she said impatiently. 'It's just that I don't understand how you could suffer for so long, without at least trying to do something about it. There are people out there who might be able to help you. That's all I'm trying to say.'

10

'I don't want us to row,' Jack told her. 'But I don't believe it's possible to stop someone having nightmares. It's not like putting sticking plaster on a cut, or fixing a broken arm, is it? And don't you think I'd have tried talking to someone years ago, if I really thought it might help?'

'All right, Jack, I hear what you're saying, and I know you don't like the idea of discussing it with a stranger – but talking to someone about it won't make it any worse than it is. You could explain how long you've been having the nightmares and how they're disrupting your sleep, so much so that you've started nodding off behind the wheel of your car. It's dangerous, Jack. Suppose you crashed? I would never forgive myself for not having tried everything in my power to make you get help.'

In truth, she was growing impatient, even asking herself whether she should bring their relationship to an end. After all, there were plenty of other fish in the sea. Jack came with a lot of baggage, and did she really need that responsibility?

'Seeing a doctor won't help.'

'Oh, and you know that, do you? Without even trying?' Molly measured her words carefully. 'We're not talking about a doctor who mends broken legs or delivers babies. But there are other doctors – who specialise in how the mind works.'

Jack didn't like the sound of that. 'You mean *a shrink?*'

'If that's what you want to call them, yes. People who know about troubles of the mind. All I'm asking is that you just go and see. Make enquiries at least.'

11

'No!' Jack had had enough. He escaped to the bathroom, calling as he went, 'Even if I went to see somebody as you suggest, they can't tell me any more than I already know. All they can do is ask me questions to which I have no answers. Or, they could drug me and probe my mind. I don't want that, and I won't do it, not even for you.'

'Now you're just being pig-headed!' Molly followed him to the bathroom. 'Look, you could tell them what happens – what you see, what you feel. Explain how it affects you. Tell them how at first it happened maybe once or twice in a month, but lately it's every week.' She took a deep breath, then said more calmly, 'If you make an appointment, then later decide not to go through with it, that's OK. You can walk away. It's worth a try through, isn't it?'

Encouraged when he gave no reply, she went on, 'Just make an appointment, eh? Will you do it, Jack – for my sake?'

Placing one hand on her shoulder, he absent-mindedly brushed the fringe from her eyes. 'I don't like the idea,' he said. 'Besides, how could I make them understand, when I don't even understand myself?' Just thinking about it, he could feel the sweat coating the palms of his hands. 'I'm not sure I can do it, Molly.'

'So, what are you afraid of?'

Momentarily taken aback by her direct question, he answered, in a soft voice, almost as though he was speaking to himself, 'Maybe I'm afraid of what's lurking there, in the back of my mind. Maybe I'm afraid of releasing some terrible thing that might be even worse than the nightmares.' He wondered what could ever be worse than his nightmares.

He grew troubled, 'I don't want to talk about it any more,' he told her. 'Not to you, and certainly not to some stranger.' Seeing her about to speak, he snapped, 'Leave me be, Molly! I'll deal with it in my own way. I've told you before – I can handle it!'

A few moments later, he emerged from the bathroom, filled with regret for yelling at her, 'I'm sorry,' he said. 'OK, if it'll make you happy, I'll promise to think about it, and that's as far as I go for now. So, does that satisfy you?'

Molly answered sulkily, 'Well, it's a start, at least.'

'OK, so now let it drop. I don't want to hear any more about it. No more nagging. No more arguments. Agreed?'

'All right, then. But if you haven't done something about it within a week, then I'll be after you again. I won't leave it there!'

Jack merely gave a grunt.

'I mean it,' Molly went on. 'I can't take much more of it – and I certainly don't want to sleep in separate beds.'

'Neither do I.'

'But it might come to that. Just look at us now. We're almost at each other's throats again, and I don't want it to be like this.'

He may be a good catch, she thought, but was he worth the aggravation?

Having washed and shaved, Jack now threw on his

13

shirt and trousers while Molly had a quick shower and got ready for work at Banbury's estate agents.

~

Over coffee, Jack was bright and chatty, but he rejected breakfast. 'I'm not really hungry,' he said. 'The boss is out on some appointment and the other four guys are all tied up with clients, so I've been asked to oversee the showrooms. I thought we might meet up for a bite to eat about twelvish My treat, so what do you say?'

Molly liked the idea of that. 'Great! I've got a viewing in Leighton Buzzard at ten-thirty, which should take me up to midday, so yes, I'm up for that.'

Jack was anxious to get away, 'So, I'll see you later then?'

After a quick slurp of her coffee, Molly asked him. 'Can I just say one more thing? Then I promise, I'll shut up?'

Jack nodded. 'Go on then,' he urged. 'One more thing, but then I've got to go.'

Molly spoke with sincerity. 'I know I've been nagging you, but it's only because I'm worried. It's been three months since I came to live here with you, and in that time, I've seen what these nightmares do to you. Even during the day sometimes, I've seen how you glance over your shoulder, almost as though you half expect somebody to be there. It does concern me, Jack, and I'd be so relieved if I knew you were seeing someone about getting help. Before it drives us both crazy.'

Reaching out, she patted his hand. 'There! That's all I wanted to say, and now I'll shut up about it. So, where do you want to meet up? I don't want to go to that scruffy little café near the showrooms. The last time we went there, I had a hair in my sandwich.'

Jack was easy. 'OK – what about the pub in Woburn Sands – the one on the corner, called the Drake? They do cracking home-cooked food.'

'How do you know?'

'Because I've had lunch there.'

'Oh, really? So how come you didn't take me?'

'Because it was a work thing, booked and paid for by the customer.' Grabbing his jacket from the back of the door, Jack slipped it on. 'I'll see you there then?'

On his way to the car, Jack looked back to see Molly waving him goodbye from the doorway.

'See you later!' he called.

Molly gave a curt nod.

A moment later, he was gone.

'You'd best keep your promise, Jack Redmond!' she muttered to herself.

En route to work, Jack thought about Molly's warning. He understood her concern, but she could have no real idea of his fears. Crawling along in the traffic, his mind went back to when he was a child. Strangers had tried before and failed to rid him of the nightmares. 'They couldn't help me then,' he thought, 'so how can they help me now, when I'm thirty?' Leaving Leighton Buzzard behind, he swung onto the A5 and headed for Bletchley.

Somewhere in the back of his mind, he slowly began to agree that Molly was right. It was only a matter of time before their relationship was damaged beyond repair, and he didn't want that to happen.

By the time he'd arrived at work and parked the car, the idea was growing on him. Making his way down to the showrooms, he felt more confident with every stride. 'I suppose I could make an appointment,' he thought, 'and like Molly said, I don't need to stay if I feel uncomfortable about it.'

Pushing open the heavy glass doors, he bade a cheery good morning to his colleagues. 'Is the boss in?' he asked the pretty blonde at reception.

Flicking out a handkerchief, the girl, called Jan, discreetly blew her nose. 'Sorry, Jack, but, Old Branagan called in to say he was heading straight for Bedford.'

'Dammit!' Jack was disappointed. 'I've got someone interested in trading his car against our demonstrator. I just need to run the costing by him.'

He gave it a moment's thought. 'That's okay. The customer isn't due until late morning – plenty of time for me to phone the boss on his mobile. All I need is a quick conversation. I've got all the figures, except for the price tag on the demonstrator.'

Placing his folder on the counter, Jack gave her an easy smile. 'Branagan's a crafty devil, though! He's known all week that we've got the schedules to work through.'

Jan giggled. 'You'll have to sort out the schedules yourself then, won't you?' She winked cheekily.

Jack winked back. 'Ah! But if I do the deal on the demonstrator, it'll be *me* who gets the commission.'

Enjoying the banter, Jan asked casually, 'Have you thought about that offer?'

'What offer?'

'You know.' She tutted. 'I thought Branagan had already mentioned it – about you running the new showrooms they're setting up in Lancashire. That's your neck of the woods, isn't it?'

'Oh, yes! I mean no, I haven't really thought about it, and no, I haven't actually been offered it yet either.'

'Yes, you have. I heard him telling you about it only the other day. He asked if you had a hankering to go back north. I heard him say it.'

'Yes, but he didn't offer me the job.'

'In a roundabout way he did.'

Jack smiled, 'Ah, but asking questions in a round-about way doesn't get answers, does it? Besides, what with the recession biting, who knows if they'll be going through with it? Soon, none of us will be able to afford to buy cars. We'll be back to our pushbikes, or Shank's pony.' He chuckled.

'So, if you *were* asked,' Jan persisted, 'you'd say yes, would you?' She hoped not, because Jack was the only really friendly bloke there. All the others treated her like part of the furniture. Car showrooms were truly a man's world, and didn't she know it.

Jack gave it a moment's thought. His answer was a resounding 'Nope!'

'Why not?'

'Because I've been there, done that.' He smiled. 'So, is the inquisition over now, little Miss Nosy?'

'Don't you miss the north?'

'Sometimes.' He shrugged. 'I suppose.'

'What about family and friends – wouldn't you like to get back amongst them?'

'I was an only child and my father died when I was sixteen,' Jack answered. 'My mother soon remarried and moved to America with her new husband. I heard later that she'd taken on three teenage children, a house the size of Buckingham Palace, and money coming out of their ears.' He gave a wry little smile. 'I never heard from her again. But it didn't matter, because even before she left she never had any time for me. I think she saw me as a waste of space.'

'Aw, that's awful!' The young woman could not imagine life without her own, doting parents.

'Truth is, I never missed her after she was gone. I'd been left to my own devices for years. So, when Dad died and Mother took off, I sorted myself out, just like I'd always done.'

When she had abandoned him, his mother left him an address, but she must have moved quickly on, because when he wrote to that address, the letter came back, stamped *Return to Sender*. He was not surprised. In the end, he set about making his own way in the world.

It had not been easy – and there'd been no chance of taking up the place he'd been offered at Manchester University, which he'd regretted for a long time – but he was proud of what he'd achieved.

When he relayed all this to the girl, she tutted. 'So, your mother turned her back on you. Well, it's her loss, not yours.' She quickly regretted her curt, throwaway remark. 'Oh look, Jack . . . one day she'll turn up on your doorstep, you'll see.'

Jack used to think the same, but it had been too long and now he had no desire to ever see her again. 'I wouldn't hold your breath,' he replied with a shrug.

'What about friends?' she prompted. 'You must have made some of those?'

'Well yes, there were school-friends, of course, but we lived too far apart to become lifelong buddies. We went to school, then we left and got on with our lives.'

'And neighbours? Did you not make friends with some of the neighbours' kids?' She could see he was impatient to be off, but did not want to let him go just yet.

Jack's mind went back along the years. 'There were no boys of my age living in the street,' he recalled. 'I knew all the neighbours though, because after my father passed on, my mother carried on working for a while. She did shifts on reception at the Kings Hotel, and it seems I was bandied about like a little parcel . . . or so Eileen told me.'

'Who's "Eileen"?' Jealousy sharpened her voice. 'An old girlfriend?'

19

Jack laughed at that. 'Hardly.' It was all coming back now. 'Eileen was Libby's mother.'

'So who's Libby?'

'My friend. When my mother went out to work, Eileen would sometimes look after me, and she'd bring Libby round with her. She'd read us stories, do puzzles with us and have lots of fun, and sometimes she'd take us to the park.' He remembered it all so vividly. 'Eileen Harrow was more of a mother to me than my own mother,' he said in a low voice.

'What about when you were older, though?' Jan wanted to know. 'Did you have friends at secondary school?'

Jack shook his head. 'Not what you might call *real* friends,' he said. 'Truth is, apart from an ongoing friendship with Libby, I was a bit of a solitary sort. I preferred my own company.'

When the visions rose in his mind, he quickly excused himself, giving her an apologetic smile. 'Sorry, Jan, I'd best get on.' One word; the tiniest memory – and they invaded his mind. He dared not let them loose. He dared not!

Behind him, the girl watched him go. 'You're a handsome devil, Jackie boy,' she murmured. 'If you'd only give us a chance, you and me could be great together.' Knowing it would never happen, she gave a heavy sigh. If Jack Redmond had clicked his fingers, he could have any girl he wanted – she knew that. Trouble was, he only had eyes for that bossy-boots Molly Davis from Banbury's. It was obvious that Jack adored his Molly, but Molly was rumoured to be anybody's, as long as they had a fat wallet. Still, there was no one more blinded than a man in love, Jan thought enviously.

~

The reminiscing had lifted Jack's spirits. He made himself a coffee, then went into his office with the idea of tackling the day's schedule. After turning on his computer, he took his coffee to the window, where he looked out across the yard and beyond, to the main road, now choked with traffic. For a while he sipped his tea and thought of Molly. Maybe he really should get help? But he'd been through all that as a child. The doctors gave him games to play and things to do; they tested his mind until he was dizzy, but nothing changed.

Nothing ever changed.

In the end the medical men told his parents he would grow out of the bad dreams, and they had to be satisfied with that. On the day Jack turned sixteen, his father was badly hurt in a factory fire and died soon after. Two years later, in 1996, his mother took off to America for her new life.

Before she left, she told Jack he was to blame for his father's early passing. 'You're the one who killed him,' she ranted. 'You knocked the stuffing out of Gordon – all that trouble from school, then the screaming in the night. There's something wrong with you, I'm sure of it! You should be locked away.' Soon after that, she packed up, lock, stock and barrel, and sold the family home, leaving her son with his late father's silver tankards and the sum of £1,000 to make his own way in the world.

Just now, going through the past, Jack knew he had to make a decision. Things could not carry on as they were. Surely the right thing to do – both for Molly and for his own peace of mind – was to face up to his demons.

'OK, Molly, you win,' he decided. 'I'll take your advice and talk to the doctor. After all, what have I got to lose?'

He suddenly felt as though an unbearable weight had fallen from his shoulders. Besides, his GP, Dr Lennox, was a very understanding man. 'That's it!' Going over to his desk drawer, Jack took out a batch of paperwork, and concentrated his mind on that. 'Decision made!'

CHAPTER TWO

BOWER STREET IN Blackburn was a quiet little street of ordinary homes and ordinary families. Like families everywhere, they all had their problems, but the mother and daughter at Number 20 had more than their fair share. On this fine brisk morning, Eileen Harrow was in an angry mood.

'If I want him in my bed, that's for me to decide – and you, my girl, should learn to mind your own business!'

The sixty-year-old woman had entertained many men in her bed these past years, and though her judgement was sadly misguided, her determination never wavered. 'I'm sorry, Libby. I know your father did wrong by you, by going off when he did, but that's all in the past – and if I can forgive him, why can't you?'

While Libby frantically searched for an answer, the older woman jabbed a finger at her. 'All right, then. Forgive him, *don't* forgive him – it's up to you. But I will not have my own daughter telling me what to do!'

'I'm not trying to tell you what to do, Mum. I only want you to be safe.'

'Why can't you forgive him?' Eileen persisted. 'If I'm ready to forgive him, you should be too.' Fired up and itching for an argument, she squared up to her daughter. 'My man is home now, and this time I want him to stay. And if you don't like it, you can clear off out of it!'

Libby remained silent, while her mother ranted on, sadly convinced that the stranger she had brought home in the small hours was actually the husband who had deserted her many long years ago.

'Well?' Eileen waited, hands on hips, for an apology. 'Do you forgive him? Is he welcome to stay?'

Libby had seen it all before. Not for the first time, she had woken up that morning to find that her mother had taken a stranger into her bed. 'Mum, please listen to me . . .'

'No! I've heard enough. Pack your bags and leave, you ungrateful girl!'

'You've got it all wrong.' Libby gently persisted. 'I don't want to upset you. Trust me, Mum.'

But when Eileen was in this kind of mood, it was hard to calm her. 'I'm only trying to help. I don't want you getting all riled up.'

'Then stop telling me I can't sleep with my own husband! If my blood pressure goes through the roof, it'll be your fault, not mine.'

'Please, Mother, you need to trust me,' Libby pleaded. 'You're not well.'

'What d'you mean, I'm not well?' The older woman rounded on her. 'You think I'm off my head, don't you? You think I'm incapable of making my own decisions. Well, you just listen to me for a minute, young lady. I know you were upset when your father left us, but now he's back – and if you're not happy with that, then you can pack your bags and bugger off!'

'Please, Mother, don't be like this.' Libby knew she must calm the older woman before it got out of hand. 'Please hear me out.'

'*No!*'

With surprising suddenness Eileen became docile. She was no longer the angry woman who had threatened to throw her daughter out of house and home. 'I'm sorry, dear,' she said, looking bewildered. 'What were you saying?'

Relieved that the moment had passed, Libby told her, 'I'm about to make breakfast for us.' She glanced cautiously up the stairs. 'When *he* comes out of the bathroom, you need to send him on his way.'

Eileen followed her gaze. 'Send *who* on his way?'

'Your friend.'

'What friend?' Not for the first time, Eileen Harrow had somehow sneaked out of the house in the early hours, desperate to find the man who had deserted them so long ago. 'Oh! You mean your *father*!' In her fragmented mind she was young again, deliriously happy because her man was home. Clapping her hands together, she giggled like a child. 'I told you I'd find him, and now I have. It was so dark, though. I got worried

I might never see him again. But then I found him and I brought him home where he belongs.'

'No, Mum.' Libby's heart sank. 'You made a mistake. We don't know this man. I'm sorry, but he doesn't belong here.' Libby hated being the one who shattered her mother's hopes and dreams, but it was her lot in life to love and protect this darling woman. 'I still can't believe you managed to sneak out when I was sleeping.' She had been extra meticulous in taking all the necessary precautions, but somehow her mother had fooled her yet again.

'Ha!' The older woman chuckled triumphantly. 'I watched where you put the key.'

'Really? Well, I shall have to be even more careful in the future.' Libby made a mental note of it. 'Right, Mum, we need to talk,' she went on. 'Once we've got rid of your new "friend" we'll take a few minutes to enjoy our breakfast. After that, we'll get you dressed and all spruced up, before Thomas runs us into town. We don't want to keep him waiting, and besides, we want to have a good look round the shops. Last time we went out, we had to rush back for your hospital appointment. Remember you saw that lovely hat in British Home Stores? Well, if it's still there, you can try it on and see if it suits you. It would be perfect for spring and summer outings.'

Reaching out, she took hold of her mother's hand. 'Would you like that?'

As with many things these past years, Eileen did not recall the hat, but she smiled at the thought. 'Am I going somewhere special?' she asked excitedly. 'Do I need a new hat?'

Libby beamed at her. Sometimes her mother's affliction reduced her to tears, but not this time, because once again she had a situation to deal with. 'Yes,' she answered brightly. 'Thomas promised to take us to the park, the first really warm day we get. It's too cold now – March winds and rain most days. But come April, we might take him up on his kind offer. So yes, you *do* need a new hat, and if that one suits you, it'll be my treat.'

With her fickle mind shifting in all directions, the older woman remembered, 'Oh, a fresh pot o' tea, you say?'

'That's right.' Libby was relieved. She went to put the kettle on.

'And remember to put *two* tea-bags in it? Last time you only put in one, and it tasted like cats' pee.' She laughed out loud. 'Not that I've ever drunk cats' pee, but if I had, it would taste just like that tea of yours.' She gave a shiver as though swallowing something horrible. 'So, this time, have you done what I told you?'

'Yes, I have.'

'*Two* teabags, then?'

'Yes, Mother. Two teabags, one sugar – the way you like it.'

'I bet you didn't warm up my cup!'

'Yes, I did that too.'

'Good girl. At long last, you've learned your lesson. You can be such a naughty child!'

Through the haze in her mind, Eileen saw a chubby

six-year-old with long, fair plaits and mucky hands, instead of a shapely, pretty woman aged thirty. 'What am I to do with you, eh?'

'Sorry, Mother.' Following doctors' advice, Libby had learned how to deal with her mother's unpredictable moods. 'It won't happen again, I promise.' Gently reaching out, she suggested in a quiet voice, 'Come on now, Mum. Don't let your tea go cold. You know how you hate cold tea.'

Unsure, Eileen moved back a step. 'Too cheeky for your own good, that's the truth of it. Drive me to distraction at times, you really do!'

'I try not to.' She gently wrapped her fingers about the older woman's hand. 'Come on, Mum.'

Eileen took a tentative step forward, only to pause again as though unsure. 'You do realise, don't you? I shall have to tell your father when he comes down.'

'If you must.'

'He'll probably smack your legs.' She jabbed her forefinger into Libby's chest. 'Oh, and don't think I'll stop him this time, because you *deserve* a smack!'

'I expect I do.'

There followed a quiet moment, during which the older woman took stock of the situation, her kindly gaze holding her daughter's attention. 'Perhaps I won't tell him,' she confided in a whisper, 'because he can get nasty when he has to give you a telling-off.' Her face softened. 'Yet he loves you, Libby. We both do.'

Choking back the tears, Libby told her, 'And I love you, Mum . . . so very much.'

Libby had small recollection of her father, who had gone away when she was still a little girl. Like a fast-fading picture in her mind, she saw a big man with blue eyes, dark hair and quiet manner; a man with a beguiling Irish accent who came home from work and went upstairs to change before the evening meal. Most times when the meal was over, he would go out – returning much later when she and her mother were in bed. Occasionally she recalled the odd, brief cuddle, but that was all. There was no memory of closeness or laughter. There were no night time prayers or bedtime stories from Ian Harrow. There was a quiet sadness about her mother then, and in the years following his desertion of them, that made Libby feel guilty, even when she had not misbehaved.

At school she was a bit of a loner. She did have one good friend, though. Kit Saunders was in the same class as her. They laughed and played, and their friendship lifted her spirit, but when the bell rang for home-time, a great loneliness came over her. Kit's dad worked shifts and was always waiting at the gates for his beloved daughter. Kit and her parents did fun things together. Sometimes they took their daughter to the summer fair and one year, they invited Libby to go with them. Kit's father won his daughter a big teddy-bear on the coconut-shy. The kind girl asked him to win one for Libby, and he did his best. It was a much smaller one, but the little bear had the funniest face, and Libby was thrilled. Oh, how she loved him!

During the day, George the bear (named after Boy

George, her favourite pop star) sat on Libby's bed, and at night he came under the sheets and together they cuddled up to sleep. He was her friend and to this day, George still sat on her bed, waiting for his cuddle.

Sadly though, Kit's family moved away and Libby lost touch with them.

The truth was, Libby never really knew her father. Her mother adored him, though. Apparently, during their marriage, Ian Harrow chose countless women over his wife. He had many affairs and once or twice even left her, but he always came back. Until the last time.

Even then, her mother continued to love him; every day and well into the night, she watched for him through the window, and afterwards cried herself to sleep. After a while, she became forgetful; she began to lose direction. If it hadn't been for Libby coming home from school and clearing up, the house would have been buried in filth. It was only a matter of time before Eileen's health really began to deteriorate, and after a while it really did seem that she didn't care whether she lived or died.

It was a cruel, heartless thing he did, deserting them. Over the years, Libby often wondered if that was why she had shut him from her mind. In a way, because of him – and because her mother increasingly withdrew into her own little world – Libby's childhood ended the day her father abandoned them.

~

Eileen Harrow's breakdown happened gradually, without her daughter even noticing. At night, when Libby lay half awake in her bed, she could hear her mother sobbing, calling out, asking why he had wanted to leave her; asking if it was her fault. Had she let him down somehow? Had she not loved him enough, or not shown it enough? And was he really never coming home? It was that which she found hardest to accept.

Libby's grandmother would come up on the coach from Manchester and stay for a time, but then she began to buckle under the strain, and her visits grew less frequent. Still grieving after the loss of her own husband, Arthur, she eventually stopped coming altogether, and died in 1992, aged seventy-three.

Libby's grandparents on her father's side didn't want to know them. They claimed it was Eileen's fault that he had strayed and they could not forgive her. They thought she should have done more to keep him happy at home. The letter they wrote was very harsh. Soon after the event, they returned to their native Ireland.

When Eileen became too confused to be left on her own, Libby quit her job as a teaching assistant and began working part-time at the local supermarket, Aston's. Thanks to their very good neighbour, the widower Thomas Farraday, Eileen was looked after, and even occasionally taken out for drives and for walks in the park.

Unfortunately, Thomas then suffered a health scare, and Libby was obliged to give up work altogether, in order to take care of her mother. That was five years ago, and now, her mother was her life. Thankfully, Thomas regained his health, and for that Libby was immensely grateful. It meant she could do a couple of hours each morning at the supermarket and get out of the house for a while.

Eileen continued to believe that her husband Ian would come home. But he never did, and Libby never forgave him, as her mother's mental health worsened.

~

'*Hey!*' Eileen's angry voice shattered Libby's thoughts. 'Did you hear what I just told you?'

'Sorry, Mum. What was it you said?'

'1 said you're not such a bad child after all,' Eileen replied sharply. 'You're just a bit mischievous at times. So I've decided I won't tell your father. At least not this time!'

Familiar with her mother's mood swings, Libby kissed her on the cheek. 'Thanks, Mum.'

'You must never do it again, though. Or I *will* tell him, I really will. And then there'll be ructions.'

'Oh, quick! Here he comes.' Libby drew her mother's attention to the figure coming down the stairs. Libby had never before seen the man – a scruffy, tousle-haired individual in his late fifties. 'Let me do the talking, Mother.'

'What's going on 'ere?' The man smiled from one to the other. 'You two 'aving a bit of a barney, are yer?' He was quick to sense the atmosphere, and equally quick to realise that the younger, pretty woman was not best pleased to see him there. Well, sod her, he thought, and sod anybody else who didn't take to him. He had a living to earn just like other folks, and he would earn it in any way he could, good or bad.

Addressing Eileen, he asked, 'This your daughter, is it? Not too keen to see me, is she, eh?'

'Ignore her, Ian.' Affording Libby a scowl, Eileen smiled up at the man. 'She always was a difficult child! As you know.'

The man gave a curt nod of the head. His name was not Ian Harrow but Peter Scott, a bully-boy and layabout. Having spent the night with the crazy old bat, all he wanted was his payment.

Looking him up and down, Eileen struggled to remember. 'I'm so glad you came to see us. You mustn't go just yet, though. Oh dear, it's been such a long time since you were last here. Please, won't you stay for a cup of tea?' Unable to remember him, she grew agitated. 'Oh, and a slice of toast and marmalade, eh?'

'What?' He saw his opportunity. 'I'm not 'ere for bloody *marmalade*!'

'Oh, well, some bacon and eggs, then.' The flustered woman turned to her daughter. 'We do have eggs and bacon, don't we?'

'Sorry, Mother,' Libby lied, hoping he might leave without any further fuss. 'I didn't have time to do a shop yesterday.' This was an awkward situation; one of many over these past difficult years.

'No eggs or bacon? Well, it won't do, my girl. It won't do at all!' Raking her hands through her hair, the older woman began stamping her foot. 'No eggs or bacon! You're worse than useless! Can't even mek a bed properly! However hard I try, you never learn, do you?' Turning her attention on the stranger, she stared him up and down. 'An' who the hell are you?'

Peter Scott gave a sly, gappy grin. 'Oh, now I see what yer at!' The grin slipped into a scowl. 'Don't play the innocent with me, you old cow,' he hissed. 'Oh, an' I can tell you now – lying in bed with you turned my stomach!'

'What d'you mean?' Looking from the man to her daughter, Eileen was obviously confused. 'What does he mean?' she repeated worriedly. 'What's he saying?'

'I'm warning yer, don't try that on me!' he snarled. 'I don't tek kindly to being conned!'

All the same, this time he thought he might have fallen on his feet. First the old one sidles up and asks him to go home with her, and now he discovers there's an even better opportunity to get away with his pockets full. Maybe after he's given the younger one a good seeing-to, an' all.

Twisting the tale, he said, 'Nice try, ladies – I'll give you that. But it won't work. Y'see, I 'appen to be in the same line of business.'

'What are you getting at?' This time, Libby sensed real trouble. Like before, her mother had obviously thought this man was her husband and promised him the earth to come back home with her. It was not the

34

first time that Eileen Harrow had scoured the streets for her missing husband, only to come across some ne'er-do-well ready to use the situation to his own advantage. 'I'd like you to explain,' she went on coolly. 'And then I'd like you to leave!'

Scott laughed – a hollow, unnerving sound that sent the older woman cowering against the wall. 'Lah-di-bloody-dah, ain't we?' Irritated, and anxious to get away, he pretended to search his pockets. 'Yer thievin' devils! Me money's gone! I can see what yer up to now! Con artists the pair of yer! And clever with it. But not quite clever enough. It's obvious that you set out to rob me blind. And I 'ave to admit, yer took me in good and proper at first, but now it's clear as day what yer after.'

Taking a step forward, he concentrated on Libby. 'You're the brains behind it, while this one' – he grinned at Eileen, who was still cowering against the wall – 'is the bait. And no doubt the police will see it the same way after I've finished.' He had to make them out as villains, or the younger one would likely call the police on him.

He outlined his interpretation of events. 'So there I was, minding me own business, when this woman latched onto me, said she needed me to 'come home' with 'er. Enticed me back here, she did, and very convincing it was too. I didn't realise I was being set up to be robbed.' He congratulated himself on being witty enough to turn the tables on them. 'I can see it all now. The two of you are in it together. Con-artists, just like I said. You set a bloke up an' leave him wi' nowt.'

'That's a lie!' Libby retaliated. 'You must have realised my mother is ill, yet you deliberately took advantage of her!'

He slowly clapped his hands together. 'Oh, very good.' He grinned widely. 'So now, what do you think to my interpretation of events?'

'I think you're a liar and a rogue. And if you reckon for one minute that anyone would believe your story, you're a damned fool!'

'Is that so?' The smile disappeared from his face. Leering at her, he hissed softly, 'Well, that's my story, word for word, exactly as it happened, and I'm prepared to tell it to anyone who wants to know.' Anger coloured his voice. 'Yer ought to be bloody grateful it were *me* she latched onto! There are men out there who might have given you silly pair a good hiding, an' more. No doubt they'd 'ave gone through this house an' took everything worth a bob or two. An' I reckon, it's only what yer deserve.'

Fearing he might get violent, Libby moved to protect her mother, 'I want you out of here – now!' she said in a low voice. The thought of him bedding her mother was sickening.

Turning his trouser pockets inside out, Scott continued to play the victim. 'There were at least fifty quid in these pockets when she picked me up, and now it's all gone. So, unless yer want more trouble than yer can handle, you'd best hand over what I've earned, along with the cash you stole from me trouser-pockets. Oh, an' don't mek the mistake o' shouting for help.' To prove the point, he grabbed Eileen and held her in a vicious grip, before abruptly releasing her when she began to struggle.

As he took a step towards Libby, Eileen startled them both by yelling obscenities. *You leave her alone!* Rushing forward, she clung to Libby with one hand, while with the other, she feverishly plucked at her hair until she resembled a wild thing.

'I'm going nowhere, not without what's mine!' Grabbing Libby by the neck, he yanked her forward. 'You'd best shut her up, or I will!' With one mighty thrust he sent her hurtling backwards.

Subdued, Eileen was sobbing. 'Who is he?' she whispered hoarsely. 'Why does he want to hurt us?'

'Don't worry, Mum. I won't let him hurt you.' Libby realised that the quickest way to be rid of him would be to offer whatever money they had. But since they had so very little, that was not really an option.

Her voice trembling, Eileen said to Libby, 'If he's here when your father gets home from work, there'll be the devil to pay!' Glancing furtively at the door, she half expected Libby's father to burst in and protect them.

'You heard her,' Libby said, squaring up to the intruder. 'My father will be home soon from the night shift. So if you know what's good for you, you'd best make tracks!' Keeping her mother safe, she added firmly, 'There's nothing for you here.'

'I'll go when I'm paid what she owes me. And fifty quid on top!' His smile widened, to show a crooked row of yellowing teeth as he eyed her up and down. 'Happen you'd prefer me to take part payment in other ways . . . if yer know what I mean?'

Libby knew exactly what he meant. 'Like I said, we've got nothing for you. So, if you don't leave, I'll have no choice but to call the police.'

'Go on, then!' he goaded. 'Call 'em now! I can soon explain how I found this poor, deluded old dear wandering the streets, prostituting herself to any man that took her fancy. Being a proper gent, I managed to find an address tucked in her pocket, and I made sure she got home safely. That's what I'll tell the police, I reckon they'll get the Social out and she'll be banged up in a home, where she belongs.'

'No one would take any notice of a man like you!' All the same, Libby was worried. If he really did what he threatened, the officials would be all over her, asking questions and snooping around. And if that was the case, who knows what might happen? Her mother must not be taken from her.

'Oh, and don't forget, there are any number of witnesses who'll back me up,' Scott boasted. 'They all saw how she offered herself on a plate to any man she came across – promising money and everything.' He added cruelly, 'Only it seems they didn't need the money as much as I did.'

Lowering his voice, he leaned forward. 'Like any decent bloke, I took pity on her, an' the fact that she's safely home proves that. So I think you know who the police will believe. No doubt they'll ask why you allowed this poor old soul to wander the dark streets in her nightwear. You put her in danger, that's what they'd say.'

Sensing Libby's concern, he went on menacingly, 'If it weren't for me, some lesser man might 'ave had his way with 'er, before throwing 'er in the canal. Wrong in the 'ead she may be, but to tell the truth, compared to some of the scrubbers we get on the streets, she's passable enough for a bit of fun.'

'You get out!' Diving out from behind Libby, Eileen suddenly threw herself at him, fists flailing. 'Get away from my girl!' The force of her attack sent him stumbling against the wall. 'What d'you want in my house? Get out! Go on, *get out!*'

Shocked by Eileen's vicious onslaught, and now with Libby joining in, Scott found himself being manhandled across the room. Libby managed to open the front door, where the two of them struggled to push him outside. 'Show your face here again,' Libby warned, 'and I'll have the law on you!'

'Yer don't say!' Grabbing Libby by the throat, he tried to push her back inside. 'I don't need no trouble with the police, so just give me what I'm owed, an' I'll go!'

When Eileen came at him again, screeching and clawing at his face, he raised his arm and, with one sharp thump, sent her backwards across the room.

'Hey! What the hell d'you think you're doing?' The man came at him from behind.

Older than Scott but strong as a bull, Thomas

Farraday grabbed the younger man by the scruff of his neck, lifted him off his feet and literally swung him down the path, straddling him as he tried to scramble up, fists bunched and ready for a fight.

'This ain't got nothing to do with you!' Scott argued, before a hammer-sized fist smashed into his mouth. It was enough to send him scampering, but not without a parting shot as he nursed his jaw: 'You want locking up! Mad as hatters, the lot of you!'

Then, as Thomas took a step forward, he ran like a crazy man, stumbling wildly in his panic to get away. From a safe distance he shook his fist. *I'll not forget this in a hurry!'* he yelled, though when Thomas started after him, he fled down the street, never to be seen again.

CHAPTER THREE

AFTER WAITING UNTIL the unwelcome visitor was out of sight, Thomas went back to find Libby trying to calm her mother, who had been deeply disturbed by the entire episode. Seated at the table, Eileen was rocking back and forth. 'It was all my fault,' she sobbed. 'I brought him here, but he wasn't the one.' She glanced up, her misty eyes looking from one to the other. 'Y'see, I thought he were my Ian. I'm sorry I caused all this trouble.'

'It's all right, Eileen, love.' Seeing how Libby was too choked to speak, Thomas came forward. 'He's gone now, and by the way he shot round that corner, he'll not bother you again.'

Calmed by his quiet voice and gentle manner, Eileen looked up with tearful eyes. 'You're a good man, Thomas.' Taking his work-worn hand into hers, she gently kissed it. 'And I'm a silly old woman. They should put me away for what I've done to my Libby.' Eileen had fleeting moments of lucidity, and this was one of them.

Glancing to where her daughter was making a pot of fresh tea and some scrambled eggs, she gave an almighty sigh: 'My lovely girl!' When she wiped her eyes, Thomas felt her sorrow. 'She never married, you know. And it's all because of me.'

Thomas gently quietened her fears: 'I'm sure she'll find the right man one of these days,' he promised. 'Besides, she's only thirty, so there's time enough yet.'

Eileen was amazed. 'Oh dear! Is she thirty already?'

'I believe so, yes.'

'So, she really is wasting her life, then?'

'No.' Thomas had a special fondness for these two women. 'Libby loves taking care of you. You know yourself, she would have it no other way.'

In her mind, Eileen was beginning to drift again. 'Thirty isn't old, but it's not young either, is it, Thomas?' When she looked away, he felt her pain. 'It was me who brought that bad man home. I didn't mean to. I was looking for my Ian. I need him, and Libby needs a father.' She gave a little sigh. 'My little girl is thirty, and all these years she's been without a daddy.' Her voice broke. 'And I've been without a husband.' She added gratefully, 'Oh, I know you've been kind to Libby and me, but you're not her father, are you, Thomas? And she's thirty already.' She looked at him curiously. 'You do know that, don't you?'

Thomas smiled. 'Oh, my! What I wouldn't give, to be thirty again!'

'You and me . . .' Eileen stroked the back of his hand, 'we're old, aren't we, Thomas?'

42

He laughed out loud. 'Aw, I don't know about that.' While he was well into his late sixties, Eileen was only just sixty. And though at times her mind was broken, she was still an attractive woman, with her high cheekbones and sparkly brown eyes. She had a kind heart and, when her intelligence was not overshadowed, she displayed a bright, appealing sense of humour.

'D'you really think Libby will find her man? I mean, you're not just trying to pacify a silly old woman, are you?'

He shook his head. 'You're not to worry, sweetheart. Libby will be all right. And you mustn't be so hard on yourself. You've had a lot to contend with.'

She smiled up at him. '*You* know, don't you?' she murmured. '*You* understand the way it is.'

'I do, yes,' he replied softly. 'I understand, because I've been there.' He reflected a moment, before going on: 'Sometimes, when you can't bear to think about the cruelty of life, you hide inside yourself.'

Eileen was amazed at how Thomas always managed to say the right thing. 'Is that what I do – hide inside myself?' She felt somehow pacified. 'I never knew that.'

Shifting positions, he sat down beside her. Sliding his arm round her shoulders, he drew her close to him. 'You're not the only one, Eileen, love,' he confided. 'At some time or another, we all have a need to hide inside ourselves.'

'Do we really?' Something in his manner made her curious.

'Yes, sweetheart, we do.'

She leaned into his embrace. 'Thomas?'

'Yes, m'dear?'

'Do *you* hide sometimes?'

He smiled, a slow, rueful smile that carried him back over the years. 'Oh yes. Like I said, we all do.'

'Why is that, Thomas?'

He took a moment to search for the right words. 'Well, sometimes, when life gets too hard for me to handle, it helps me to go to a quiet place, somewhere deep inside, where nobody else can follow.'

For reasons he would rather not say, Thomas knew all about that. 'It's my own little haven, y'see?' He glanced down into her upturned brown eyes, and his heart was pained. 'Are you feeling better now, m'dear?'

Eileen's smile was beautiful. 'Yes, thank you, Thomas. You always help me.'

He smiled back. 'Well, that's good. I'm always glad to help, as you know. And don't ever forget, I'm always here for you and Libby. You know that as well, don't you?'

'Mmm.' Already her mind was shifting.

From across the kitchen, Libby heard their conversation. Deeply touched by his genuine kindness, she listened while buttering toast. These two people were not angels, by any means. They each had tempers when riled and they took no prisoners. Yet they were kind and generous, and beautiful in spirit.

Over the years, since she was a little girl, Libby had looked up to Thomas, who had proved to be a great comfort to her mother. Libby had strong affection for this dear man, and the friendship was between Thomas and her mother was a joy to see.

Their innocent chatter made her yearn to have a man of her own. To be making plans for the future. To be someone's sweetheart. To walk down the aisle, plan a home, and be a mother. And most of all, to share the burden that life had become. And yet, she had coped, because of her deep, abiding love for her mother. No one had wanted this sorry situation, but they still had each other, and the ever-watchful Thomas.

Like Thomas, she understood about that special hiding-place where no one else could follow. Libby had often visited that special place inside herself, to dream and wish and hope. It was a wonderful, brief respite from the way her life had evolved. Though when she came back to reality, nothing had changed. Nothing ever would. But for that short, precious time, when carried along by her imagination, she was free to dream.

In many ways, Libby considered herself blessed. She had her health and strength and so did her mother, apart from her slowly deteriorating mental state; although thankfully, Libby was able to make her days as normal and enjoyable as possible.

The two of them had a pretty home, paid for by the man who later abandoned them. She and her mother were warm and cosy, and they shared a deep bond of love. One way and another, there was enough coming in to feed and clothe them both, even though they had to watch every penny.

Libby often reminded herself that there were many people worse off than them. She counted her blessings. Life threw challenges at you: some you could deal with and some you couldn't. Life was no easy ride for anyone, she knew that. She also knew that all you could do was to get through the best way you could.

'Breakfast is ready, Mum. Thomas, would you like some scrambled eggs? I've made plenty.'

As the three sat and enjoyed a hearty meal, Eileen began worrying again. She was sad because her darling girl was nearly thirty years old and still not wed. So there were no children or grandchildren to love. Eileen truly believed it was all her fault, even though both Libby and Thomas tried to convince her otherwise.

'It's like Thomas said – I just haven't met the right man yet,' Libby assured her cheerfully. 'One day I'll be filling the shelves in the supermarket, and just like on the TV ads, some handsome fella will pick up the tin of beans I accidentally dropped, and before you know it, I'll have met my future husband and father of my ten children.'

'Hey, you'd best not have ten children,' Eileen teased. 'I won't be able to fit them all on my knee!' But in her more lucid moments, Eileen knew the truth: her daughter had been robbed of marriage and children, and all because of having to look after her.

'I had a husband,' Eileen now announced. 'When we first married, we were so much in love we never needed anyone else. Then we had Libby, and everything was perfect . . . for a time.' She discreetly wiped away a tear. 'After we had the baby, my Ian began to change. He was restless – didn't seem to want us any more. Sometimes he went with other women. I found out and I faced him time and again. He kept saying he loved me, and I had to believe him. I so *wanted* to believe him!'

A look of despair was etched on her face. 'In the end I stopped worrying, because I knew I had to put up with it, or lose him. I pretended it wasn't happening, and we were much happier. Later though, he left me anyway.'

When her voice broke and she began to stare into her teacup, Libby told her, 'You don't need to think about all that, Mum. It's all water under the bridge, and I don't like you being upset.'

Eileen gave a sad little nod. 'I have to say it,' she told her. 'He's been gone so long, and I need him here with me! I need answers. I need to ask him why he did it.' She grew agitated. 'It must have been my fault. I must have done something wrong.'

This time it was Thomas who intervened, his voice stern but kindly. 'It was *not* your fault, my dear. If you think back, you'll remember how it really was. Your husband *did* love you – he would have been crazy not to. But he liked to play the field. We all knew that, and we all wondered how you managed to put up with it for so long. The truth is, for whatever reason, he liked other women. One was never enough. *You* were never enough. His own little daughter Libby was not even enough to keep him faithful. When he left, it was not your fault, Eileen. It was his. You must never forget that.' It hurt him to see this darling woman so terribly sad.

'He's right, Mum.' Libby agreed with his every word. 'It's common knowledge – Father was a womaniser. You stood by him, and yet he still went away, leaving us both behind, and me only six years old. Like Thomas said, it was nothing you did. Dad liked other women. It was just the way he was, that's all.'

'Ah, but you never knew about that woman next door, did you?' As was her way, Eileen suddenly brought the discussion to a different level. 'Claire Redmond, her name was.'

Libby was intrigued. 'Yes, I do remember her,' she confirmed. Sometimes her mother took her completely by surprise.

Thomas recalled the neighbour in question – a loose woman who liked other men, even before her husband died. 'What was her son's name, now . . . ?' he pondered. 'Jim? Joe? Oh, goodness! My memory's getting worse by the minute.'

'Jack!' Libby's voice rang out. She had not forgotten him and never would. 'His name was Jack, and he was my best friend.'

Thomas scowled. 'From what I remember, Jack's mother was a real flighty sort – go with any tom-cat that howled, she would!' He added softly, 'Shame about what happened to her husband. Gordon was a nice enough bloke – struck down with a heart-attack two days after that big fire he got caught up in, and him only forty-two. It just goes to show – we never know what's round the corner, do we, eh?'

There was a moment of quiet, before Eileen spoke

again, and what she had to say came as a surprise to both Thomas and Libby. 'Claire Redmond was a bad woman.' She wagged a finger at Thomas. 'She threw herself at my Ian!'

Nervously rolling her teacup in her hands, she leaned forward. 'You were a bairn at the time,' she told Libby, 'and I took you with me to babysit for little Jack. Later, I found I'd left my coat behind, so I put you in your cot and nipped back – and there they were in the hallway. Your father and Jack's mother – going at it like two ferrets, they were!'

Rendering the other two speechless, she went on. 'I was so ashamed. My own husband – cavorting with her, and right on our own doorstep!' She gave a deep sigh. 'So maybe I'm really *not* to blame after all.'

'That's right, Mum. You were *not* to blame.' Libby was used to her mother switching from one subject to another, but this time she was shocked. The thought of Jack's mother and her own father 'going at it like ferrets' was not a pleasant one.

'If I remember rightly,' she said, 'Jack's mum went away and never came back.'

'That's right, dear. His poor father passed on. Two years later, young Jack comes home from school to find the house with a "Sold" sign outside. Soon after, his mother packed her bags and took off with her American boyfriend, leaving young Jack to fend for himself.'

Thomas still recalled that day, all those years ago. He also recalled the desolate look on the boy's face as he walked past his window. 'What mother would do such a dreadful thing, and just a few days before the boy was about to leave school?' He tutted loudly. 'First his father gone, and then his mother. Then he finds himself with no roof over his head. What a dreadful start to his young life! No one cared tuppence about him.'

'We did – he could have stayed with us until he found somewhere,' Libby said, rather sadly.

'Happen he was too proud.' Thomas too would gladly have given the lad a home.

'Or maybe he wanted a fresh start,' Libby mused. 'Maybe he wanted to put as many miles between himself and Blackburn as he could.'

Thomas agreed. 'As I recall, he was a sensible, decent sort of lad. More than capable of making his own way in life too, I shouldn't wonder.'

Eileen smiled. 'He was such a quiet baby . . . pale-looking and good as gold. And then he turned into a fine, handsome young man.'

Thomas nodded at Eileen's memories of Jack, but he recalled Jack as being a chubby baby, with a smile to brighten the day and an active curiosity about everyone and everything.

All this talk of Jack made him strong in Libby's mind. For a long time she had hoped he might come back, but then a new family moved in next door, and she resigned herself to the idea that she would never see him again. To this very day, she missed him. She missed his company and his quiet smile, and the way he always took it on himself to take care of her at school.

Once, after an older girl had bullied and upset her, Jack had shyly kissed her on the mouth, before shooting off quickly, as though having shocked himself. That was the first time he ever kissed her. And the last. Thinking of it now, she involuntarily raised her fingers to her mouth, gently brushing her lips. The memory of Jack's mouth on hers was surprisingly vivid.

'Libby!' Her mother's raised voice broke the spell. 'I was talking to you.'

Mortified, Libby was quickly attentive. 'What is it, Mum?'

'Oh, dear, I've forgotten now, but it doesn't matter. Must've been something and nothing.'

Like Libby, Thomas was miles away, back in the past, thinking of the tragic Redmond family; and particularly of young Jack. 'What age will he be now?' he mused. 'As I recall, he were just a bit older than Libby, so he must be over thirty now.'

'Oh, dear, is it really that long?' Eileen was surprised and saddened at the speed with which the years had flown away.

'I wonder where he went.' In truth, Libby had never stopped wondering.

Her mother wondered too. 'I hope he's all right.'

'I expect he's wed,' Thomas chipped in, 'wi' a couple o' children running round his backside.'

As always, Eileen had a short span of concentration. 'Libby, now I remember what I wanted to ask you,' she said.

'Good. So, what was it, Mum?'

'Do *you* ever feel guilty about your father?'

'Not at all, no.' She was used to her mother flitting from one subject to another.

'Don't you want him back?'

'Not now. He chose someone else over us and left.' Libby was more bitter than ever. Convinced that her father's womanising had damaged her mother's mind, she had been disgusted to learn that he had even had a fling with Jack's mother.

'Don't you love him?' Eileen asked.

'I didn't even *know* him, not really.' Nor did she want to, 'Don't forget, I was only a little girl when he left.'

When Eileen again grew silent, Libby wished she hadn't voiced her true feelings. 'I'm sorry, Mum. I didn't mean to be so hard.'

Eileen understood. 'You were right,' she answered. 'He did hurt us both, very much.' Her pretty brown eyes misted over. 'It's just that, well . . . I really miss him, that's all.'

'I realise that,' Libby said kindly, 'but it was a long time ago and, like Thomas said, you could never have changed him.'

After her father went away, he was kept alive by the photographs lovingly placed about the house by her mother. And also by the stories her mother would tell over the years, about how it used to be, and how, one day, Ian Harrow was bound to come home. But he never did.

'It's best if you don't think about the bad things any more,' Libby suggested now.

'You didn't know, but last night, when you were fast asleep, I went to find him,' Eileen confided. 'I sneaked out and walked the streets – and there he was.'

Sensibly , Libby let her talk. It was the only way.

Eileen mumbled on: 'I hoped he might be sorry for what he did to us. I wanted it to be like it was before . . . well, you know, don't you, love?'

'Yes, Mother, I think I do.'

'When I found him, he was angry with me. At first he tried to send me away, but I told him if he would come home with me and be like he was before, I would forgive him. I even promised him money. He was bad, though, wasn't he? He came back, but he only wanted to hurt us again.' Her voice broke. 'Oh, Libby, why would your father do such a thing?'

Realising she was drifting away from reality, Thomas felt obliged to help. 'Listen to me now, m'dear. That man you brought home was *not* your husband.'

'Who was he, then?' Eileen looked at them both, perplexed.

'You should never have gone out, Mother,' Libby said firmly. She had believed the precautions she'd taken were enough. Thomas had even fitted a gate at the top of the stairs. And yet again, her mother had outwitted them both.

'I'm sorry, Libby, I won't do it again.'

'Good. I'm glad about that.'

'The bad man who hurt us just now. Was *that* your father?' Her confusion thickened.

Libby suddenly found it hard to hold back the tears.

She was losing her mother again. 'No, Mum. That man was a stranger. Thomas sent him packing.'

Inside her mind Eileen struggled to put the pieces together. 'Who was he, then?' she asked worriedly. 'Why was he here?'

'There's nothing for you to worry about, m'dear.' Gently intervening, Thomas put her mind at rest. 'He came in off the streets, wanting a handout. He was a rogue, and now he's gone.'

'I don't want him to ever come back!'

'You don't need to worry, my darling, because he won't be back.'

'Not ever?'

'No. Not ever.'

'Do you promise?'

Thomas nodded, his eyes moist with sorrow. 'I promise. With every bone in my body.'

'Thank you, Thomas. You're the best friend to me and Libby,' Eileen whispered, and in an impromptu move that surprised the other two, she leaned forward and pursed her lips for a kiss.

With aching heart, Thomas took hold of her hands, and drawing her close, he kissed her quickly, with great tenderness. 'I'm always here for you,' he promised hoarsely. Then, addressing Libby, he stood up to leave. 'Thanks for that nice bit o' breakfast. Went down a treat, it did.'

Libby nodded. 'Mum's right,' she acknowledged. 'You really are a true friend.' She had been touched by the way her mother had asked him for a kiss, and he responded, appearing to be deeply moved.

Thomas assured her, 'What I did was only what any right-minded bloke would do. Now then, ladies, don't forget: if you need me . . .'

'We know where you are,' Libby finished, and showed him to the door, where they bade each other good day.

Thomas walked the few steps along Bower Street to his own little house next door, thinking about the vile creature he had sent packing. 'He'll not be back,' he muttered. But like Libby, he had a feeling it would not be the last time Eileen would go wandering off. 'We shall have to keep a sharper eye on her in future.'

He gave an involuntary shiver. The sun was bright, but there was no warmth in it. 'You should've put your coat on,' he chided himself. 'Catch your death o' cold if you're not careful!'

Cheering up, he made his way through the little wooden gate and on down the garden path, pausing to see if the flower-buds were peeping out. 'Too early yet!' he chuckled wryly. 'They've got more sense than me. Like as not, they won't pop their heads up for a while yet.'

Letting himself into the house, he closed the door behind him. It was only a few steps along the passageway to the living-room. Once there, he dropped his weary body into the depth of a big old armchair. When it creaked beneath his weight, he laughed out loud. 'Sounds like I'm not the only one getting old,' he remarked to the empty room. 'Old and worn, me an' the chair both.'

Rolling up his shirt-sleeves, he noticed a dark, elongated bruise on his wrist. 'I'm too bloody old to be rugby tackling fellas, that's for sure!'

He gave a deep, rumbling laugh. 'Saw the bugger off though, didn't we, eh? Me an' the lasses – we saw the bugger off good and proper!' For the first time in a long while, he felt useful. Moreover, he felt proud to have dealt with such an ugly situation.

His mood sobering, Thomas gazed at the fire-grate and the dark coals flickering there. He felt safe in this little house; sheltered from the changing world and the harshness of life. This home was where he had been most happy, with his late wife. It had always been a deep disappointment that he and Rose were never able to have children. If they had, his life and hers would have been all the sweeter. Maybe then, she'd still be with him, grandchildren on her knee.

Growing melancholic, he got up from the chair and ambled over to the sideboard, where he studied the array of photographs displayed there. His eyes settled on one in particular – of a pretty young woman seated on a swing near the rose-beds in Corporation Park.

He recalled the day clearly. It was high summer and they'd been married for two years to the very day. The gentle breeze lifted her long fair hair, just as he was about to take the picture. She laughed, he clicked the button, and she was captured for ever. This photograph had always been his favourite one of her. They were young then, and she was so beautiful.

He had always wondered what she saw in him – an ordinary-looking bloke with few prospects. But oh, how he loved her, and still did . . . to this very day, in spite of everything life had thrown at them.

Collecting the photograph, he carried it to the chair, where he sat down and stared at it for what seemed an age, until the tears ran freely down his weathered old face. 'I know what Eileen meant when she said she missed her husband,' he told the image, 'because I miss you, every minute of every day.'

After a time he went to the back window and looked out. 'See that!' He turned the photograph, imagining she might see what he'd done to the garden. 'I've set the flowers either side of the path, the way you like it,' he said proudly. 'And look at the potting shed . . . I've created a bed of your favourite red geraniums along the front. Should be lovely, come the summer.' He gave himself an imaginary pat on the back. 'Give it another month, an' our little back garden will be ablaze with colour, you wait and see.'

Glancing up at the skies, he chided himself, 'Hark at me! Telling you what it looks like and how pretty it'll be. I expect you can see more than I can, from up there with the angels.'

His sorry gaze lingered on the shifting clouds, following their progress across a kindly sky. 'I do miss you, Rose,' he murmured. 'I even miss you nagging at me when I made your tea too strong. I miss our cuddles, and seeing your pretty face in the mornings when I wake, and I miss your chatter and laughter. I know I'll never hear that again, and it makes me really sad.'

When the tears threatened again, he told himself sharply, 'You stop that, you silly old devil! She's gone, and you can't bring her back. It's the way it is, and that's that. Some of us are destined to go, and others are left behind to soldier on, and like it or not, that's a fact of life.'

He chatted for a while, telling her, 'Eileen next door snuck out again. She went looking for her two-timing husband. Brought a real bad fella home this time, she did. But thankfully, we managed to get rid of him without too much trouble.'

He lapsed into thought for a time, before softly confiding, 'I must confess, Rosie, I really do like Eileen. In her clearer moments, we seem to understand each other. We've both suffered a loss and we're both lonely – though of course she's a bit luckier than me, because she's got her daughter Libby, while I've got no one.'

A gentle sadness marbled his voice. 'Yes, I know she's damaged and I know she's a handful, but it's nice to be able to take care of someone, and those two lovely people next door are more like family than neighbours. During the day, when Libby goes to work and I nip round to keep Eileen company, I find myself laughing with her over silly little things. We sit and have a cup of tea and I let her chatter on, because she likes to talk, and it does my old heart good.'

He relayed the gist of the recent conversation about Jack Redmond, remembering how Rose used to claim that Jack's mother was unfit to have children, while mourning the fact that infertile women like herself were denied the opportunity of ever becoming a mother.

'The truth is, young Jack were thrown to the wolves,' Thomas declared angrily. 'If you'd still been here, I know you would have offered him a home, my sweet Rosie, but he were a proud young fella, and I don't believe he would have accepted any kind of charity. Just now, me and the girls next door, were wondering what might have happened to him, and whether he found a better life after leaving these parts.'

He scratched his head. 'Listen to me, talking away as if you're sitting there listening to me! But y'see what I'm saying, sweetheart? It's good for me to pop in next door. It keeps me up with what's going on, and it gives me summat to think about. Moreover, it's nice for me to look after Eileen of a morning. We have a laugh. We gct on really well together, and you know what?' He gazed directly at his late wife's photograph. 'Eileen and Libby make me feel I'm needed, if y'see what I mean?'

While his gaze lingered on her pretty face, his old heart flooded with guilt. 'I'm really sorry, my lovely. I don't mean to make you jealous, or hurt your feelings or anything of the kind, but I do love Eileen. Oh, not in the way I loved you. I could never love *any* woman like I love you.'

He gave a quiet smile. 'I'm not saying we never argued, because you know very well we did, and there were times when you drove me to distraction.' He did not want to think badly of her; to him, she would always be his first and only real love. 'I've always loved and adored you, and I always will.'

Pressing two fingers on his lips, he transferred the kiss onto her photograph. 'The thing is, we none of us know what's round the corner. Fate can be a giver or a taker. Sometimes she's kindly, and sometimes she causes terrible pain. Things happen and we'd rather they didn't – and however desperate we are to change them, we just can't.'

Returning the photograph to the sideboard, he went across the room, heavy with regrets, and as always, wishing his wife was still there. Sinking into his familiar, cosy armchair, Thomas let his mind wander back over the years.

There had been so many wonderful times which he would not change for the world, but there were other, more recent memories that brought him little comfort. He also had a deep regret that he and his wife had not been blessed with children. And now, he was left to face the future alone.

He had always been a practical man. He believed there was a reason for everything; though for the life of him, there were times when he struggled to fathom what that reason was. Overwhelmed with emotion, he leaned forward in the chair, spread his hands over his face and, frantically rocking back and forth, he began to cry. When the dark memories flooded his mind, the sorrow was more than he could bear. 'I miss you, my lovely,' he whispered. 'And I'm so sorry.'

MIDNIGHT

In that crippling moment, he thought of everything he had suffered since his woman had gone. First, the raw shock of it all. Such pain. Such grief. And then the unending loneliness.

The trauma of losing her would never leave him. Grief and pain he had learned to live with. But the loneliness was the worst punishment of all.

CHAPTER FOUR

'Y OU'RE LUCKY THE specialist had a cancellation and could fit you in so quickly.'

'Don't be afraid to say it, Molly,' Jack reminded her. 'He's a *psychiatrist*!'

'Look, Jack! Don't let's go through all this again. Just go and see him. For my sake, if not for yours. Neither of us have had a good night's sleep in ages!'

'No need to get agitated, Moll. I haven't said I won't go and see him!' Jack wondered what he might be letting himself in for, and he was not looking forward to seeing the psychiatrist. I think you're over-reacting. I know I've kept you awake, but like I said, I'll move into the spare room. It's not a problem for me.'

Molly would not hear of it, 'You're wrong! It *is* a problem – for *both* of us!' Snatching up the breakfast-plate, she slid it onto the sink-top. 'I've told you before: sleeping in separate bedrooms would be the beginning of the end of our relationship.'

'Huh! That's not saying much for our relationship then, is it?'

'We're already drifting apart, Jack. I can't help but wonder how long it will be before I'm out of your life altogether.'

'That won't happen. Not if I have anything to do with it.'

'Look, Jack. I know it isn't easy for you, but you must go and see him, even if it's only to talk.' She paused, recalling all the things he had told her, about the childhood drawings, and the dark images. 'I don't see what *you* see, when you're dreaming,' she conceded quietly, 'but I've seen how the nightmares affect you. You have to talk with someone who might be able to help you. This is your chance, Jack,' she coaxed. 'What have you got to lose by keeping the appointment?'

When Jack gave no answer, Molly grew angry. 'For pity's sake, Jack! What the hell is wrong with you?'

'You don't understand.'

'Then tell me!'

She placed her hands over his in a gesture of reassurance. 'I'm frightened of losing you, Jack. I'm frightened that if you don't get professional help, there might be no way back.'

Jack gave a harsh little laugh, 'That's a bit dramatic —*no way back*!' He knew what she meant, but wouldn't admit to it.

In truth, there were times when he thought the same. Lately, he found it increasingly difficult to cope.

'JACK!'

Molly's raised voice startled him.

'Will you keep the appointment, or not?'

Collecting his plate and cup, Jack got out of the chair to place them in the sink. 'Look,' he explained, 'if I seem reluctant to go, it's just that I went through a lot of this stuff when I was a kid.'

He remembered it as if it was yesterday: the long hours in a stuffy room; the questions he found hard to answer; the fruitless tests and meaningless suggestions, and later the snide remarks from the other kids at school.

Afterwards, for a time the nightmares went away, but they soon came back, stronger than ever.

He had promised never to put himself in the hands of strangers again, so he learned to live with his fears. He became clever at putting on a front for his parents and teachers. When the dreams took him, and he woke with the darkness and the images still clinging to him, he would walk the floor of his bedroom until he was able to relax into a kind of shallow sleep. They never knew. And he never told them.

Consequently, the sessions with the child psychologist eventually stopped altogether. But not the dreams and not the darkness, because they were still there, in that other place. The place where his mind took him.

Over the ensuing years, he had hidden his secret well. Until Molly came into his life and began to sleep with him.

'You win, Sweetheart.' Walking over to the sink, he put his arms around her. 'As soon as I get to the office,

I'll talk to the boss and arrange an extra-long lunchtime.'

'Good! And I'll do the same.'

'Why would you do that?' he asked defensively. 'To check up on me? To make sure I get there, is that it?' He did not want her too involved.

Molly protested, 'No! It's just so you won't have to go on your own, that's all.'

'But that's just it,' Jack told her. 'I *want* to go on my own.'

'No! That's not right. You need me there.'

'Molly, listen to me. I prefer to be on my own.' Sometimes, she was like a dog with a bone. 'I don't want to worry about you being there – if I freak out, or anything. You see, once the therapist starts digging into my brain, who knows how I might react? Like I said, I've been there before, so I know what I'm talking about.'

'All the more reason for me to be there for you.'

'No, Molly – the subject is closed. I appreciate the offer, but I'm going on my own, and that's an end to it.'

'All right, I'll stay away – but if you want me, give me a call or text me, and I'll be straight over.'

'I can tell you now, I won't be calling you. Like I say, I know what's coming, and I'm probably better equipped to deal with it now I'm older.'

A short time later, they left the house. Within the hour, Jack had dropped her off at the estate agents in Woburn, before travelling on to the Bletchley showroom, where he clinched a deal with a long-standing customer.

'You've made the right choice, Mr Gallagher.' With the papers signed and the monies paid, Jack led the client outside, where the shiny new Lexus was parked and waiting.

'I doubt there'll be any problems.' Handing over the car-keys, he then shook the buyer by the hand. 'If you think of anything you've forgotten to ask, just give us a shout.'

The customer was a weasel of a man, but while he looked somewhat lost in such a big car, he appeared more than capable as he skilfully manoeuvred it out of a tight spot, before driving off at some speed.

Jack rubbed his hands. 'Another satisfied customer,' he thought, feeling very pleased with himself. 'Another sizeable commission.' But when he remembered his appointment in a couple of hours' time, his sense of achievement fell away.

'What's wrong with *you*?' Jan the receptionist had noticed how he seemed on top of the world when he walked by her with the customer, and now he looked as though the weight of the world was on his shoulders. 'Lost one of your boy-toys, have you?' she quipped. 'Don't be sad. There's another delivery in today.'

'That's right.' Jack gave her a cheeky wink. 'One out, another in. Keeps the wheels turning, so they say.'

'Oh, I see.' She tutted. 'So does that apply to women too – one out, another in?'

'I never said that.' He was used to her teasing.

As he hurried back to the office, she called after him, 'At least when you sell a car, you can look forward to a commission! Not me, though. I smile and make the tea. I answer the phone, run about and take a lot of stick from you lot. But *I* get no commission.'

Jack leaned out of the office door, 'Ah, but you get the unending gratitude of the team, and a big smile from yours truly. What else do you want?'

'Do you really need me to tell you?'

Jack laughed out loud. 'Not just now.'

'Later then?' She gave him a saucy smile.

'Behave yourself, you!' He went back into the office, still smiling at her naughty banter.

A short time later, having filed away the last of the paperwork from the sale, he made his way to the main office and tapped on the door.

'Come!' The voice was small, but the man seated behind the desk was built like a buffalo, with a short, thick beard and dark-rimmed spectacles. 'I see you've clinched that deal this morning? Well done, Jack!'

Hoisting himself out of his seat, the boss, Branagan, strolled across to where the office window looked into the showroom. 'So, what can I do for you?' Hands clenched behind his back, he commented, 'Well, now! For a man who's just earned himself a handsome commission, you don't seem too pleased with yourself. Is there a problem?'

Jack explained, 'I need to beg some time off this afternoon – an hour, possibly two.'

Stuart Branagan became curious. 'Might I ask why?'

'Doctor's appointment,' answered Jack.

'Really? Is everything OK?'

Jack already had an answer. 'It's nothing serious – well, at least it's serious to me, because it's quite painful. I strained my back some time ago. I just need my GP to take a look so he can give me something for the discomfort, that's all.'

'Strained your back, you say?' The manager was instantly on his guard. 'You haven't been lifting stuff on these premises when you're not supposed to, have you? Because if you have, there'll be no comeback on the company. You know the rules, Redmond!'

Jack was quick to reassure him. 'No, it's nothing I've done here. I don't know how I did it, but it's beginning to really play me up. My doctor will probably prescribe anti-inflammatories, that's all. I won't be away long. An hour. Two at the most, depending on traffic.'

Branagan gave a crude laugh. 'Too much nookie with that girlfriend of yours, is it?'

Jack ignored his unwelcome remark.

Seeing that Jack was not amused, the big man went on to remind him, 'Don't forget we've got a delivery late this afternoon. It'll be all hands on deck.'

'Don't worry. I'll be back in plenty of time.'

'Mmm!' Branagan was none too pleased, but he needed Jack, especially as he himself had only been with the company for a short time and was still learning the ropes. Moreover, with the under-manager having left a fortnight back, Jack's experience and expertise were invaluable to him, at least for now.

'Very well. But make sure you're here when that delivery arrives.' With that, Branagan swung round on his heels and, without another glance at Jack, returned to his desk.

As Jack closed the door behind him, the older man muttered, 'You've become far too big for your boots in these showrooms, Redmond! It's even got to the point where the staff would rather go to you for advice than come to me.'

He had a habit of sucking his bottom lip when rattled, and he was rattled now. 'Undermining my authority, that's what you're doing. Well, I know your little game.'

He watched as Jack retreated into his office. 'I've already got the man to fill your shoes, Redmond!' he mumbled spitefully. 'So the sooner I can shift you up north, the better.'

His new son-in-law Jamie was the sort of person he needed to work under him. Unambitious, but hard-working. Ready and able to make the sales, but not too keen to take on managerial responsibility.

Oh, yes. Once he was rid of Jack, he would choose his staff carefully. Capable salesmen who, as long as they got their commission, were not too bothered if someone else took all the glory.

When he realised the receptionist was looking at him, he smiled sweetly and gave a condescending nod. If he hadn't dropped the blinds before returning to his work, he might have seen the rather crude sign she made to him.

Jack saw it, though, and smiled to himself. Having

already been obliged to discreetly mop up the new manager's mistakes, Jack held much the same opinion of Stuart Branagan as Jan did. 'Little sergeant-major!' he mumbled, 'hunched in his office, ordering tea and biscuits, and putting on airs, while the minions out here have to work twice as hard to keep the place going.' He had hoped he might get on with the new manager, but no matter how he tried, he could find no respect for him.

'All right then, Jack?' That was Bill West, a young newcomer, wet behind the ears but eager to make a name for himself.

'Fine thanks, Bill. And you?'

'Not sure.'

Jack understood. 'Been thrown in at the deep end again, have you?'

The younger man nodded mournfully. 'You couldn't help me out, could you, Jack? Only I've mixed my appointments up again. I don't want to tell the boss-man, or that'll be his excuse to have me out the door.'

He went on quietly, so as not to be overheard: 'Trouble is, I've got this customer arriving in five minutes . . . he wants a trial run in the four-by-four. But when I checked my notes just now, I realised I've gone and booked Mr Tomlinson in at the same time, and I can't get hold of him to change the appointment. He's not answering his phone.'

'What's he coming in for?'

'To talk about finance, on a trade-in against a new car.'

'Go on then.' Jack could see he was beginning to panic. 'Be sure and make a good job of selling that four-by-four, and I'll deal with your Mr Tomlinson. Have you done your work on the finance?'

'Yes. It's in my desk-drawer – second down on the left.'

'And do you have his first name?'

'Er, yes. It's Jason, I think.'

Jack had a piece of advice for him. 'First rule of the game, Bill. Make a mental note of the client's first name. Read the signs, and if it's all going well, then you adopt the friendly approach . . . but not *too* friendly, if you know what I mean?'

Bill nodded, 'I really do appreciate you doing this for me, Jack.'

'That's OK. As it happens, I've got piles of paperwork to check and file, but because I need to take an extra-long lunch-hour, I'll be staying on late to make up. So, I'll do the paperwork then.'

'Aw, thanks, Jack. You're a pal. I owe you one.'

As it turned out, Bill's first appointment was done and dusted in record time. With Mr Tomlinson arriving half an hour late, the young man was thrilled that everything had fallen so neatly into place. However, buoyed by his first-ever big sale, he was too excited and too gushing to concentrate on the matter in hand. Consequently, the second customer walked away without signing.

'What did I do wrong?' he asked Jack.

As always, Jack gave it to him straight. 'Sale or no sale, Bill, once you've dealt with one customer, you need to clear your mind and concentrate all your attention on the next one. You have to make every customer feel as if they're the only one that matters.'

Then, not wishing to curb Bill's enthusiasm, Jack slapped him on the back and assured him, 'Don't be too down-hearted, though. Mr Tomlinson came here because he liked our product. I dare say he'll be back. They usually are.'

Bill thanked Jack and went away to consider his advice. Jack's words had pricked his bubble, but he had learned a valuable lesson today. One he would never forget. And for that he was grateful.

~

As the morning wore on, Jack grew more edgy. The hours passed all too quickly, and then it was time to leave for his dreaded appointment. He was on his way out, when Jan called to him, 'Going anywhere nice for lunch?'

'Hardly!'

'Want me to come with you?' she asked, fluttering her eyelashes saucily.

'No, 'cause I need you to keep an eye on young Bill,' Jack told her, worried that he might have been a bit too harsh with his advice.

'Why? What's he up to?' Jan was curious.

'He's not up to anything as far as I know, but I reckon he might need a friend and a cup of tea . . . when you're making one.'

By the time she turned to look where Bill might be, Jack was already out the door and heading for his car.

~

Once inside the car, he sat awhile, wondering if he should go or not. There was no denying he was nervous – and he had every right to be. Molly was right, though. If he didn't master this thing, it would master him.

More than anyone, he knew the score. The nightmares had gone on for too long. Maybe now that he was older, he could handle whatever the sessions threw up. Also, since his relationship with Molly was taking a battering, it was time to seek help. Time to trust a stranger again; enough to put himself into their hands. Today could be his chance to root out his fears and hopefully put a stop to the torment.

The alternative did not bear thinking about.

CHAPTER FIVE

DOCTOR LENNOX WAS waiting at the clinic to greet Jack.

The GP was a handsome fellow in his early sixties and with numerous letters after his name. 'As I explained in our little telephone chat, I'm not qualified to deal with these particular issues,' he said, 'but Mr Howard, on the other hand, is one of the best in his field. You'll be in safe hands with him.' He suddenly caught sight of the man in question. 'Ah! Here he is now.'

A tall, bony man with sweeping eyebrows and a look of authority came striding up to Dr Lennox, and greeted him as a valued old friend. 'Good to see you, Sam.'

Having briefly renewed his acquaintance with the older doctor, he then turned to Jack and shook him by the hand. 'You'll be Mr Redmond, no doubt? I'm Alan Howard.' Taking stock of Jack, he saw a responsible, accomplished man, just as Dr Lennox had described.

He also saw the shadows beneath his eyes and the tension in his features, and could tell that he was deeply troubled.

'Dr Lennox tells me you've agreed to let him sit in on the session?' The psychiatrist allowed the whisper of a smile. 'If you've changed your mind, we'll just send him away.'

Jack assured him it was fine. 'I've known Dr Lennox for a few years now,' he confirmed. 'I would be happy to have him stay – if that's all right with you?'

'Of course. We don't apply rules as such.' Howard's voice was unusually soft, almost mesmerising. 'I'm here to help, and that means I'm prepared to do whatever is necessary. So, if having your trusted family doctor on hand puts you at ease, I have no objections whatsoever.'

In truth, having another person sitting in on the session was not something Howard would normally allow, but he knew Sam Lennox very well and trusted him implicitly. Also, he knew that Lennox had deep concerns regarding his patient, and wanted to see for himself how Jack reacted to this treatment.

'I don't mind telling you, I'm not looking forward to this,' Jack admitted. 'The sooner it's over, the better.' He could feel his hands beginning to sweat, and somewhere in the pit of his stomach a dozen rats were gnawing at him. The only thing that kept him there was fear. The fear of not knowing. The fear that if he didn't go through with this right now, while he had the chance, he might well live to regret it later.

Howard fully understood Jack's misgivings. After all, it was tantamount to stepping into the unknown – for everyone concerned.

After a quick word with the receptionist, Howard was ushering Jack and Lennox along the winding passageway to his consulting room, 'Here we are. Everything's ready.'

Jack took stock as they went inside. The room was small, with a high ceiling and pastel-coloured walls. The furniture was minimal. There was a tall, double filing cabinet in the corner, a long couch along one wall, and in the centre of the room, a small desk, displaying a lamp, and one solitary file, which Jack assumed must have his name on it. In front of the desk there were two chairs – one upright, one easy.

While the walls were soothing to the eye, the furniture was heavy in style and finished in darkest-brown leather; the same sober colour as the curtains which framed the two long Victorian windows, through which the daylight dimly filtered in.

There was a unique sense of peace about the room. It helped put Jack at ease, in spite of every nerve in his body crying out for him to run from there. To run from whatever might be revealed. Because if it was revealed, then it would actually exist – and until now he had been able to convince himself that the place he visited in his dreams was only the figment of a vivid imagination. And that hopefully, one day soon, the dreams would vanish, as though they had never been.

The soft voice interrupted his thoughts. 'There is nothing for you to worry about,' said Mr Howard. 'We'll just talk, you and me. You'll talk and I'll listen. You say as much or as little as you feel comfortable with. If you say stop, we'll stop. Is that all right, Jack? Does that put your mind at rest?'

When Jack merely nodded, Howard gestured to the armchair. 'You sit here, please, Jack.' He then glanced at the older man. 'The couch for you,' he instructed light-heartedly.

The doctor made no reply. He made his way to the couch and settled down. He was content with his vantage point. From here he could follow the procedure without being a disturbance to anyone.

A few moments later, when all were seated, Mr Howard asked Jack to tell him about himself. 'Your background . . . where you were born, family – that sort of thing.'

For years, Jack had made every effort to shut his past out, but now he cast his mind back. 'Well, I'm an only child,' he started. 'I was lonely, I remember that.'

'Was your relationship with your father a happy one? What I mean is, did you get on better with him than with your mother?'

Jack took a moment to clarify his thoughts. 'Sometimes, when she was in a bad mood, I was frightened of my mother. Oh, I'm not saying she beat me, because she never did. But she had such a quick temper, you see? My father was more gentle. Sometimes he took me to football matches – we supported Blackburn Rovers – and sometimes he took me fishing. He was a good man . . . a hard-working man.'

For one fleeting moment, a deep sadness threatened to overwhelm him. 'I was sent home from school one day. At that time I was coming up to my GCSEs. My mother was hysterical, so Eileen next door had come in and was sitting with her. She told me that my father had been taken to hospital, that he was hurt bad after being trapped in a fire at the factory where he worked. She said another man had died.'

He paused before going on quietly, 'Two days later, my father died too.' He had not let himself think about all this in any detail for such a long time; it was painful talking about it now.

'My mother cried a lot. She didn't want me near her. It was as if she blamed me for what had happened. So Eileen took me in for a time. Her daughter, Libby was my best friend. After school, we went on long walks across the fields to Cherry Tree, where we would sit in the field and talk about things – Libby was a good listener. Sometimes if the weather was really hot, we'd paddle in the brook, and go home with wet feet.'

The thought of her made him smile. 'Libby wasn't like the other kids at school. Unlike them, she never laughed at me or called me names. But she did not like my drawings. She said they frightened her and she didn't want me to show them to her any more.'

The psychiatrist saw the smile and asked, 'You really liked Libby, didn't you?'

Jack thought about that and was surprised at his own feelings. 'Yes, I did, she was a wonderful companion. She always had time for me. Sometimes, after Eileen had gone to bed, me and Libby would sit and talk for hours when we were teenagers.'

'And how was your mother coping with the tragic loss of your father?'

Jack's mood darkened. 'She was never the same after dad died. She took on extra shifts at the hotel where she worked, and she started to go out with different men. I can understand it, now I'm older – she must have been lonely. She and I barely had a conversation. I planned to go to university and worked hard at school, but Mum didn't seem to care about my plans one way or another. She met an American bloke called John Towner or Tooner, I can't quite recall because she only said his name once, when she introduced us. I was not all that interested. Anyway, it wasn't too long before she went off with him. That was when the idea of university took a back seat, because I found myself out on the street and had to take responsibility for my own welfare.

'Were there no relatives you could go to?' asked Mr Howard.

'No. I knew I could have had a home with Eileen and Libby, or with another neighbour Thomas Farraday, but it was too close to where I used to live with my parents. Two weeks before I finished school, our house was sold and I left Blackburn for good. I couldn't get away quickly enough. I was worried though, about the future. I wasn't really sure about anything, and in the end I came away in such a hurry I left without saying goodbye to anyone. I came south, found a job and gradually made something of myself.'

He shrugged his shoulders. 'That's my life in a nutshell. Nothing special. Nothing more to tell.'

'Oh, I think there's a lot more to tell.' Alan Howard had been making notes all the time Jack was speaking. Pushing them aside, he said, 'That's plenty of background for me to be going on with.' He wondered whether maternal deprivation was behind Jack's condition. Certainly his mother's indifference to his welfare and emotional well being could have completely undermined his true state of mind. Only time and gentle questioning would reveal the truth.

'Now, I'd like to spend a few moments looking at the dreams that trouble you. Are you all right with that?'

Jack's heart began to race. 'Yes,' he said.

'I can't say how long this first session will last,' said Howard. 'It all depends on whether you want to go on, or whether I feel it's time to bring it to an end, for whatever reason.'

Jack voiced his fears: 'What if I get . . .' Reluctant to say the word, he came to a halt.

'Yes, Jack?' A quiet prompting was enough.

'What if I get . . . *trapped?*' He imagined himself alone and enclosed in that terrible place.

'I won't let you get trapped. That's why you're here – to bring you out of that prison and set you free. To understand exactly what's happening to you, because once we understand, we can deal with it, you and me – together. Now I'd like you to just relax . . . it might help to close your eyes . . .'

While Jack settled more comfortably into the chair, Alan Howard spoke softly, slowly, deliberately lulling his patient into another place; a place where he might confide his fears.

'Jack?'

'Yes?'

'Why did you seek my help?' Reaching across the desk, the psychiatrist switched on the recording machine.

Feeling safe in this man's calming presence, Jack told him, 'I have these nightmares. I've always had them. They frighten me.'

'Are the nightmares always the same?'

'Always. Sometimes in the day, I can't get them out of my head. Other times, I make myself shut them out. If I didn't, I wouldn't be able to think. I wouldn't be able to do my work.' He paused, a feeling of dread creeping over him like a dark, suffocating cloud. He continued in a low voice, 'Sometimes, I think they might drive me crazy.'

'You say you've had them for as long as you can remember?'

'Yes.'

'Can you recall exactly when they started?'

'No.'

'When you were at school, did you have them then?' He was trying to pinpoint the age at which Jack's nightmares began.

Jack's breathing quickened. He would never forget the awful times at school, when he was afraid of everything and everyone. Sometimes, when the other children were pointing at him and whispering behind his back, he hid in the toilets.

'Jack?'

Jack wasn't listening. The memories and the images were too strong. He felt himself being drawn back. There were no voices here. Only the silence, and . . . *something else*, something bad. He knew it was there, but he didn't know what it was.

'Jack, can you hear me?' Mr Howard was aware that Jack was sinking deep into the past, but that was a good thing. Glancing at Dr Lennox, who was content just to listen and learn, he gave a little nod, as though to reassure him that everything was going well.

When Lennox acknowledged this with a discreet smile, Howard returned his full attention to Jack.

'Are you ready to talk with me, Jack?'

'Yes.'

'Did you tell your teachers about the dreams?'

There was a tense moment, and then Jack's voice, firm and decisive: 'No! I never told them anything.' He remembered something, though. 'Once, when we had a drawing lesson, I made a picture of my night-mare. The teacher was angry with me. She made me stand up in class, while she showed my picture to the other children. She said my picture was nonsense, that I had not been listening to her, and that I would have to stay behind and draw another picture – one that made sense. The other children teased me about that – but not Libby. She was my friend.

'Jack?'

'Yes?'

'What else did your teacher say about the drawing?'

'She said I had bad things in my head. She tore the drawing up, and the children laughed at me.'

'So . . . the teacher asked you to draw a particular thing, and you drew your nightmare instead. Why did you do that, Jack? Were you really asking for her help, do you think?'

'I wanted her to see, that's all. But she called my mother in and made a big fuss.' As he went deeper into the past, Jack's voice became more childlike.

'In what way did she make a fuss?'

'She said the drawing was disturbing, and that I was disobedient.' He gave a knowing smile. 'I think my drawing frightened her.'

'And what did your mother say?'

'She said I ought to listen to the teacher in future, and not draw rubbish stuff.'

'Did you ever draw like that again, either at school or at home?'

'Never!'

'So, what else did your mother say . . . about the drawing you did, and why the teacher was so very angry?'

'When we got home, she kept asking me what the drawing was. When I said I didn't know, she got into a rage, yelling and screaming, demanding to know what it was that I'd drawn, why I had drawn it, and if it really was like the teacher said. She demanded to know where

I had seen such a place as the teacher described. She said I'd better get these bad things out of my head, or they might have to put me in a home.'

'Did she tell your father?'

'I think so, 'cause later on I had to see the school psychologist. But I never told him the truth.'

'Did you ever talk to anyone else about the nightmares?'

'Only Libby, just once. She said I should just forget about it, that it wasn't real.'

'Was that a hard thing to do, Jack? Keeping it to yourself?'

'Very hard, yes.'

'Tell me about Libby.'

'She lived near us on Bower Street.' Jack's face broke into a smile. 'She was very pretty, and she was good-natured. All the boys liked her but she wasn't interested in them. She preferred to hang out with me. She was a tomboy. I think that's why everyone liked her. She could play football, and run like the wind. She climbed trees and swung from the branches, like a monkey.'

He gave a small chuckle, 'Libby was fun. She made me laugh. Sometimes, she even made me forget the bad things.'

'But you never again spoke to her about the bad things?'

'She didn't want me to.'

'And you never told anyone else?'

'Never!'

'Was that because you thought they wouldn't believe you?'

'I didn't want the other kids to think I was weird.'

Mr Howard opened the top drawer of the desk, from where he collected a larger writing-pad.

'You're doing very, very well, Jack,' he said, his voice warm and encouraging. 'Now, just let yourself go back, to when you were inside the dream. My voice will go with you. I'll be with you, every step of the way . . . Now, Jack, I want you to tell me how you feel . . . what you see. Describe the scene Jack.'

Jack let the other man's voice lap over him, invasive yet hypnotic, and incredibly comforting. 'Tell me where you are back there, Jack,' the voice continued. 'When you're ready, I'll be waiting to bring you home. But first, you need to tell me *everything*.'

For a long moment the silence was palpable. There, in that dim, quiet room, nothing else existed for Jack except what was happening in his mind at that moment. He felt his arms grow heavy, sensed himself going even further back in time, before his school-days, back to the source of his fear. Yet this time, he was not so afraid. This time, he had someone with him. This time, they would see. They would know what he knew.

Still in his boyish tones, he described his surroundings. 'There's a window, high up. I can't reach.' He raised an arm to indicate the window. 'The skies are black. There's a big, golden moon, but there's no light. It just hangs there, like a shiny ball.' He caught his breath in fear. 'Oh, look! Something else is here.'

Pressing into the chair, he curled up and began to cry. 'Go away! Leave me alone!'

'Who else is there, Jack?' Mr Howard was drawing feverishly, his voice was calm, authoritative but ready to call a halt if need be.

'They're looking at me!' His voice shook with terror. *'They're looking at me!'*

Like a child in pain, he called out, over and over: '*Mummy*!' He was trapped here . . . there was no way out. '*I want my mummy*!' The eyes had seen him. They had seen him – and now his cries heightened to hysteria.

'Jack!' The voice was firmer now, insistent. 'I'm going to count from three to one, and when I reach one, you'll be back in this room with me, safe and sound. So here we go: three . . . two . . . one. Now open your eyes.'

Jack clung onto the hand that now reached out. But the shock, the fear, was like a living thing inside him.

It took a while for Jack to realise he was back. Even when he opened his eyes and saw that he was safe, the relief was not instant. He felt heavy inside, as though someone, or something, was holding him back.

'It's all right, Jack.' The same easy voice that had brought him back spoke again. 'Take another minute now, Jack. Just relax.'

The curtains were opened to let in more light, as Jack told Mr Howard about the eyes watching him. And the awful feeling that he was in danger.

The two doctors listened intently as he explained where he had been and the things he had witnessed.

'Same as always,' he told them. 'It was like before, but today I felt as if there was someone else there – someone gentle who did not wish me harm . . .' He then fell silent, and Mr Howard wisely did not press him further.

After a while, because he thought Jack had endured enough for today, Mr Howard rang his assistant for some coffee and biscuits. A few moments later, while the other two men enjoyed the refreshments, Jack himself had no appetite. All he wanted was to get as far away from there as possible.

'You did well, Jack.' His GP had been fascinated by the session, although at times he felt out of his depth.

His colleague was satisfied with the way things had progressed. 'It was an excellent beginning,' he declared, sipping his coffee.

Drained and nervous, Jack listened to what he had to say.

Mr Howard began pacing the floor. 'Fascinating!' He said it twice. 'A first session is usually a probing experiment, but this one was very graphic. Very telling.'

'In what way?' Jack was sceptical, yet in the strangest way, he believed Mr Howard understood.

'You gave an amazingly vivid indication of what you were actually feeling. Now, Jack, I'm going to ask you a very important question. Think before you answer.'

Jack was instantly afraid. 'What kind of "question"?'

'During any of your nightmares, can you ever remember calling out for your mother?'

Jack was surprised by the question. 'No, never!' He was certain of it. 'Why do you ask?'

'Because today, in the midst of describing what you saw, you became extremely distressed and you called out for your mother. You began to panic and cried out for "Mummy", just as a very young child in trouble would do. Are you sure you don't recall ever doing that before?'

Intrigued, Jack cast his mind back. 'No,' he said. 'I don't remember thinking about my mother. All I ever wanted was to be out of there.' He was struggling to understand the other man's thinking. 'What does it all mean, exactly? What are you getting at?'

'I'm not saying this *is* the case,' Howard cautioned, 'but there is a distinct possibility that this time, you regressed back to when this all began. You told me beforehand that you could not be certain when it all started, but that you had suffered the nightmares for as long as you could remember.'

The psychiatrist started to pace around the small room as he outlined his thoughts. 'It's early days yet, and we must not get ahead of ourselves. By the same token, we also need to consider every possibility if we're to help rid you of these distressing images. Now, let us suppose that a traumatic event *really did* happen to you, in your early infancy – that, as I am beginning to suspect, your nightmares are *not* a figment of the imagination, but result from an *actual experience.*'

'What?! How can that be?' Jack could not accept such a shocking idea. 'It's too awful! If something like that had actually happened to me, I would remember it, surely?'

'Not if you were a small child. Not if the shock was too traumatic for you to cope with. I understand your anxiety, Jack, and as I mentioned before, I could be wrong, so now, let's take time to clearly analyse the facts as we have them.'

Unlike Jack, he was convinced that he had hit on a shocking truth. 'Firstly, you described the images, which appear to be consistent in every case. Is that correct?'

'Yes.'

'In each and every case, you're trapped and afraid. Eyes are watching you. Someone is there – you can sense their presence. You desperately need to get out of that place, but you are physically unable to do it – am I right?'

'Yes.'

'Well, maybe the reason you can't get out is because you're too small and helpless.'

'We don't know that! I mean – I didn't *feel* like a small child.'

'But you were desperate to get out, and for some reason you couldn't. All right, let's look at it another way. Were you aware of your hands being tied? Or of being secured to anything, in any way?'

Jack had never dwelt on anything like that before, but he now concentrated his mind. 'I'm reaching up and shifting about, so no – I don't feel as though I'm restricted.' Unwillingly, he felt himself drifting back. 'But I can't get away. *I can't get out!*'

'Jack, can you give some quiet thought to what I'm saying? I believe we can assume that at least one of the reasons why you could not get yourself out of that place, was that you were a small child. Maybe you were too little to find your way back to safety. So you did the one thing you were able to do. You cried out, calling for your mummy to help you. The fact that you were able to speak suggests you were at least two years old, maybe three.'

Jack had to admit that the explanations made sense. Yet he was deeply disturbed by these new revelations. If he had been a small child at the time, what on earth was he doing in that hellish place?

There had been someone else there – he knew that now. So who was it? Did they help him? He couldn't remember. The idea that someone, for whatever reason might have taken him to such a terrifying place was too shocking.

'I don't understand!' He clambered out of the chair. 'No one would put a small child in such a position. I can't believe that!'

When his confusion threatened to erupt into anger, Mr Howard spoke calmly. 'Like I said, Jack, this is just one suggestion. Nothing can be ruled in or out at this stage. But we have to discuss every aspect as we go along. Only that way, can we uncover the truth.'

Jack took a moment to digest what had been said. 'So, what you're saying is, these nightmares could be happening for any number of reasons. The idea of me being a child in a real situation is just one possibility. On the other hand, they may simply be a figment of my imagination.'

'That's exactly right. Our understanding of dreams is very limited. They are, in the main, a condition of the subconscious. The reasons for regular nightmares such as your own are many, and what we're doing with you now is simply delving. Searching for the source of your own particular torment. Pausing, he then continued sincerely, 'Like it or not, we owe it to you to consider the possibility that your nightmare could stem from a real episode.'

Jack had a question: 'If I can remember everything else, why can't I remember calling out for my mother?'

'Mmm.' Mr Howard weighed his words carefully as he went on: 'Maybe the stronger memories, such as the images, and the terror you experienced, shut out everything else. The cry for help was as natural as the images were unnatural. All these years, you retained the memories of actual images, the physical impact on your senses, such as the darkness and the watchful eyes. These were the source of your torment. Your cry for help, however, was intuitive. You felt no need to retain it within yourself.'

'So, what happens next?' Jack felt tired. Beaten. More than that, he was afraid of the unknown. Especially now.

In truth, he was already regretting having agreed to come here, and now all he wanted was to get away and never come back.

Molly was wrong. This had not helped. All it had done was to shatter his confidence even more.

A short time later, having said his goodbyes, Jack hurried off in the direction of the car park, while

92

behind in the office, Mr Howard examined the drawings he'd made. And the more he studied that dark, intimidating place, the more he began to fear Jack's sanity.

On passing a builders' skip, Jack paused to take the new appointment card from his jacket pocket, tore it into small pieces, and threw it into the skip. 'I won't be needing *that*!' he muttered. In spite of the doctors reassurances it was impossible for him to accept even the remotest possibility that the nightmares might not be a dream after all, but based on a *real* experience.

Now, because of the confusion in his mind, and the awful implications of what the psychiatrist had said, he was deeply insecure, and his fears were tenfold.

There were so many questions. If he *had* been haunted by a real experience as a child, then where was the place he saw in his nightmares? What was he doing there and what was it that filled him with such terror? Someone else had been there, he was sure of it now. But *who* could it have been?

One thing he knew for certain. He would not rest, until he found out the truth but, he would need to do it *his* way.

Whatever the cost.

Running across the street, Jack cut along the alley and went down towards the car park. He was both excited and nervous, because at long last he had come to a decision, one which had played on his mind for some time, but which he had set aside because of Molly.

His plan now was to face his demons. He was

determined to get to the root of it all – however much he was afraid of the truth. Going to the psychiatrist had at least given him the push he needed. He was ready to go back now. As far back as the beginning.

He had to believe that the truth could never be as terrifying as the nightmares.

Molly would not like it, he knew that much. He also knew that now his mind was made up, nothing – and no one – would stop him.

CHAPTER SIX

AT EVERY OPPORTUNITY, Branagan delighted in reprimanding Jack in front of the others, and this time was no exception. 'You were meant to be back here within two hours, but it's nearly three o'clock!' he boomed, making sure the rest of the staff could hear him. 'That is *not* what was agreed. The others have been run ragged, covering for you. I've half a mind to take this out of your salary, Redmond.' Leaning forward with his hands on the desk, he glared up at Jack. 'Right then! Let's hear your explanation.'

Jack was in no mood for a fight. 'I'm sorry the others had to cover for me, Mr Branagan. But I had a doctor's appointment, as you know. The thing is, it went on longer than I anticipated.'

He was angered by the other man's threats. 'As for taking a bite out of my salary, I believe that would be unwarranted. I've never before asked for time off. I always stay on to clinch a sale . . . even if it takes me beyond my working hours – overtime, as you must

95

know, is not paid. I shall be staying late tonight to make up the time, and, as far as I'm aware, no one has ever before been made to cover for me.'

When the other man appeared taken back by his outright and honest reasoning, Jack swiftly went in with his proposition. 'You've been asking if I might be interested in taking on the new northern showroom. Well, I've been giving it some thought, and the answer is yes. If it's still available, I'll do it. Just say when and I'll be ready.' There, it was said. One way or another, with or without the job, he was on his way north.

'Good grief, man!' Stuart Branagan almost leapt over the desk. Rushing round to shake Jack by the hand, he gushed with praise. 'I've always known you were the right man for the job,' he said. 'All that about docking your salary – it was all just hot air – it's been a stressful day. I value you too much, and you know it. There's not a man here who has the experience or the number of sales under his belt that you have. Good decision, Redmond!'

Gripping Jack's hand in his meaty fist, he almost shook it off. 'Well done, that man!'

From the reception desk, Jan saw the exchange and was curious. 'Cor! Branagan looks like the cat that got the cream,' she murmured to herself. 'I bet the old bugger got Jack to accept that job up north. He's been trying to get rid of Jack from the minute he sat his fat backside in that manager's chair. I reckon he's jealous. That's because Jack's too good. Too well-liked and respected, and he's stealing that fat little toad's limelight. Hmh!' Disgruntled, she went off for an unofficial fag-break. And if Branagan came after her, she was ready for him!

Beside himself with excitement, the manager was delighted to be seeing the back of Jack, even though he was the best salesman he had ever encountered. Branagan was well aware that he himself only had this job as manager because, for whatever reason, Redmond had previously turned it down. That was a humiliating position to be in.

'Very well, Redmond, you get on with your work for now, and I'll make a few calls . . . see how the land lies. As you know, we understand the new showrooms will be up and running within the month, with the first consignment of vehicles being delivered towards the end of June. I do believe they now have a full contingency of staff, with the exception of the manager.'

He gave a little snigger. 'I think they've been waiting for you, Jack. It'll be a feather in your cap, eh? More responsibility, more money and a secure future.'

Jack thanked him, and made his excuses to leave. 'I'd best get on.'

'Yes, well, we do need to get this business signed and sealed while the iron's hot.' What he really meant was, before Jack had time to change his mind, 'So I'll call you in when I've had some feedback from Head Office. All right?'

Jack made for the door. 'Thank you, yes. I'll be about.'

As Jack closed the door behind him, Branagan

punched his fist in the air. 'YES!' Not wanting to let the grass grow under his feet, he set about making his calls. 'The sooner I've got Redmond's signature on that contract, the better!'

~

At 5.30 p.m., half an hour before closing time, Jan told Jack, 'The boss wants to see you in his office, after the others have left.' She had already guessed what was going on. 'I'm thinking he's talked you into accepting that post up north. Would I be right, Jack? Have you gone and said yes?'

When Jack gave a nod, she groaned. 'I knew it! I knew he'd wear you down eventually. Don't go, Jack! Don't let him win. You know he's been determined to get you as far away from here as possible, because you were offered the manager's job here before him and you turned it down. Your presence here is a constant threat to him. Please, Jack! You won't be happy, away from everything familiar.'

Jack sighed. 'You're right, I *will* miss everything familiar,' he smiled at her, 'especially you and your weak tea and cheeky comments. I'll miss all of you, but my decision has nothing to do with *him*. It's what *I* want.' His thoughts turned inward. 'It's something I have to do. Something I should have done years ago.'

Disheartened, she went to get her jacket and handbag, ready to go home. 'We'll all miss you, I know that.' It wouldn't be the same here without him. Somewhere

98

in the back of her mind, and despite the presence of Molly in his life, Jan had deluded herself that one day, she would persuade Jack to take her out, and he might even grow to love her. But that would never happen now. Tomorrow, she decided, she would switch her attention to Bill West, the new young recruit. 'He's a bit wet behind the ears,' she muttered into her compact, while painting her lips bright pink, 'but he'll mature, and when he does, I'll be there to teach him a thing or two.' The naughty thoughts cheered her up no end.

~

When the others were making their way out, Jack went into the main office, as requested. 'Good man, Jack! Sit yourself down,' said Branagan. He could hardly hide his delight at the thought of Jack being sent 200 miles away.

Reaching across the desk, he grabbed a document. 'Technology, eh?' His smile was luminous, 'The contract was emailed through a few minutes ago. I've been advised to ask that you take it home and read it inside out and upside down. So, here it is, Jack.'

Branagan handed the document to him. 'Look through it and make notes on anything that catches your attention and that you might want to talk about. Tomorrow Curtis Warren himself is travelling up from London. He wants to have a meeting with you.'

In theory, Curtis Warren, the company's big boss, had already given his approval of Jack, whose reputation went before him, as an accomplished and trusted employee, having been awarded 'Employee of the Year' status, two years running.

Jack was not surprised to be told of the big chief's arrival. He had worked with the man some years back, and knew how thorough he was. He told Branagan, 'I'll have my queries ready for the morning – if there are any.'

'There are bound to be niggles,' the other man said. 'But I'm sure you won't let a few lines on a page stop you from grabbing the best opportunity you're ever likely to get.'

Annoyed by the other man's arrogance, Jack replied coldly, 'I don't accept that this is "the best opportunity I'm ever likely to get", but you can rest assured I'll read every word and make notes as warranted. I won't deny, I would like this position. But when all is said and done, I mustn't be too hasty. I mean, I'd be a fool to jump out of the frying-pan into the fire, don't you think?'

His mind was already made up, but he didn't want to give the other man the idea that it was all a done deal. He wanted him to sweat on it until the morning. He wanted him to believe that he could take the job or leave it – that he wasn't all that bothered either way.

A few moments later Jack left the building, the contract secure in his grasp, while Branagan remained, pacing his office in a fret, saying, 'Arrogant bastard! One way or another, I'll be rid of you, Jack Redmond! You see if I don't!'

He had no way of knowing that Jack was as determined to sign the contract as he was determined to be rid of him.

~

That evening, when Jack dropped the bombshell of his plans to move north, Molly was quick to show her disapproval. 'If you do this, you do it on your own!' she raged. 'I want no part in it.'

Devastated that he had not thought to discuss such an important matter with her before making his decision, she told him, 'If you want my opinion – which you obviously don't – I believe you're making a big mistake. But it doesn't matter to you what *I* think, does it? I thought we were a couple, that we talked things over together. And what about the session at the clinic? I don't suppose you even went, did you?' Her voice shook with anger.

'Yes, I did go to the clinic. In fact, it was because of what happened there that I know now I have to go back – back to the beginning, where I grew up.'

'That's nonsense!' she burst out. 'What will you be going back to? You're not thinking straight, Jack. You've been gone from your hometown for too many years. What makes you think there's anything there that can possibly explain what's happening to you now? Oh, I get it! *That's* why you've accepted the manager's post up there. You tied the two together and came up with an answer to all your troubles. You've made what could

101

be the biggest decision of your life, without even bothering to consult me. That tells me I'm not important enough in your life. That's right, isn't it, Jack?'

'No!' Going across the room to her, he pleaded with her to calm down and listen to what he had to say. 'Please, Molly. Come and sit down. I'll tell you what happened at the clinic.' Taking her by the hand, he led her to the sofa, where he sat her down beside him. 'Like I said, I did go to the clinic.'

'And?'

'And it was a long session. Mr Howard asked me a lot of questions. I told him about the images – how they made me feel . . . everything.'

Molly softened a little. 'That was good. So, what did he say? Did he have any advice? When is your next appointment? You *are* going back to see him again, aren't you?'

Avoiding her questions, Jack went on, 'After a while, he asked me to close my eyes, and suddenly I was back there . . . in that place – only this time it was more vivid than before. Everything was so powerful, Molly.' Reliving the ordeal in his mind, he inwardly shivered. 'I could hardly breathe.'

Before she could start on her questions again, he went on quickly, 'Afterwards, he said the descriptions I gave were very strong. He said I had done something which he claimed was very significant. When he told me about it, I was shocked.'

'What do you mean?'

'He said . . . I cried out.'

102

'But we already know that.' Molly had lost count of the times she had been shocked awake by his cries.

'Molly, I'm going to ask you something, and I want you to think very hard before you answer.'

Her curiosity was heightened. 'Go on, then.'

'You've been with me for over a year now. You know more about my dreams than anyone else. So, was there ever a time when you heard me call out for my mother?'

Molly shook her head. 'I don't think I've ever heard you cry out for *anyone* – certainly not your mother. So, is that what you did? How strange. What did he make of that?'

'He said it was significant, that we'd made some kind of breakthrough,' Jack explained. 'Now, it's changed everything. I'm finding it even harder to cope with. It was the way I called out for her, like a small child.' He mimicked the cry that Mr Howard had portrayed. 'He said it was the voice of a child, not much older than two or three years of age.'

'But, what were his conclusions about the night-mares?' Molly digressed. 'Did he know why they were happening – and does he think he can help you?'

Jack remembered the psychiatrist's cautious approach. 'He said he couldn't be certain what the cause was at this stage, but that we needed more sessions before we could root out the truth. He said we would have to be patient.' Something made him hesitate from divulging too much of what Mr Howard had said. 'He warned that different possibilities will come up – some right, some wrong – and that we have to deal with them as they occur. He said it would take time.'

'And that's *it*?!' Molly was not satisfied. 'So far, then, he has no real answers?'

'Like I said, it's bound to take time.'

From the tone of his voice and the way he was hesitating, Molly knew there was more. 'You're not telling me everything, are you?' she accused.

Jack paused. He was reluctant to reveal how his dreams could be rooted in reality.

'So, are you still planning on moving up north?'

'With you, yes, I hope so.'

'I've already said – if you go, you go on your own. Why should I leave everything behind – my job at Banbury's, my family and my house – which in case you've forgotten, my brother is renting at the moment? I expect you want me to sell that too, don't you?'

'That would be entirely up to you.' He had never interfered in Molly's private arrangements. 'I'll probably sell this house and buy a home for us up in Lancashire. It makes sense.'

Molly didn't agree. 'Look at it from my point of view, Jack! It all seems a bit rushed, don't you think? This morning there was no mention of any of this, and now suddenly you're in a tearing hurry to up sticks and turn our lives upside down. What's happened, Jack? Why is it so urgent that you move away?' She grew increasingly impatient, 'You *are* holding something back, I know it!'

~

Jack held his silence, unsure whether to confide in her. He didn't know if it would change her mind about moving away, or if it would make her dig her heels in even more.

Reluctantly, Jack told her how the psychiatrist had suggested that his dreams might not be the product of a fertile imagination, but could be based on a traumatic event that took place in his early childhood. Even as he said it, Jack felt a shiver run down his back.

'Oh, I see.' Molly was ready for an argument. 'That's why you want to go back up there – to delve into the past and torment yourself even more.' She could see how determined he was. 'You're not thinking straight, Jack.' When she flounced off to the kitchen to put the kettle on, he followed her.

'Oh, but I am! And I've got you to thank for that. You did right in making me see someone, because now I know what I must do.' Putting his hands on her shoulders, Jack turned Molly to face him. 'For the first time, I have something to go on. I need answers, and now I'm hopeful that maybe – just maybe – I'll find out the truth.'

On the way home from work, Jack had thought long and hard about the series of events that had led him to these crossroads. Sharing his deeper thoughts with her, he said, 'Don't you think it's strange, of all the places in the country where we could be opening a new showroom, the company chose to build it in Lytham St Anne's, just a thirty-minute drive from the street where I grew up?'

Molly did not believe in fate; she preferred to think there was a rational explanation for everything. 'There's nothing "strange" about it, Jack.' She gave a mocking little laugh. 'It's quite simple. The company chose to build the new showrooms in Lytham because they did their homework and decided a car-showroom was needed there. It's business, Jack – plain and straight. It's not some kind of celestial plan that's meant to get you promoted and send you back to where you were born so you can find out if your nightmares are real.'

Jack was not altogether surprised by her cynicism. 'So, why have you been asked to run the new showrooms, when there are any number of other people at Curtis Warren's who are more than able to handle the responsibility?'

Agitated, Molly began pacing the floor. 'It's all academic anyway, because you're not accepting the post. Or if you do, I won't be going with you.'

'You can't mean that, Molly?'

'Yes, Jack, I can, and do! And I want an answer right now.' She swung round to face him. 'Have you already signed the contract?'

'Not yet, no. I'll be handing it in tomorrow, signed and sealed, subject to Curtis Warren's approval.'

'Without even asking me?'

'I'm asking you now, Molly. I want you with me.'

'I take it this means you won't be attending the clinic again?'

'There's no need. I know now what I have to do.'

'Will anything I say make you change your mind?'

'Please, Molly.' Jack put his two arms about her. 'Don't do this.' Drawing her close, he spoke softly. 'We belong together, you and me. I don't want to be without you. I want us to be married – to have children one day.' He gave a nervous chuckle. 'I want us to grow old together – you with your silver hair and me with my white beard and walking-stick. When we meander down the street, people will say, "Look! That's the old couple with all them grandchildren."'

Molly couldn't help but laugh. 'You're crazy, you are.'

'You're right. I am – crazy for you.'

'Then tell them you don't want the job. Stay here, Jack. Attend the clinic. There's no need to go chasing the past. Eventually it will all come right, you'll see.'

Frustrated, Jack held her at arm's length, 'Do you love me, Molly?'

'You know I do.'

'Then why can't you help me do this?'

'Because it's wrong!' Angry at his dogged determination, she broke away from him. 'We're happy here, aren't we?'

'Well, yes, but we can be happy elsewhere just as well.'

Ignoring his comment, she pointed out, 'Look, we have each other and we have our work. We've built a good life here together, and we've got plans. Why spoil it all now? Especially when you've finally found someone who can help you.'

Torn two ways, Jack paced back and forth across the kitchen, hands in his trouser pockets, and a look of desperation about him. Everything seemed to be falling apart between them, and he had to believe it was his fault.

'Won't you at least try to see it from my point of view, Molly?' he asked. 'You of all people know what it's like with me. These nightmares are ruining my life – spoiling what we have! I need to clear my head, and I can't do that unless I go back – to where it all began.'

He turned his back to her, his mind racing. 'If I don't try to find answers, Molly, I'll never rest. I'll never know! This is my chance and, more than anything, I want you there with me.'

The sound of footsteps made him swing round, only to find that Molly had gone.

'Molly?'

Calling her name, he ran up the stairs two at a time, to find her in the bedroom, packing her suitcase. 'Don't do this!' Jack was devastated. 'Stay tonight at least. We can talk it through.'

Molly turned to him, her voice calm and cold. 'If I do stay, will you change your mind about leaving here?'

For one desperate moment, Jack would have promised her the world if need be, just to keep her there. In his deepest heart though, he could not lie to her.

'I'm sorry, Molly. I love you so much, and don't want to lose you, but this is one time I need to do what my instincts tell me. So no, I won't – I *can't* – change my mind.'

'And I can't uproot myself just because you've got

this crazy idea in your head. Tell them you don't want the promotion. Go back to the clinic. In the end, it *will* work out. I know it will.'

Falling silent, Jack cast his gaze to the floor, and she knew she had lost. 'All right, then. Do what you want. That's fine by me!' Slamming shut the suitcase, she swung it off the bed, pushed by him and ran down the stairs. At the bottom, she turned and looked up at him. She saw a man determined. A man who refused to give in to her. And what she saw, she did not like.

Without another word, she stormed out of the house, down the path and, throwing the suitcase into the boot of her car, she climbed into the driving seat, and slammed shut the door. Taking her frustration out, she switched on the engine, thrust home the gearstick and, putting her foot down hard, shot away without a backward glance, even though she knew Jack would be watching her every move.

~

From the upstairs window, Jack followed her movements. He knew from past experience that it was no good arguing with her. Yet long after she was out of sight, he remained at the window, hoping that he would eventually see the nose of the car peep round the corner on its way back. Then after a while, he realised that Molly was not coming back, and he was shattered.

Later, feeling tired and emotionally drained, he climbed into bed for an early night. He didn't sleep, however; he simply catnapped, his mind alive with thoughts of Molly. It was not often that he went against her wishes. Should he have let her persuade him to abandon the idea of going north?

When the doubts began to set in, he angrily chided himself, 'You *are* doing the right thing, Jack!'

Unable to settle, he went downstairs and made himself a mug of tea. For a while he examined his actions from Molly's point of view. His emotions were mixed. He wanted her back, and most times he would do anything to settle an argument – but not this time. With or without her, he meant to go ahead with his plans. If he was proved wrong and there *were* no answers, would he be any worse off than he was now? Maybe not – except for losing Molly, and that was hard.

Jack was aware that he had set himself on a lonely path. After all, changing his workplace, moving to the other end of the country, risking a permanent break between himself and Molly – these were huge decisions.

Doubts began to niggle. 'Am I setting myself up for a fall?' he asked himself. 'Can Molly see something that I can't? When all's said and done, I don't really know where I'm actually headed, and when I start overturning stones, who knows what I might find – if anything?'

Once he had burned his bridges, there might be no

way back. It was a frightening thought. Yet even with all the doubts, he knew in his heart that he had no choice, but to try.

For as long as he could remember, he had suffered disturbed nights, his sleep constantly haunted by these terrifying images. For the first time ever, an opportunity had presented itself to free himself of his demons. Nothing was certain; nothing was guaranteed. But the opportunity was in place. If he turned his back on it now, he would regret it for ever.

Jack tied his dressing-gown tighter around him. Looking up at the wall-clock, he realised it was midnight. 'Midnight is a lonely place,' he murmured. Memories of the past stalked his mind. Vague memories – some good, some not so good.

After his father died from injuries suffered in that fire, his mother had changed. Claire Redmond began to drink, to yell and scream at every little upset. Jack became the butt of her ill temper. There were cruel rumours about her going with men. She was even called a slut. For Jack, this was a lonely time. Yet he understood, even as a schoolboy, that she was suffering, that her husband was lost to her. Along with the security she had enjoyed.

Like his mother, Jack felt the pain of his father's passing. Yet while he tried every which way to help his bereaved mother, she was not there for him when he needed her most.

He had long forgiven her for that, but he had felt lost. Just a boy. In a way, while his mother had lost her man, Jack had lost *both* his parents. His pain was almost unbearable.

Later, when his mother, Claire met the wealthy American she gave no thought to her son, but simply walked away from Jack and her old life in Bower Street, without a backward glance. Her new man, John Towner only met Jack once, and did not invite him to join his own children in Minnesota. Jack was eighteen, alone and afraid. Left behind, to pick up the pieces.

When he left Blackburn, he had no idea where he might go. All he knew was that he had to get away, because there was nothing left for him there.

Thrust into a big wide world, he learned the hard way – to make his own decisions and do what he believed to be the right thing. Just like now; when his every instinct told him to go back, to where it all began.

Some instinct made him think of Libby, and a warm feeling crept through his troubled soul. She had been his friend next door, his friend at school, and his confidante through the bad times. He wondered if she was still there; in the street where they grew up. Still a tomboy, with her mop of autumn-coloured curls. Was she married, with children? Or maybe she had fulfilled their shared dream, of travelling the world, to search for adventures that could not be found in homely little Bower Street?

'My friend, Libby.' Even now, the very thought of her brought a sense of comfort. And he remembered her mother – dearest, kindest Eileen.

There was Thomas too. He was ever the good

neighbour. These kindly, honest people paraded through his mind and lifted his heart, despite his sense of guilt at having left them behind without a word.

The more he thought about moving back, the more he felt he was making the right decision. And even though Bower Street held some bad memories, he found himself looking forward to visiting his hometown. He hoped it was not too much changed.

CHAPTER SEVEN

MOLLY HAD INTENDED to drive straight to her parents' house in Bedford, some ten miles away from Leighton Buzzard, but five minutes from the motorway bridge, she changed her mind. Still bristling from the heated row with Jack, she knew her parents would quiz her, and she wasn't in the mood to be nagged at just then.

She thought of her brother. At least Brian wouldn't nag her – although she knew he wouldn't be too pleased about her turning up on his doorstep like this.

Turning right, she slipped through Husborne Crawley and made her way to Ridgmont, where her own house was now rented by her brother Brian, in order to pay the mortgage while she lived with Jack.

Tears clouded her eyes as she reflected on her heated discussion with Jack. She even pulled over to the side of the road and considered going back to make it up with him. But then she thought it might be best to let him stew for a while.

'Stubborn devil, Jack Redmond, that's what you are!' Angry now, she wiped away the tears, plucked a tissue out of her bag and blew her nose. 'Damned stubborn!'

Slipping the engine into gear, she set off again. 'My Brian will understand.' Though she wasn't even sure about that, 'Men! What do they know!'

Travelling along the main road, she passed the church and drove to a house on the right – a cottage with flower-baskets hanging from the wall, and a well-tended, pretty garden behind. 'Brian had better not lecture me!' Molly declared aloud. 'I'm not in the mood for another fight!' Her hackles were up already.

Parking the car behind her brother's, she recognised a third car as belonging to her brother's friend and workmate, Mal. She was disappointed because she needed to unburden her troubles onto her brother, who at times was the only one who understood her. 'I expect they're talking about work,' she thought. 'So with a bit of luck, Mal won't be here too long.'

It wasn't that she didn't like Mal, because she did. He was a good bloke, and a good friend to Brian. In fact, he was a good friend to all the family. She and Mal had even been sweethearts at one point, and after breaking up they had remained firm friends.

Wheeling her suitcase along the path, she rat-tatted on the front door. 'Brian! It's me – open the door!'

There was silence, then the sound of running steps, and the door was flung open to reveal a lean young man with an unruly mop of fair hair. Dressed in black Levis and a check shirt, he looked somewhat flustered.

'Hi, Mal!' Molly greeted him with a big smile. 'You took your time getting to the door, didn't you?'

On seeing it was Molly, his face broke into a wide grin. Darting forward, he took her in his arms and almost squeezed the life out of her. 'My favourite girl! Where've you been all my life?'

Giggling like a schoolgirl, Molly pushed him away. 'Back off, Mal!' She was used to his flirting. 'It's only been a few weeks, but anybody would think you hadn't seen me for years.'

'Even a few *days* without seeing you is too long,' he teased.

Molly rolled her eyes. 'So where's my baby brother?'

'Browsing over a hot construction plan. Come to chuck him out, have you?'

Molly laughed. 'It's *you* I'll be chucking out if you don't behave yourself.'

'Oh, don't be like that. Especially when I've been dreaming about you every night.'

'I'm warning you, Mal. I'm not in the mood for games.'

'I'm not playing games. I mean every word.'

'If you don't get out of the way, I might just accidentally drop this suitcase on your toes.'

'Oh well, if you're in *that* kind of mood . . .' Turning towards the sitting-room door, he yelled at the top of his voice: *'Brian! It's your long-lost sister . . . come to throw you out for not paying the rent!'* Grabbing Molly's case, he led her down the passage and into the sitting-room, where Brian was already scrambling out of the armchair.

Molly's brother was shorter than the other young man, with long dark hair tied back to the nape of his neck.

'Molly!' Grabbing off his rimless spectacles, Brian laid them on the table, on top of what looked to Molly like an unfolded plan of sorts. 'What brings *you* here?' He gave her a bear-hug.

'Well, that's charming, I must say!' Molly chided him. 'Here I am, come to see you, and that's the kind of greeting I get.'

'She's brought her case,' said Mal. 'Looks to me like she means to stay. It's your own fault, matey. I expect you've been skipping the rent again, spending it down the pub.'

'Don't be daft.' Though Brian looked worried all the same. 'I pay my rent by standing order and, as far as I know, I haven't missed a payment – well, not for a while, anyway.'

'Don't take any notice of Mal,' Molly reassured him. 'You know what he's like.' Then she asked pointedly, 'Are you going to offer me a drink, or what?'

Sensing that Molly needed to talk with her brother, Mal leapt in with the offer, 'Coffee, tea – or something stronger?'

Brian had a better idea. Folding up the plan, he said, 'Look, why don't we give this a break and pop across to the pub for an hour? We could get a snack. And

Molly can tell me why she's turned up with a suitcase in one hand and a face that would turn milk sour.'

He could see by her subdued manner that she'd had some kind of upset, which he deduced as being a row with the ever-patient Jack. Brian knew his beloved sister had strong opinions, and right or wrong, she was a woman who liked to get her own way. Normally, Jack took it all in his stride, but Brian suspected that this time, the big guy must have refused to be pushed around.

'You and Jack have had a falling-out, and you want to stay here for a while,' he speculated. 'Am I right?'

'Well . . . yes. But only for a day or so, until Jack sees sense,' Molly answered.

'So this time Jack stood up to you. Good for him!'

'Whose side are you on?' Molly could do without his comments. 'Look, am I welcome here or not? If not, I'll leave you to your building plans and go to Mum and Dad's.'

'It's your house,' said Brian, 'so of course you can stay here!' He gave her a cheeky wink. 'But only if you make breakfast.'

'In your dreams!' she said, laughing. Her spirits were always lifted when she was with her brother. 'I'll throw you out on your ear if you mess with me.'

'She will too!' Mal chipped in. 'She's a strong woman, your sister. We belong together, me and her. But will she listen? No, she won't.' He grinned. 'She does fancy me, though – I've always known it.'

Everyone laughed at that. But Mal meant every word.

He really did love Molly. She only had to say the word and he'd marry her tomorrow.

When Molly was about to retaliate, Mal teased her, 'No! You can't deny it. You've left Jack to be with me – that's the truth, isn't it?'

'As if!' joked Molly. Although she would never admit it, she was fond of him really.

Mal was also staying the night, but happily agreed to sleep on the living-room couch. 'Anything for you, my beauty,' he said, giving Molly a knowing wink.

Molly ignored his teasing and went about her business. It took her just a few minutes to unpack the necessary items from her suitcase – pyjamas, toothbrush, toiletries, and a complete change of clothes for the morning.

She switched on her mobile and tucked it into her jeans' pocket in case Jack thought to call her.

She half-regretted running out on him, but he just wasn't giving her a fair say. He was determined to change his entire life, just so he could go chasing ghosts from the past. It was a recipe for disaster. Why did he have to be so damned stubborn?!

She put most of the blame on that psychiatrist, for planting the idea in his head that the nightmare was not part of his imagination, but something more sinister.

Taking the last garment out of the case, Molly threw it onto the bed, wishing she'd never persuaded Jack to see that bloody shrink! Look what it had led to!

She felt wronged. 'What the hell is he thinking? All

he has to do is stay put and attend the clinic. But no – he wants to dump me, after all I've done for him!' Though if she had stopped to think about it, she'd have realised what she'd actually done for him didn't really amount to much.

Sliding her pyjamas into the drawer, she then slammed it shut. She didn't intend staying here long. Just long enough for Jack to come to his senses. Turning to the mirror, she smiled at her reflection. 'It'll be all right,' she told herself. 'Jack will give in. He'll see it my way.'

In the past, he always had.

~

Later, the trio walked across the street and along the path to the pub.

'What are you two working on?' Molly asked. She now felt more relaxed, though her mind continually went back to Jack.

'We've bought a derelict barn,' Brian replied. 'Mal caught sight of it on his way back from a costing job, the other side of Leighton Buzzard.'

Mal took up the story: 'You could hardly see it through the trees. It sits in a beautiful setting, though. Well away from the main road.'

'It's an investment,' Brian explained. 'Ripe for development.'

On entering the pub, he gestured to the far corner. 'Right, you two – sit yourselves down. I'll get the drinks.'

Mal led Molly to a table in the corner by the window. 'This is the best spot,' he said, pointing to the garden. 'Some of the flowers are just beginning to blossom.'

Molly looked out the window. 'Oh, it's really lovely!' The fence was dressed with wicker hanging-baskets, dripping with colour. The border around the lawn was alive with masses of dahlia blooms.

Molly was on edge because Jack hadn't even rung her mobile to see if she was all right. She was tempted to ring him, but he would need to make the first move, because she had no intention of going along with his radical plans.

Brian was soon back with the drinks, which he placed on the table. 'A pint of the best for Mal, and a light shandy for you.' He pushed the glass of shandy in front of her. 'When you've had that, I'll get you another, and another, and when your tongue loosens, you might tell me what's been going on.'

When Molly merely shrugged, Mal decided to change the subject and told her more about the barn. 'It's smack bang in the middle of a field. The bank is sloping, and when you follow it down, you come to this brook. Oh, I don't mind telling you, Moll, the location is as pretty as a picture – just like you.' He leaned forward and lowered his voice: 'It's the perfect place for you and me on a lazy day – and maybe a dozen of our offspring playing round our feet.'

Molly laughed out loud. 'That'll be the day – I don't think!'

'You're a cruel girl, Molly Davis. In fact, I don't think you even deserve my affection.'

'That's all right,' she quipped, 'because I don't want it. Well, not in the way *you* mean.'

Collecting the menus from the bar, Brian threw them down on the table, 'We've got to be quick. They're closing the kitchen soon. Fish and chips, that'll do me!'

'Me too!' That was Mal's favourite meal.

Having lost her appetite since the upset with Jack, Molly chose a baked potato with salad.

Mal was open-mouthed. 'That's not even enough to keep a sparrow alive!'

'Well, it's enough for me.' Molly closed her menu.

A short time later, when the food was before them, Molly opened the conversation: 'About this barn . . . have you already bought it?'

Mal swallowed a chip. 'Lock, stock and barrel.'

She asked her brother, 'So, did you get it for a good price?'

Brian nodded. 'Not bad, but it wasn't dirt cheap either. It's virtually derelict, so it needs a lot doing. And, as we're naturally looking for a profit, we're having to count our pennies.'

Molly thought the setting of the barn sounded lovely. 'What are your ideas for it – I mean, in terms of size and that?' Never having had much interest in broken-down buildings, she had no idea of what it might entail, but she hoped to stop Brian fishing for an explanation as to why she was there. Unfortunately, her little ploy didn't work, because it wasn't long before the conversation shifted to Jack.

'So what's been happening between you two?' Brian asked as he put his empty glass on the table. 'If you don't mind me asking.'

'Well, I do mind.'

'Oh, well, please yourself.' Brian knew she would have to talk about it at some point. She would seek his sympathy, and she would want him to side with her. That was Molly's way.

For a moment the mood was quiet, but then Mal chirped up, 'When we've finished our meal, why don't we take home a bottle of plonk, and finish the evening in the privacy of your front room?' His question was directed at Molly.

'What, so the pair of you can pry into my affairs?' She took a long swig of her shandy. Then another, and afterwards she sat back in her chair. 'I might tell you – but only when I'm good and ready.'

After two more shandies, she suddenly burst out crying. 'He won't listen to me. He's got these ideas in his head and he just won't listen!'

Realising she had drunk too much, Brian knew it was time to leave. 'Come on, Sis.' Sliding an arm under hers, he gently raised her out of the chair. 'Time to go.'

Molly didn't argue. She was tired and emotionally drained.

Back at the house, Molly fell asleep in the chair, while the two men took another look at the plans for the barn.

Later, she woke to find that the day was beginning to fade and the night was already creeping across the skies. 'Why didn't you wake me?' She was none too pleased.

She considered calling her parents to see if Jack had tried to contact her there, but she wisely dismissed that idea.

'I thought it best to let you sleep it off.' Brian apologised, 'Me and Mal got lost in the smaller details.' He gestured to where the plan was laid out on the table.

Irritated, Molly made for the kitchen. 'I don't suppose Jack phoned while I was asleep?'

Brian didn't even look up. 'Nope.'

'Hmm!' She didn't know whether to be upset or relieved. 'Do you two want tea, or coffee?' She poked her head round the door.

Studying the merits of a tricky decision, both men declined the offer. 'Give it ten minutes and I might just take you up on it.'

'Please yourselves!' After preparing herself a chocolate drink, Molly took it outside to the garden, where she sat on the swing-seat and lost herself in misery.

Brian soon appeared. 'I'm done in,' he said. 'I'm off to my bed.' Thinking it might be best to leave her to her thoughts, he kissed her good night, and strode off towards the house.

A few minutes later Mal emerged, carrying a mug of coffee. 'OK if I sit down beside you?' he asked nervously, recalling her mood earlier.

Molly shrugged her shoulders. 'If you want.'

He sat beside her, gently sending the swing into an easy motion. For a time, they both sat there, with Molly deep in thought, hardly aware of Mal sitting beside her.

Mal, on the other hand, was very much aware of her closeness. But he kept his silence, and swung very gently back and forth, comfortable with himself. After a while they made their way indoors.

Mal seated himself at the kitchen table and was the first to speak. 'What's wrong, Molly?' he asked tenderly. When she made no reply, he went on, 'You can talk to me. I'm not a telltale. I won't repeat anything you say. You know that, don't you?'

'I suppose.' Her voice was dreary as she checked her mobile phone for messages. Nothing!

He gave a nervous little chuckle. 'I'm not really the idiot I seem to be at times. It's just that, well, sometimes when I'm caught up in certain situations – like when you're around – it's easier to play the fool than to let people know what I'm really feeling.' He dared to let his guard done. 'You know how I feel about you, don't you, Molly?'

She turned to look at him. 'I'm sorry, Mal, but what we had is long over. You have to accept that.'

There was a short, difficult silence, before Mal asked, 'Do you really not have any feelings at all for me? Not even the tiniest little drop?' He made a pinch with his fingers.

'No. I've already told you. You and me, we've been over a long time now.'

'For you, maybe. Not for me.' God! Why did he say that?

Molly inched away. 'Stop it! Please, Mal.'

'I will . . . if you give me an answer.'

'What kind of answer?'

'Why are you here?' he asked outright.

'Not for you, that's for sure. Sorry, Mal, but it's Jack I love.'

'Is it over – with you and him?'

'No.' In fact, she wasn't sure. She wanted to go back and make it up with him, but her pride was getting in the way. It would mean giving in to him, even when he had no respect for her opinions. What basis was that for a long-term relationship?

Jack was wrong. If he did what he said and left his life here, he would be leaving her too, but that didn't seem to matter to him! She still loved him, but what should she do? She didn't want to lose him.

Suddenly she was crying. Softly at first, and then uncontrollably.

'Ssh, Molly, please don't cry.' Mal's tender voice soothed her. 'Whatever it is that's upset you, I'm sure it can be put right. There's always a way.'

'Not this time.' Deep down, she knew that.

It hurt Mal to see her like this. Sliding his arm about her shoulders, he drew her close, surprised and delighted when she didn't pull away but relaxed into him. 'Jack doesn't want me any more,' she whispered brokenly. 'I don't know what to do.'

Putting his own feelings aside, Mal reassured her,

'I'm sure he does want you.' His lips caressed her hair. 'He'd be crazy not to.'

It took a moment before Molly answered thoughtfully, 'He's changed.'

'In what way?'

'I don't know him any more,' she sobbed. 'I don't even know if we've really broken up. I don't know what he's thinking any more. We had a big argument and I walked out on him.'

'Oh, I see.' Mal was lost. He couldn't believe he was actually holding her in his arms. He wanted to kiss her. To tell her how much he needed her. How desperately he wanted to take care of her.

Suddenly Molly rounded on him. 'No, Mal! You *don't* see! You don't know anything about it. How can you?'

Mal took a deep breath, 'You're right. I'm sorry.' He'd forgotten how quickly her mood could turn.

Slightly repentant, Molly explained about how she and Jack had rowed because he was planning to move away. They'd offered him a manager's post at the company's new showrooms in Lytham St Anne's, and because it was near where he grew up, Jack wanted to go there. He decided it all, without even discussing it with me. I thought we were partners.'

'But, it's not so bad, is it – getting promoted and sent to pastures new?' Mal pointed out. 'Some people would find that exciting. Or don't you want to go with him – is that it?'

'Maybe I do, maybe I don't, but it's not that simple.'

She found it comforting, talking to Mal. He didn't answer back, and he didn't put her down. He listened, and right now, that was all she needed.

After a while, tearful and angry, she scrambled off the seat and ran away, towards the house. Nervously, Mal followed her. On opening the kitchen door, he could hear her softly crying. He found her in the sitting-room. She was on the floor in front of the fire, hugging her knees and crying bitterly, unaware of his presence.

'Hey . . . don't go upsetting yourself like that,' he said. Kneeling, he reached out and pressed her into his arms.

'It hurts me to see you so upset, Molly.' Deeply moved, he leaned his face against hers, tenderly stroking her hair and murmuring reassurance. Easing him away, she looked at him, her curious, intense gaze affecting him deeply. 'I won't let anyone hurt you,' he whispered. 'I love you, Molly. I always have, ever since we were kids . . .'

Molly was deeply touched by his loyalty and friendship. Unlike Jack, he had always put her first. Smiling through her tears, she kept her gaze on his face. He dared to read the signs, and slowly, half-afraid she would turn away, he kissed her on the mouth.

In that very private moment, it felt right between them. Even though Jack lingered in her mind, Molly felt safe with Mal. She felt as if she didn't know Jack any more. Mal, on the other hand, was like an open book. She knew him. She knew how kind he was, and how much he truly loved her. He would never clear off to the other end of the country, and leave her behind.

When she now felt two strong arms gently laying her down, she made no protest. Even when his kisses grew demanding and passionate, she didn't mind. She needed someone to hold her. Someone who cherished her, above all else.

She gave herself to Mal, freely and willingly. There were no regrets; at least not for now. Not in the heat of the moment.

Later, though, there might well be a price to pay.

CHAPTER EIGHT

Aᶠᵗᵉʳ ᴀ ʀᴇꜱᴛʟᴇꜱꜱ night, Jack clambered out of bed. He showered, shaved and dressed, and with Molly strong in his mind, he ran downstairs and looked up the phone number of Molly's parents.

Twice he dialled the number, and twice he replaced the receiver before the number rang out. 'Come on, Jack!' he chided himself. 'You need to sort things out with Molly.' He had to make her understand how much going north meant to him.

He took a moment to make a cup of coffee and to feed two slices of bread into the toaster. When the bread popped up, he threw it onto a plate and smothered it in full-fat butter – a long-held weakness of his. He then took time to enjoy his breakfast, while thinking what to do about Molly.

Fortified by his toast and a second cup of coffee, he picked up the receiver and tapped out the number once more. This time he let it ring until someone answered.

'Hello?' He recognised the voice at the other end.

It was Pauleen, Molly's mother. A staff-nurse at the local cottage hospital, she was a busy, amiable person – sometimes overwhelming, but in a nice way.

'Hello, Pauleen. It's me – Jack.'

'Oh, hello, Jack. Everything all right is it?'

Not knowing how much Molly might have told her, Jack played it safe. 'Yes, everything's fine, thank you. But I wonder if you could please put Molly on the phone. I'm off to work in a minute and need to arrange for us to meet up at lunch-time.'

There was a pause, during which Jack heard her answering someone. 'No, dear. You go ahead. I'll just be a minute.' Returning to her conversation with Jack, she told him, 'I'm sorry, Jack, but what makes you think Molly might be here?'

'Are you saying she's not?'

'That's exactly what I'm saying, dear.' She was beginning to get worried. 'What's happened? Have you had an argument and she's run off? I know how impetuous she can be. Don't worry, she'll be back with her tail between her legs.' She gave a loud tut. 'I have no idea why she would tell you she was coming to us.'

Having heard her quiet remark to a third person, whom he assumed to be Molly, Jack simply asked, 'Will you do something for me, Pauleen?'

'You know I will, if I can.'

'Thanks. Look, I'll be at the coffee shop in Bletchley around one o'clock. Molly knows the one. If she *does* turn up at your place, will you please tell her I'll be there for about half an hour?'

'Yes, of course I will.'

'Thank you, Pauleen. I appreciate that.'

Replacing the receiver, and convinced that Molly had been standing right beside her mother, listening to every word, Jack felt a rush of anger. 'All right, Molly. I know you were listening. If that's the way you want to play it, there's nothing I can do. Meet me, or don't meet me. I've held out the olive branch. It's up to you now.'

He hoped she would meet him, because he hated the way things were. 'I want you and me to have a future together,' he murmured. 'We really need to thrash this out.'

With the call made, and hopefully Molly aware that he wanted to see her, he turned his thoughts to the imminent meeting with Curtis Warren 'Who knows,' he muttered as he went out the door, 'they might not want me in the new post, after all. If they turn me down, that's the end of *that*.' He smiled a sad little smile. 'No doubt Molly would be well pleased.'

One way or another, with or without Molly alongside, he meant to pursue the idea put forward by the psychiatrist. It was an astonishing and frightening thought, but he was determined to follow it through.

He hoped the outcome of this morning's meeting would be in his favour. A definite approval from the big boss would be the first step in a journey that could either save him, or damn him.

~

At ten thirty, Jack was behind his desk, feeling reasonably confident, but not taking anything for granted.

Just as he was beginning to wonder if they had cancelled the interview, he noticed a black Lexus driving up to the front of the building, and he recognised the man inside as Curtis Warren, the boss himself.

'Hey!' Jan the receptionist poked her face round his office door. 'I expect you've already seen him, have you?' She made a sad little face. 'If he approves the posting, don't take it, Jack. I'll miss you too much. We all will.'

Jack smiled, 'Let's not jump the gun, eh?' he warned. 'We don't know for sure that I'll get it.'

'Oh, you will.' Like everyone else there, she knew it was a foregone conclusion. Catching sight of Stuart Branagan making his way to Jack's office, Jan slunk away. 'See you later, eh? And good luck.'

A few moments later, Jack was summoned to the main office.

'Sit down, Redmond,' Branagan commanded. 'You already know Mr Warren.' Warren was a tall, well-built man of confident stature.

'Great to see you again, Jack.' Reaching out, he shook Jack by the hand. 'I understand you're ready to take on the responsibility for the new showrooms. Am I right in thinking that is still the case?'

Jack nodded. 'You are. I have with me the signed contract. If you want me there, I'm ready to go.'

'Mmm. Well, there are a number of reassurances we

need from you. Firstly, Do you understand that this is a long-term responsibility?'

'I do, yes.'

'And are there any reasons why you might not be able to stay the course, if the job was offered to you?' He gave a knowing smile. 'Obviously, we're concerned about domestic arrangements – that kind of thing.'

Jack was brusque but respectful. 'First of all, can I say I was led to believe that the post was already offered – subject firstly to my acceptance, and then to your approval.'

The other man smiled again, only this time his smile was genuine. 'That is absolutely true, yes. In fact, I was the first to suggest you for the posting. I've known you for a long time, Jack. Having worked together for some years, I believe you're the right man for the job. I know from experience, you won't let us down.'

His smile faded. 'As you can appreciate, this new venture is costly, and needs to be monitored at every step. We have to be sure that it's going to work. In other words, we don't need any hidden agendas, which is why I put that question to you just now.'   .

'I appreciate that. But you should know me better than most, and what I'm saying is, there *are* no hidden agendas – at least not on my part.' His deeper meaning did not escape them.

Curtis Warren looked him in the eye. 'Unfortunately, Head Office still remembers a certain occasion some four years ago, when you actually turned down a posting very similar to this one, and later on, the job Mr Branagan is doing so ably now. So, you can understand why we need to be sure it's what you want this time round.'

'You can be sure. You have my word on it.'

From the receptionist desk, Bill West and Jan watched with great interest. 'Looks like he's getting a right grilling,' Jan commented, secretly pleased. 'I know Jack, and he'll only take so much before he tells them to shove it where the sun don't shine.'

'Remember, it's a managerial post,' Bill reminded her. 'You don't easily turn your nose up at an offer like that. Well, I know *I* wouldn't!'

Jan made him a promise: 'Your turn will come,' she said confidently. 'You're made for promotion.'

'Are you saying I suck up to the big guys?'

'Not yet, no. But you will.'

'Hmph! Thanks for that. I thought you and I were on the same team?'

'We are. Only I'm happy just being a dogsbody, while you and Jack are meant for higher things.'

'Hey, that's a really nice thing to say. Thank you, Jan.' Bill gave her an appreciative glance.

'I really don't want him to go,' she said woefully.

Bill grinned. 'I knew it! You've got your eye on Jack, haven't you?'

Jan blushed bright pink. 'Don't be silly!' It was the truth though.

Seeing how embarrassed she was, Bill said, 'Sorry, I shouldn't have teased you like that. None of us want Jack to go – he's the backbone of this place. I've only been here for a few weeks, but even I've noticed what a waste of space Branagan is. Jack does twice as much work and shoulders too much responsibility. Our so-called manager squats behind that desk, like a fat king summoning the minions. I've yet to see him dirty his hands, or even make his own cup of tea. He doesn't even pull his considerable weight when the salesmen are run off their feet, or someone is away sick.'

Jan was horrified. 'Ssh! You'd best not let him hear you, or you'll be out on your backside before you can say "Jack Robinson"!'

Just then, a customer arrived and Bill rushed to attend to her, all the more eager because she was young and easy on the eye.

Half an hour later, Jack emerged from the main office. Jan held her crossed fingers behind her back, hoping that he had turned the new posting down, or that the powers-that-be had changed their mind, for whatever reason.

The look on Jack's face said it all. 'Oh, Jack! You got it, didn't you? Say something, dammit!'

Jack leaned over the desk, smiling from ear to ear. 'Yes, I got it, Jan, my little darling! I want everyone to come to the Red Lion tomorrow night. *It's time to party!*'

'Congratulations, Jack!' she was genuinely pleased for him. 'We're not losing you just yet though, are we?'

'Not yet,' he reassured her. 'There are a number of things to be put in place before I can move up there. Somewhere to live, for one.'

Buoyed with a sense of accomplishment, Jack went

about his work with renewed enthusiasm. Suddenly, his life was changing, and he was both excited and anxious. This was not just an ordinary move; it was far more important than that. He felt as though he was on a runaway train and didn't know where it might stop.

Time alone would tell whether he'd made the right decision.

~

Just before one o'clock Jack drove to the little café in Bletchley, impatient to tell Molly the news. He was apprehensive as to how she would take it, now it was a done deal. Would she understand? Maybe overnight she had thought about it, and was ready to give way on her decision. He hoped so. Either way, for him there was no going back.

The café was a small, family-run business, with home-cooked food and a smile served with it. Jack found it a welcome oasis in the storm of life. He ordered a coffee while waiting for Molly to come.

'Well, here you are again, Jack – deep in thought as usual,' said Maria, the friendly waitress. She glanced about. 'No girlfriend today, then?'

He returned her smile. 'She'll be along shortly.'

'Same as usual, is it?' She got her pad and pen ready. 'Or would you rather wait for the young lady?'

'I'll wait,' he decided. 'Meantime, I'd love one of your special coffees.'

After two cups of coffee Jack realised that Molly wasn't coming. With a sinking heart he paid the bill, and left.

En route to the office, he wondered if he should try to get hold of her at her workplace. Or maybe he should call Pauleen again. Perhaps she didn't tell Molly he'd called earlier. Or maybe Molly just wanted to make him suffer.

Once inside the office, the manager approached him. 'You're late back from lunch again, Redmond. Don't think you can start taking liberties, just because you're leaving.'

'Sorry, Mr Branagan. I got caught up, but I'll make up the time, as always.'

'See that you do.' With a face that told its own story, he stomped off.

'He's jealous as hell because Curtis Warren likes you.' Eagle-eyed Jan didn't miss a trick.

~

Once inside his own office, Jack called the estate agency where Molly worked.

'Banbury's Estate Agency, Julie Hart speaking.'

'It's Jack here,' he answered. 'Could I possibly have a quick word with Molly?'

'Sorry, Jack. Molly rang in to say she wouldn't be in today.' Julie gave a knowing little chuckle. 'I don't know what the pair of you got up to last night, but she sounded somewhat the worse for wear.' Seeming to have suddenly realised something, Julie paused to ask, 'Didn't you already know she wasn't coming in to work?'

'No. I had an urgent meeting, so I had to leave early,' he lied, to allay her suspicions.

'Well, I'd give her a ring at home if I were you.' She tutted. 'Our Molly did *not* sound a happy bunny.'

Jack went along with her chatter. 'You're right,' he said pleasantly. 'That's what I'll do. Thanks, Julie.'

'You're welcome.' There was a click and the phone line went dead.

~

Throughout the afternoon, Jack was run off his feet, but the minute he got a break, he rang Molly's mother again, only this time it was her father who answered. 'Hello, Ted. Is Molly there?'

'No, she is not. And from what Brian just told me, she's in no fit state to be anywhere. I'm sorry, Jack, but don't you think it's about time you and Molly sorted your differences out, once and for all?'

'That's why I want to speak with her,' Jack answered honestly. 'I'll try to contact her at Brian's. Thanks, Ted. Sorry to have bothered you.'

He rang Brian's landline number. 'Is Brian there, please?' he asked. He suspected it might be wiser to speak with Brian before he asked for Molly.

''Fraid not. He's in a meeting at his office this afternoon. I'm Malcolm Salter, his business partner.'

'Oh, I see. The thing is, Malcolm, I need to speak to Molly. She is still there, isn't she?'

'Yes.'

'Could you ask her if she'll come to the phone, please?'

There was a pause, during which Mal seemed to be considering Jack's request. Then he said, 'OK. I'll go and get her.'

After a few moments, Jack was relieved to hear Molly's voice down the line. 'What do you want, Jack?'

'I want *you*, sweetheart. I need you to come home. I'll try to get away early from work. I can come and collect you, if you want?'

When she gave no answer, he was hopeful. 'I'm sorry we had that row. I love you, Molly. You know that, don't you?'

'Have you turned down that promotion?' she asked sharply.

'No. I've accepted it. You knew I'd made up my mind.'

'So, everything I said, everything I feel about this business – none of it meant anything to you?'

'Of course it did – it does! I know the score. I want to go and you want me to stay. But we're intelligent, mature people. Surely we can find a middle way. We need to sit down and thrash it out, or we'll never find a solution. Please, Moll. Come home. Let's try again.'

'I'm not coming home, Jack. We're finished, you and me.'

'Don't say that! You can't mean to throw away

everything we've built up, just because I accepted the promotion?'

Suddenly Molly launched into a screaming attack: 'It's never just been about the promotion anyway – it's the fact that you don't care what I think! Look, Jack – I mean what I say. Some time tomorrow, when you're at work, I'll come and get the rest of my belongings, and that's an end to it. I don't want you calling me, and I never want to see you again. You'd better believe it, Jack. No more contact; no more talking. I don't want you any more. It's over. Have you got that?'

Before he could answer, she slammed down the phone, and he was left with her harsh words ringing in his ears.

Molly ran back up the stairs and into the bedroom. Concerned for her, Mal followed and he was surprised when Molly instantly wrapped her arms round his neck and drew him down onto the bed. 'Make love to me,' she urged, tantalisingly straddling him, 'I don't need him when I've got you.'

Mal held her off for a moment. 'Do you mean that, or are you just saying it because you're angry with Jack?'

She laughed out loud – a harsh, spiteful sound. 'I'm angry, yes. But not because of Jack.' Her tone softened. 'I'm only angry that I ever left you in the first place.'

That was all the encouragement he needed. 'You're really never seeing him again?'

'Never!'

'If you really want him, Molly, you know I would step aside.'

'You'd better not!' She pressed her body into his. 'I'm yours now, Mal. And don't you ever forget that.'

Mal heard only what he wanted to hear. He adored her, and she knew that. But even then, for the sake of Molly's happiness, he really would have let her go, although it would have crippled him to do so. He prayed she was not lying to him, like last time, when she broke his heart. He had to trust her now, because life without her was too empty.

But Molly had no conscience. No shame. Jack was still her priority. Yes, he needed bringing under control, but she already had that in hand. Emotional blackmail was a powerful thing.

In her arrogance, she truly believed that now Jack had been given a glimpse of what life would be like without her, he would give in and abandon his plans. Like all men, he would lick his wounds, then he'd be all over her, begging her to come back. Meantime, she would enjoy Mal and his puppy dog devotion, in every way possible. Live for the minute, that was her motto.

When she now suddenly responded to Mal's touch with a crazed, sensual energy, he foolishly believed it was his own prowess that had aroused her in such an exciting way.

But then, that was exactly what she wanted him to think.

CHAPTER NINE

Having worked a week of four-hour shifts to cover for another woman who was taking a short holiday, Libby was thankful when Friday afternoon came.

'Glad it's the weekend are you?' asked Madge Lovatt, the supervisor. A smart, single woman in her late fifties, she had ten years of dedicated service under her belt. Well respected by all the staff, her fair-minded manner brought out the best in people.

'Yes, I'm off now,' Libby replied as she walked between the aisles towards her.

'I see you've got your mother's ginger biscuits, then?' Madge gestured to the package in Libby's hand. 'I must admit, I'm rather partial to a ginger-nut myself.'

'I'd be shot at dawn if I went home without them,' Libby joked. 'The minute I open that gate she'll be looking for these biscuits. She'll have them out of my hands before I know what's hit me.'

'Does Thomas still look after her?' Like most of the staff at the supermarket, Madge knew of Libby's burden, and she was filled with admiration. The young woman's dedication to her ailing mother was commendable.

'He does, yes.' When Libby entered the staff cloak-room, Madge went with her. 'D'you know what, Madge – I really don't know what I'd do without Thomas. He's such a good man – the best friend ever. I can leave Mum in his care and be content that no harm will come to her.'

Madge was impressed. 'That's wonderful.' After several disasters involving the opposite sex, she had long ago lost her trust in men. But from what she'd heard about Libby's neighbour, he was obviously an exception to the rule. 'How old did you say he was?'

Libby gave her question a moment's thought. 'I'm not altogether certain. He's never really let on, but I reckon he's in his late sixties.'

'Ah, that's a shame. I'm looking for a good man – and for a minute there I thought I'd found him, but late sixties . . . hmm.' She gave Libby a comical glance. 'A bit wrinkled round the gills, is he?'

Libby laughed. 'No, actually, he's not! In fact, he's not a bad-looking man at all. He's tall and well built, with a smile that would melt snow. Added to which, he has a heart of gold, and a mountain of patience.'

'So, a man like that – he must have a wife tucked away somewhere.'

'No – not as far as I know, anyway.'

'How's that?'

'Sad story, really. His wife packed her bags one day and cleared off, without so much as a by your leave.'

'Got family, has he – children and the like?'

'No. He's all on his own.'

'No baggage then, by the sounds of it.' Madge glanced about to make sure no one was listening, as she asked with a twinkle in her eye, 'You say he's well built?'

'That's right.' Intrigued by the other woman's curiosity, Libby went on, 'He likes walking, and he has an allotment. I expect that keeps him fit.'

'Mmm . . . a good-looking, active man who grows his own veg – it gets better and better!' Leaning towards Libby, she asked confidentially, 'D'you reckon he's fit' – she blushed – 'down under, if you know what I mean? Or has it been dormant for so long, it's neither use nor ornament?'

Shocked and amused, Libby collapsed into a giggling fit. 'How would *I* know?' she chided. To even mention Thomas in that way, was embarrasing.

'You do understand, I wasn't being smutty,' Madge assured her. 'It's just that, well – if you must know, I'm on the lookout for a fella, only they all seem withered and brain-dead, or they've got a face that would frighten a horse.'

'Well, I can promise you, Thomas doesn't fit any of those descriptions. He's just a regular bloke who keeps himself to himself, and he's got a kindly heart. If it wasn't for him, I wouldn't be able to work. That means Mum wouldn't get her little treats, and life would be less comfortable financially.'

Madge was impressed. 'He sounds very interesting,

your Thomas. Obviously, your mother enjoys being with him while you're at work.'

Libby smiled. 'Mum adores him. Thomas makes her laugh, and he's always got some outing planned – like a trip to the shops, or a walk in the park. Apparently, they talk about when they were young, and if Mum is having one of her forgetful days, he reads the signs and treats her gently.'

Madge thought it over. 'D'you reckon he fancies your mother?'

'Don't be daft!' Taking her jacket out of the locker, Libby shrugged it on. Fastening her buttons as she walked, she assured Madge, 'He's just a really good friend, to me and my mother both.'

'Ah, but your mother is a good-looking woman. When you brought her in here the other week, we all thought she must have been a stunner when she was younger.'

'Yes, she was.' Libby had seen the photographs, and was struck by how attractive her mother had been as a young woman. 'She'll always be beautiful to me,' she said, a little wistfully.

'I'm sure she will.' Madge understood. She could only imagine how hard it must be for Libby to deal with the current situation. 'I meant no offence, talking like that about your friend Thomas. He sounds like a really decent bloke.' She gave a weary little sigh. 'They're few and far between, I can tell you.'

'It's all right, Madge,' said Libby. 'No offence taken.'

'So, what have you got planned for this weekend?'

'Well, if it's warm enough, I've promised Mother a picnic in Corporation Park.'

'Oh, how wonderful! It's so lovely there, and peaceful. You can always find a quiet spot by the man-made lake, where you can feed the ducks and watch the children playing. Or there are plenty of quiet little nooks in the gardens, where you can while away the time, listening to the birds.'

'You can meet up with us, if you like.' Libby had always assumed that Madge preferred her own company, but after this conversation, she was not so sure. Maybe the reason she had never married was not because she didn't want to, but because her standards were too high. Maybe Madge was not prepared to settle for less than the perfect man.

'Thank you, Libby. I appreciate that, but I'm on duty here tomorrow. I have some urgent paperwork to be getting on with. See you on Monday – have a great weekend!'

But after Libby was gone, her thoughts returned to Thomas. 'By the sound of it, he's a man with a heart. I wouldn't mind a man like that,' she sighed. 'A man who would love me and take good care of me.'

She rolled her eyes at such dreams and fancies. 'You're an idiot, Madge,' she told herself. 'You're long past all that now, so get used to it!'

As Libby walked home, she thought about what Madge had said, about Thomas fancying her mother. She chuckled to herself. If Thomas were to make advances to Eileen, her mother would probably clip his ear.

~

At that very moment, Thomas emerged from his kitchen with a tray of goodies. Taking them out to the garden where Eileen was waiting, he told her, 'We've got a couple of cheese sandwiches and a piece of Battenberg cake. How's that?'

Shifting forward on the bench, Eileen cast her gaze over the tray's contents. 'Oh, Battenberg!' she clapped her hands like a child. 'Lovely, Thomas!'

'Good.' He set the tray on the table between them. 'Well, at least I've managed to put a smile on your face.' He had been concerned earlier, when they were in the park, that Eileen seemed unduly restless. But then, she often got that way. One minute she was right as rain, and the next she was like a naughty child. He was not overly concerned, because over the years, he had learned how to pacify her.

Now, though, he did as he always did when they were having tea in the garden. He poured the tea and made sure to add enough milk to cool it down. When Eileen took up the spoon and began frantically shovelling sugar into the cup, he gently took away the spoon. Then, taking his empty cup, he filled it with tea, slid the cup over to her and spooned in two sugars. 'You don't want to be rotting your lovely teeth,' he told her.

'You know what Libby would say if she saw you putting all that sugar in your cup.'

Making big eyes, Eileen looked towards the gate. 'She didn't see me, did she?'

Thomas shook his head. 'No, she didn't see you.'

Suddenly, from somewhere in the garden, the angelic tones of a songbird filtered through the air. 'Oh, listen . . .' Eileen put her finger to her lips. 'Isn't that beautiful?'

But Thomas was not listening to the birdsong. Instead, he was looking at Eileen, and his old heart was turned over with love. 'Yes, it is beautiful, my darling,' he whispered, 'but not as beautiful as you.'

Leaning over, he drew the fleecy blanket further across her knees. 'Be careful with the tea, now. Don't drink it too quickly, or you might scald yourself.' While she sipped, he held his hand under the saucer.

'I'm not a baby. I won't scald myself.' When she smiled up at him, he wanted to hold her and kiss her, and tell her how much she had come to mean to him. But he would never tell her. Not when Eileen was so very poorly. He felt ashamed, to be thinking of her in such a way.

The truth was, he had come to love this delightful woman, and the more he witnessed how helpless she could be, the more he felt he should take care of her. But he would then remind himself that it was not his place. He had no right. So, for everyone's sake, he kept his feelings to himself.

Libby was doing a marvellous job with her mother, but it saddened him to see her so tied down. He had always thought she should have a life of her own, with a husband, and children running round her feet. Yet here she was, a vibrant young woman, devoting her life to looking after her sick mother. Life was very cruel, he thought.

~

By the time Libby arrived to collect her mother, Thomas had her ready and waiting, and clutching a bunch of wild flowers. 'Me and Thomas picked these,' Eileen announced proudly. 'Oh, Libby, we had such a good time.' Turning to Thomas, she urged him, 'We did, didn't we, Thomas?'

'We certainly did,' he said grandly. 'What's more, we fed the ducks, and afterwards we drove into town and had fish and chips.'

'And mushy peas!' Eileen clapped her hands together.

Thomas laughed, 'Yes, we did. And, if the weather permits, we'll do it again next week.'

'We could go on one of them boats, couldn't we, Thomas?'

'Ah, well, I don't know about that.' Thomas thought it best not to make promises. 'That would be up to Libby,' he said. 'But first, you and Libby have got this whole weekend to enjoy.' He went with them to the door.

'Thank you, Thomas.' Libby could see how happy her mother was. 'I really appreciate what you do for us.'

'It's my pleasure,' he told her sincerely. 'I'm sure you already know that. And besides, what a sad, lonely old man I'd be, if I didn't have you two to keep me on my toes!'

Libby gave him a kiss, and not to be outdone, Eileen did the same. 'I love you,' she told him, and he answered with a smile, 'I love you too,' as he gently ushered her out of the door. 'Both of you.'

Worn out by the busy day, Eileen soon fell asleep in front of the telly. Coming in from the kitchen, Libby gently touched her on the arm. 'Ready for your bath, are you?'

'I don't want a bath.' Eileen was adamant. 'I'm not dirty, so why do I need a bath?'

Recognising the signs of an argument in the offing, Libby said reassuringly, 'No, Mum, you're not dirty, and no one said you were. If you don't want a bath, a wash will do just fine.'

'I'm tired!'

'So, we'll make it a quick wash. Then I'll put you to bed. Agreed?'

Eileen's answer was to settle herself in the chair and prepare to go back to sleep.

'Mum?'

'What now, child?'

'I'm ready to take you upstairs.'

'Why am I going upstairs?'

'Because it's gone ten o'clock, and you're falling asleep in your chair. Wouldn't you rather sleep in the comfort of your bed?'

Rubbing her eyes, Eileen looked up at her daughter. 'Libby?'

'Yes, Mum?'

'You're a good girl.'

'Well, thank you.' She had abandoned ever trying to follow her mother's train of thought. 'So now, are you ready to go upstairs?'

'If you like.'

'Come on, then.' She helped Eileen out of the chair, before taking her step by careful step up to the bedroom. Having decided that her mother was too weary to go into the bathroom, she then got her into her nightgown and seated her on the edge of the bed. 'You sit there a minute,' she said. 'I won't be long.'

She hurried to the bathroom, where she quickly ran a measure of both hot and cold water into a bowl, before swishing it about with her fingers. Gathering flannel, soap and towel, she hurried back to the bedroom and helped her mother to wash.

Settling her into bed, she switched on the nightlight. Libby knew only too well how her mother feared the darkness. Not for the first time, she wondered about this fear. 'Maybe there isn't a reason,' she thought. 'Maybe it's just one of those instinctive, irrational fears that can never be explained.'

Libby wondered if there had ever been a time in her mother's life when there was no fear of the night, or the shifting shadows; no pressing need to have a light on in her room. She knew her mother was not the only one to fear the dark. Still, it was a curious thing, all the same.

Exhausted, she climbed into her own bed and slid down under the duvet. Within minutes, she was fast asleep.

While her daughter slept soundly, Eileen was beginning to toss and turn. Waking with a start, she lifted herself up against the pillow, her wide eyes scouring the room. Everything seemed as it should be – so what had startled her awake? What was it? *Who was it?*

Apprehensive, she glanced about the room until her gaze was drawn to the window. With her heart pounding, she got out of bed and ran to open the curtains. 'Go away. Leave me be!' She whispered it over and over, her voice trembling uncontrollably. 'Please . . . go away.'

She told herself there was nothing to be afraid of, but the dark memories – crippling images engrained in her soul – tormented her. *He* was out there, watching her. Wanting to hurt her. She knew it.

In the adjoining room, Libby was woken by the screams. Scrambling out of bed, she raced next door, only to find the bed empty and her mother nowhere in sight.

Hurrying onto the landing, she called out, *'Mum!'* She checked the stair-gate, but it was intact, just as she had left it.

'Mum, where are you?' Stepping over the stair-gate, she ran downstairs to quickly check the doors back and front. All was secure. She searched all the rooms – even

the toilet, where Eileen had hidden before – but there was no sign of her anywhere.

Covering the stairs two at a time, Libby headed for the bathroom. That too, was empty. Returning to her mother's bedroom, she searched again, under the bed and in the cupboards – but still there was no sign of Eileen.

Intent on calling the police, she turned towards the door – and it was then that she heard the low, whimpering sounds.

They were coming from behind the long curtains at the window.

'Mum?' She went forward, speaking softly, knowing how quickly her mother's mood could change. Confusion became fear. Fear escalated into violence – against others, and against herself.

'It's all right, Mum. I'm here.'

Easing back the curtain, she found Eileen crouching on all fours, her stricken eyes peeping over the low window-sill.

'He's there,' Eileen whispered hoarsely. '*He's* out there . . . waiting for us!' She made a shivering sound. 'Get back, child! He mustn't see you!' Frantically clawing at her daughter's bare feet, she tried desperately to draw her back. 'Come away from the window!'

Libby tried to calm her. 'There is nothing out there, Mum,' she coaxed. 'Please believe me. You're safe enough here – *we're* safe enough.'

'No! He's hurt. He knows we're here. He's been here before.' When she swivelled her gaze upwards, Libby was shocked at the terror in her mother's face.

Reaching up, Eileen grabbed hold of Libby's hand. 'Close the curtains,' she implored. 'I don't want him to hurt you – it's not your fault. Come away, child – come away!'

She drew Libby down beside her. 'Ssh. Ssh, now. He's listening. He can hear us, you know.' Her whole body was shaking with fear.

Grabbing both ends of the curtains, Libby swished them shut. 'Come back to bed now, Mum.' Shaken by the experience, she coaxed Eileen to her feet. 'Has he gone now?' Eileen whispered. 'Are we safe?'

Choked with emotion, Libby assured her that she was safe now, that no one could see them, and that there was no one out there.

'Mother, listen to me,' Libby said as she lay on the bed beside her. 'Just now, when you thought you saw something – will you tell me about it? Please, Mum – describe what you think you saw.' She had to get her talking, opening her heart and mind. That was the way. Over the years, she had been advised by the people who knew best that it was all right to gently question.

Visibly nervous, Eileen mumbled, 'No, it's a secret. He's listening. He's *always* listening. It's too late, you see. *Wicked!* Wicked, that's what it is!' Then she was crying – deep, racking sobs that broke Libby's heart.

For what seemed an age, Eileen wept – until all the fight and fear seemed to ebb away. Then she suddenly asked Libby, 'Why are you in my bed? I can't sleep with you in my bed!'

Libby breathed a sigh of relief at this abrupt change

of mood. She played along: 'I thought we might talk, that's all.'

'Naughty girl! I'm very tired. You must go back to your own bed.'

Knowing that her mother had completely forgotten the incident at the window, Libby said, 'I'll leave you to sleep, then. Goodnight, Mum.'

There was no answer. Eileen was already asleep.

~

For Libby, though, there was no rest now. Whatever her mother imagined she had seen, it had somehow got to her as well.

So, what terrible person had her mother imagined? Who did she think was 'out there'? And why was this person so 'wicked'?

All these years her mother had been losing her sense of reality, but there was never anything that Libby could not handle, or explain at least to some degree. Tonight though, she could find no explanation for the state of terror she found her mother in. Something, whether real or imagined, had truly spooked her. Libby would not easily forget seeing her mother crouched in fear behind the curtains, convinced that something 'wicked' was out there.

A disturbing thought suddenly came into Libby's mind. What if it was not the first time her mother had suffered this particular trauma? What if she had experienced it all before, and suffered in silence? And what if she had *not* screamed? What if she had crouched by the window all night long, not daring to move or call for help? 'He's been here before.' Her mother truly believed that.

Libby herself could not accept the possibility that some unknown stalker was out there, spying on them. As far as she was aware, neither she nor her mother had any enemies. So, why would anyone want to hurt them?

These past years, Eileen had suffered many attacks of paranoia, but this time it was different. It felt more real. And what did she mean when she told Libby, 'I don't want him to hurt you – it's not your fault'?

Deeply troubled, Libby turned over and sank into a restless sleep.

CHAPTER TEN

'*M*OLLY!' LAYING THE receiver beside the telephone, Brian hurried to the bottom of the stairs. He waited a moment, then when there was no sign of her, he called again, this time more loudly: '*Molly, get down here, will you?! Jack's on the phone, and my toast is going cold!*'

Molly appeared at the door of her bedroom, 'What does he want?'

Already frustrated with her having stayed with him longer than he'd expected, Brian thumped the banister with his clenched fist. 'How would I know?! You should answer your mobile, then he wouldn't need to call the land-line!'

When she came running down, he lowered his voice so Jack could not hear. 'Don't you think you should put the poor devil out of his misery? Meet up with him, for crying out loud! All he's asking is that you talk things through.'

'Hmph!' She raised her voice so Jack might hear.

'As far as I'm concerned, there *is* nothing to talk through!'

Brian shook his head in despair. 'Honestly, Sis, you can be a nasty piece of work when you set your mind to it.'

Making a face, she was about to go over and pick up the phone, when she changed her mind, deciding that it wouldn't do any harm to keep Jack waiting.

From the doorway, Brian watched in disbelief as she calmly stood over the telephone, obviously enjoying the moment. 'Are you going to speak to him or what?' he deliberately spoke loudly before giving a wry little smile as Molly spun round, gesturing for him to clear off out of it. Which he did.

Snatching up the receiver, Molly was irritated. 'Yes? What is it you want now?' Determined to make Jack suffer, she called out to her brother, 'Brian? Where's Mal?'

'Gone – as you well know!'

For Jack's sake, she feigned disappointment. 'Oh, and he never even gave me a kiss goodbye.'

Brian made no further comment. Not for the first time, he had been shocked by his sister's behaviour. If he was Jack, he'd have been long gone. Because Molly was his sister and his landlady, it put him in a bad position; so much so that, he had secretly started looking for somewhere else to live. Though, if this development deal came through, he might even find himself in a position to put down a deposit and actually buy a place.

He could see that Molly was just using Mal to make Jack jealous. He had always been aware of his sister's shortcomings, but lately, he had seen a side to her that had truly disgusted him. He would not interfere in her life, but once he got himself another place, she would hear a few home-truths from him – and so, for that matter, would Mal. His mate was a good bloke, but he was too trusting, and too besotted with Molly, to see what she was really like.

Torn between the devil and the deep blue sea, he wanted to warn Mal to be on his guard. On the other hand, if he told him the brutal truth – that Molly had no real feelings for him – he might risk Mal falling out with him, and he didn't want that. Not when the man was like a brother to him, and especially not now, when they had committed themselves to working on this big project together.

Brian felt that the sooner he was out of Molly's house, the better. He had never thought he would say it, but living under the same roof as his big sister was just too uncomfortable for words.

Now, on hearing Molly play the injured party, he decided to skip his now cold toast and make a run for it, before she came off the phone and turned her spite on him. Within minutes, he was out the door and gone.

Brian just didn't get it. Mal and Jack, both infatuated with his sister. 'Jack's either hopelessly in love and can't see the forest for the trees, or he's hoping to change her selfish ways.' Then he said out loud, 'You've no chance, mate! Best get rid of her while you can.' He jumped on his motorbike and revved it, hard. 'If you don't, she'll make your life a misery.'

The thing was, when they were younger Molly was an OK sister. But somewhere along the line, she'd become hard and selfish.

~

The conversation was not going Molly's way. 'So nothing I've said has changed your mind, Jack?' she asked in a hurt voice. 'You're still hell-bent on leaving me?'

'Don't put it like that, Moll.' Jack felt guilty, but he was not about to undo all his plans, at least not when she refused to even discuss a middle way. 'We can go up north together – make a new life. Get married sooner rather than later. I'm ready for that—'

'*Are* you, now?' Molly's voice shook with anger. 'Well, *I'm not*! You think you can just click your fingers and expect me to throw away my job, but you have no intention of doing the same for me. The answer is no. Unless you ask for your old job back and drop this idea of chasing ghosts, I want nothing more to do with you.'

Jack had been trying to see it from her point of view. 'What if I didn't accept the post permanently?' he suggested. 'What if I was to ask for a trial period of, say, three months? It's not unknown for an employee to do that and still retain his old position. Think about it, Moll. Three months would maybe give me enough time to search for answers. It will at least give me a chance to do some delving – to go back to my old stamping-ground and search for the answers I so badly need.'

'You won't find any answers there, Jack. You're not the only person in the world who suffers from night-mares, but other people learn to live with them. So why are you so determined to ruin our lives by going on this wild goose-chase? Why can't you stay where you are, and maybe spend a weekend or even a couple of weekends up there? You'll soon find out that there are no answers.'

'That's not what the psychiatrist hinted.'

'Yes! That's exactly it. He just *hinted,* and you jumped on the idea, like the fool you are.'

Jack chose to ignore that spiteful remark. 'But I need you to support me, Moll. It's important to me. One way or another, will you give me the time to find out if there is any truth in what he suggested – that my nightmares are rooted in real events that I can't shut out?'

None of what Jack had said had made any impres-sion on Molly, except to fuel her rage. 'I wish I'd never suggested you going to see him!' she snapped. 'The idea was for you to get some closure of sorts. Not to leave me and go searching for something that isn't even there.'

'Well, whether you like it or not, this is something I have to do. It might be the solution I'm looking for, and apart from that, when the promotion came up and it was offered to me, it was too good an opportunity to turn down. Surely you can see that, Molly?'

When she remained silent, he asked her again, 'So, are you prepared to meet me half-way?'

'No.' Molly would not give way an inch. 'I won't move up there with you. Nor do I intend playing the little wife-in-waiting. Putting my life on hold, while you take off on a whim No, Jack! I want nothing to do with any of it.'

'Which means you want nothing to do with me. Right?'

'If you want to look at it that way.'

'You really don't want to marry me – that's the truth isn't it?'

'Yes, you're right. I don't want to marry you, Jack. Not when you're so pig-headed and selfish, you can't even do what I want.'

'But this isn't altogether about *you*.' For a fleeting moment, Jack actually began to wonder if he really was being selfish, but after he had gone her way as far as he could, and still she was unable, or unwilling, to meet him half-way, what was he to think?

'This is a big decision for me,' he reminded her. 'I need to find some peace of mind, if I can. You trying to hold me back tells me only one thing.'

'What's that?'

'We don't have a future together. We don't have the kind of partnership that makes for a happy marriage. Perhaps we never did. Here am I, trying to find a middle way, but you're only interested in what *you* want. You're not even trying to see it from my point of view. You don't respect my feelings, or any decision I make, unless it complies with yours.'

After this tussle of wills, he was beginning to see more clearly. 'You obviously don't understand that this is a last resort for me. Sometimes, I feel as though I'll be cursed with these nightmares till the day I die. You may be right, and maybe there aren't any answers – but at least this way, I'm trying to do something, and I desperately want you with me.'

'Huh! Well, that's not going to happen!'

Jack could see he was fighting a losing battle. 'Won't you even consider coming with me, just for a week or so – to see how the land lies? And if, for whatever reason, it doesn't work out, we can think again. Say you'll give it a try at least?'

'Sorry, Jack, but this conversation is at an end.'

'I'm sorry too. I'm sorry we couldn't reconcile our differences.'

'Your fault, not mine,' she insisted.

Jack shrugged. 'If that's how you feel about it, I won't bother you again. But if you do change your mind, you know where I am.'

'Oh, but I think you're the one who must change *your* mind, Jack.' She played her last card. 'I think you should know . . . Mal Shawncross has asked me to marry him. And I'm going to say yes.'

'I see.' Jack knew about Mal from Brian. He also knew how much Molly meant to him. 'Mal's a good bloke,' he told her quietly. 'Brian says he adores you, Molly. I'm sure he'll take good care of you.'

'He *will*, yes!' Molly was furious that her plan had backfired. 'Is that all you have to say?' she demanded.

'Aren't you even going to try to fight for me, and make me change my mind?'

'What's the point? If you agree to marry Mal, you obviously don't want me, and now I'm done arguing and talking. Like you, I need to get on with my own life.'

He felt betrayed, yet oddly relieved. 'I'm glad for you both,' he said – and was surprised to find that he meant it. Then, there was little else for him to say, except, 'Bye, Moll. Thanks for everything. Take care of yourself.'

When he replaced the receiver, Molly threw a tantrum. Furious that her little ploy did not get the result she wanted, she upturned the small table, sending the phone crashing to the floor. 'You'll regret doing this to me!' she yelled. 'You bastard! I hope it all goes wrong for you!'

~

At Curtis Warren Motors, the morning had been frantic. The new stock had attracted a good turnout, which continued right up to lunchtime.

'I've never known it so busy.' Jan was kept on her toes behind the desk.

'It must be the new promotion,' Bill decided.

Jan had other ideas. 'Nah. I reckon they've heard that Jack is leaving, and as he normally trims his own commission to make a good deal, they thought they'd best get in before he goes.'

'I would *never* cut my commission!' Bill bragged. 'I need the money.'

'Why? Have you got a wife and six kids hidden away somewhere?' Jan found him easy to tease.

'No way! I need the money because I mean to have my own showrooms by the time I'm thirty.'

Having emerged from his office to deliver a batch of mail for the post, Jack overheard his remark. 'I've no doubt that you'll do it too,' he told Bill. 'In fact, it wouldn't surprise me to find that some day you own a string of showrooms right across the country.' He drew an imaginary sign in mid-air: 'Bill West – Autos to the Stars.'

Bill blushed. 'Don't take the mickey, Jack. It's my dream. I know it'll take time, but I *will* do it!'

Jack kindly reassured him, 'I wasn't taking the mickey. I really meant it, Bill. You've only been here a short time, but already you've proven yourself to be a born salesman. You've got a knack for making the right deal, and that only comes naturally. Many others have to learn the hard way.'

'A born salesman!' Bill was highly flattered. 'Do you really mean that?' His boyish smile lit up the room.

'I do mean it, yes – and I'm not the only one who thinks so.'

'The customers are of paramount importance and good judges. They like and trust you. They know you won't flannel them into buying a car they don't really want.'

Bill returned the compliment. 'You taught me that,

Jack,' he admitted. 'You showed me how the customer is more important than anyone else. 'Look after them and they'll look after you.' That's what you said.'

'There you go, then! Keep that in mind, and you won't go far wrong.' Picking up his coffee, Jack took it back to the office.

'I wish he wasn't leaving,' sighed Jan. 'I'll really miss him.'

'We all will.' Bill had no doubts about that. 'I suppose he's got a lot to think about, mind you, what with moving up north to take on such a highly responsible position.'

'Yes, but if you ask me, Jack's got a lot more on his mind than work just now.' While Bill was always looking for the next customer, Jan enjoyed keeping her eyes open and her ear to the ground, for any juicy snippet of gossip. Leaning forward, she lowered her voice to a whisper: 'He's got woman trouble. After what I overheard earlier when he was on the phone, I reckon he's about to chuck his girlfriend for good. And about time too, if you ask me!'

'Why do you say that?' Against all his instincts, Bill was intrigued.

'Mind your own business.' Jan regretted even mentioning it. 'I'm not telling.'

'Ah! Now you're beginning to wish you hadn't tittle-tattled . . . You like him, don't you? I mean, you *really* like him! In fact, you fancy him rotten!'

'Keep your voice down, or he'll hear you!'

'Admit it, then.'

'All right, I won't deny it.' She glanced to where Jack was seated in his office, head bent over a pile of paperwork. 'Who wouldn't like him?' she murmured. 'He's a good bloke.'

'Yes,' Bill taunted her, '*and* he's about to receive a top-of-the-range company car. *And* he's on his way to becoming a boss-man, with an outrageously generous salary.'

'It's got nothing to do with any of that. Like I say, he's a good bloke, and there aren't many of them around.'

~

Later, with the rush having slowed down, Jack arranged for his calls to be covered, while he took an hour out for lunch. 'If it's urgent, just call me on my mobile,' he told Jan.

Getting into his car, he drove off towards Leighton Buzzard's town centre. After parking, he made his way to Banbury's main rivals, Johnson & Everett. For once, it was quiet there, for which he was grateful. He was also pleased to see a familiar face behind the desk. Having met her through Molly, he greeted the young woman with a smile.

'Afternoon, Tess,' he said. 'You're looking good, I must say.' Daintily built, she was a pretty woman with a thick cap of black hair and a set of perfect teeth that dazzled when she smiled – like now.

'Jack Redmond!' Scrambling out of her chair, she

171

came round to him. 'How lovely to see you. What are you doing here?' Peering out of the window, she asked cautiously, 'Is Molly with you?'

'So she's not told you, then?' Jack asked.

Tess sighed. 'I sort of heard, but I wasn't sure. What's it all about, Jack? You and Molly . . . well, I mean, it seems crazy that you two should split up. One minute I'm thinking of buying a new outfit for the wedding, and the next I hear there's been a rift.' She gestured for him to sit beside her on the couch in the waiting area. 'So, is it final? Have you really broken up?'

Jack was wary. Though he had much respect for Tess, he knew how close she was to Molly, and he warned himself not to say too much. Or he might live to regret it.

'It seems so, yes,' he answered.

'But *why?*'

Jack gave a shrug. 'It might be best if you were to ask Molly that.'

'I did, but she wasn't very forthcoming.'

'Well then, maybe we should just leave it there, eh?'

'If you say so.' Tess looked him in the eyes. 'Are you wanting me to speak with Molly on your behalf, is that it?'

'No, of course not.' Jack kept his guard up, 'Molly and I have already talked it through – several times.' He quickly changed direction. 'The thing is, I've come here to ask that you put my house on the market.'

She gave a low whistle. 'Does Molly know you've come to us?'

'No.'

'She won't be best pleased, will she?'

'I thought about that, but with the way things are between me and her, I'm sure she wouldn't thank me if I asked her to sell my house. Especially when she knows I really am making the move away.'

'Where to?'

'Distant parts.'

'Ah!' Tess gave knowing smile. 'Now I understand. So, am I right in thinking you would rather I didn't say anything to her about you giving us the sale?'

Jack nodded. 'I've a feeling it might be better all round if you just took the business, and made as little fuss as possible.'

'Yes, of course. I promise you, I can be very discreet when needs be.'

'Good.' He dug into his jacket pocket. 'Here are all the particulars, and here's a set of keys. Please feel free to show people round the house whenever you like. Give me a ring when you've taken a look, and we'll talk about prices. OK?' He looked at his watch. 'Got to get back to the office.'

'Right, I'll take it from there, then,' said Tess. 'I'm sure it won't take long to find a buyer. Houses in that road are well sought after, as it's near the train station.' She could see he was impatient to be on his way. 'We'll be in touch, then. I'm sure we'll have good news for you soon.'

'Thanks,' said Jack. 'See you, then!'

He left with a slight feeling of anxiety. Had he done the right thing? He reassured himself with the knowledge that Tess was a first-class businesswoman. For that very reason, he could trust her to be discreet around Molly. And besides, the agency had an excellent reputation. He knew Tess wouldn't do anything to jeopardise her position of responsibility.

However, he was unaware that her colleague Tina Morgan, new in the back office, had recently been recruited from Banbury's, where Molly worked. Unfortunately she had overheard everything. Even as Jack made his way out of the front door, Tina was dialling Molly's number.

~

Having recently secured a substantial house-sale, and earning an excellent commission along with it, Molly was just handing out some house details to a grey-haired gent, when the phone rang.

'Can you get that, Molly?' Hayley, the scatty receptionist, was just on her way out the door. 'I'm sorry, but I'm already late for my lunch-date. If I don't get a move on, Pete will just clear off. He's got no patience at all, miserable git!' Before Molly could object, Hayley was out and running down the street.

Molly finished dealing with her customer and snatched up the receiver. She gave her usual business-like greeting, her tone changing when she realised it was Tina – who was eager to impart her snippet of gossip.

~

Later that afternoon, Jack came out of the office and chatted with Jan at the main desk. 'Well, that's a long day almost over.' He gave a long-drawn-out sigh.

'You sound weary, Jack. That's not like you.'

'It's just that I have so much going on in my life at the minute, I haven't had time to properly sort out my thoughts. What I wouldn't give to leave it all behind, just for one week. Imagine – no paperwork, no phones ringing; nothing to worry about. Just lying on a beach, with the sun beating down on my head. What absolute bliss!'

'Don't forget the girl lying next to you!' Jan said eagerly. 'How about taking me with you, eh? You can stroke sun-oil on my back any time . . . wherever we are.'

Jack laughed. He was going to miss her sense of humour. She never failed to make him smile.

He was still smiling, when the doors were flung open and Molly rushed across the room to confront him. 'Laughing at me with your new woman-friend, are you?' she shouted, her voice shaking with rage. 'I expect you're telling the bitch how you took your business to someone else. Isn't it enough that you sent me packing, without rubbing my nose in it!'

Hearing the fracas, Bill and his colleague came running,

but Jack already had her by the arms and was holding her at bay. 'For God's sake, Molly, you've got it all wrong. If you've got a grievance, let's talk about it like adults. Come into the office, and we'll sort it out.'

When she began shouting obscenities, Jan thought to calm the situation by telling her, 'We weren't laughing at anyone. We were just talking.' She had been deeply offended by Molly's earlier comment. 'And I'll thank you not to call me a bitch!'

Molly replied by clearing everything from the desk with one sweep of her arm. 'It wouldn't matter to me whether you were his bitch or not. You're welcome to him!'

Quieter now, she turned on Jack. 'I'm glad it's over between us,' she hissed. 'As for what you did – asking a rival agency to sell your house – that was just spiteful. But you know what? If you'd asked me to sell your house, I'd have said no anyway.'

Caught in Jack's iron grip, she looked into his face, into those strong, mesmerising eyes that had once gazed on her so tenderly, and suddenly she was sobbing – quietly at first, then helplessly, her whole body shaking with emotion as she leaned into him.

Caught unawares by her change of mood, Jack coaxed her into the office, where he closed the door and sat her down. 'What's caused you to fly off the handle like this?' he asked. 'It can't just be the fact that I went to another agency. You just said yourself that you wouldn't want to sell my house anyway. So, come on, Moll. What is it?'

For a moment, Molly let him stew. She still wanted him back, but even now, it had to be on her terms. She took a deep breath, before confessing reluctantly, 'It's just that, well . . . I still hoped you might come round to my way of thinking. Then, when I found out that you'd actually put your house on the market, I just lost it.'

'I'm sorry. Perhaps I should have told you earlier, but I thought it was for the best.' Jack now realised he should have known the news would reach Molly.

'I don't want you to leave, Jack. I love you. I want us to get back together. I want you to forget about taking up the new job—'

Jack interrupted, 'I'm sorry, Moll. I won't do that. I've signed the contract and even now they're making a short-list to fill my old position. It's all settled, and I have to say, I feel lighter of heart than I've felt for a very long time. I really believe the recent series of events – you badgering me to see someone about my nightmares, then this vacancy coming up in Lytham – it all seems to fit.'

'You could still say no,' Molly persisted. 'You just said, they haven't got anyone to replace you yet, so you could tell them you've changed your mind . . . that you're staying put. It's not too late. Look, Jack, I've been thinking. Maybe the psychiatrist you saw was not the right one for you. So, go to someone who knows what they're talking about, and in time, you're sure to find the answer you're looking for.'

Jack was adamant. 'I do love you,' he told her, 'but

to my mind, love is sharing. It's helping each other. It's a two-way thing.'

'But that's exactly what I'm saying!' She grew excited. 'I understand you. I understand about the nightmares. That's why I made you go and see someone, because I wanted them to end. I wanted to help you. But now everything's got out of hand. You listened to some idiot who didn't know what he was talking about. Then you get it into your head to go back, to where you think it all began. I so want it to be like it was before. I don't want to be on my own, Jack. You're leaving, without a thought for me. You're uprooting your whole life, and I know you're bound to regret it.'

For what seemed an age, Jack let her words soak in, and all he could hear was 'I' this and 'I' that. '*I* want it to be like it was before . . . *I* made you go and see someone . . . *I* don't want to be on my own.'

All he could hear was what *Molly* wanted. Not for one minute did she ever stop to consider what *he* wanted. What he desperately needed.

'I can't stay,' he told her quietly. 'It can't be like it was before.'

When she opened her mouth to speak, he gently shushed her. 'Molly, I know you understand about the nightmares, and I know you badgered me into seeing someone about them, and for that I am truly thankful.'

'*But?*' The harsh question was also an accusation. 'Go on – tell me! Why can't you stay? Why can't it be like it was before?'

Jack knew then, that it really was over between them.

'I *have* told you,' he reminded her, 'many times. Over and over. But it seems not to have sunk in, so I'll tell you again. I cannot live with these nightmares for the rest of my life, and believe it or not, when it was suggested that they might actually be a memory, rather than my imagination, I have to tell you, Molly, something inside me knew that it was the truth. That the nightmares really do stem from something that actually happened.'

'NO!' She had never accepted the theory and she didn't accept it now. 'That can't be! The things you see must be awful beyond words. You wake up covered in sweat and terror. You make strange noises, like some wild animal . . . and when you finally come out of it, you're gabbling about the darkness, the full moon, and eyes staring at you . . . and unspeakable things that frighten me.'

Getting out of her chair, she looked at him as though seeing a stranger. This time she spoke softly, as though not wanting others to overhear. 'You know what, Jack? I've always wondered, but now I know for certain. You're losing your mind! There's no other explanation.'

Jack was deeply shocked. 'I think you'd better leave.' Her accusations, her changed attitude, had unnerved him.

She went on, 'You really are out of your mind, I can see that now. So go ahead, do what you like. I want no part of it.'

Heading for the door, she turned, her face set like stone. 'Goodbye, Jack. Go and chase your ghosts. I really don't care what you do any more.' But what she said and what she thought were two different things.

Jack watched her leave, stunned by her cruel words. 'So I'm a crazy man, eh?' The awful thing was, he could almost believe her, but lately he had learned how vicious she could be when things did not go her way.

'That was a spiteful thing for her to say.' He thought about it for a moment, and was tempted to admit, she might be right.

That was why he had to go on this journey – to prove that he was as sane as anyone else.

Outside in Reception, they were still feeling shaken by Molly's stormy entrance. Jan was talking with Charlie, one of the sales team. 'What was she thinking,' Charlie said, 'coming in here and causing such a scene?'

'She's crazy!' Jan answered. 'I wouldn't mind smacking her one. Calling me his bitch!' She let her mind linger on that for a while, and a slow smile lifted her face. 'Come to think of it, I wouldn't mind being his bitch!'

~

The last two people to leave the building were Jan and Jack.

'I'm sorry about all that,' said Jack, referring to the nasty comment Molly had made. 'She hasn't always been so spiteful. It's my fault she's in such a rage.'

'That's not true!' Jan had a habit of speaking her mind. 'You can't blame yourself for her bad temper. We can all throw a tantrum when things don't go our way, but she was totally out of order. She just marched in and went straight for you. Thank God the boss wasn't here.

She didn't give a toss about getting you into trouble, did she? She obviously meant to have a row, and there was no stopping her.'

'She was right, though. It must have hurt, me taking my house sale to a rival company. But I thought it would be less hurtful to her.'

'Well, there you are, then So, like I said, her behaving like that was out of order.' Jan picked up her keys and shoulder-bag. 'Come on, let's get out of here. Look, if you don't mind me saying, your *ex*-girlfriend is nothing but a spoiled brat. Sweet and sugary when things are going right for her, then a cat in hell when she can't have her own way. For what it's worth, I think she showed you her true character today.' She tutted loudly, 'I bet even now, you still feel sorry for her?'

'I do a bit, yes.'

Jan chuckled. 'She was right about one thing.'

'What's that?'

'She wasn't far wrong when she called me a bitch.'

'Why do you say that?'

'Because she's a woman, and she knows deep down that I fancy you. If I thought I had a chance with you, it would be claws drawn at noon and no mercy.'

Jack laughed, 'You're a feisty sort, I'll give you that.'

'Right, I'm off now,' said Jan. 'Mind how you go, eh?'

~

On the drive home, Jack couldn't get Molly out of his mind. He kept thinking of the good times, and the guilt was like a clenched fist in his chest. Did he still want her? Or was he well rid of her?

There was a time, not very long ago, when she was his saviour. She had been there for him in his darkest hours. She had comforted him when he was low, and listened to him when he needed to talk things through. They were friends and lovers, and he had actually believed their relationship was too special to flounder.

Lately, though, he had seen a side of her that had shaken him. Maybe he had only now seen the real Molly. The Molly who by nature had to be in control. The Molly who had a nasty, vicious side when she was unable to pull all the strings.

When he actually thought back, Jack realised that he had always danced to her tune. But not this time, because he must follow his instincts and take this new promotion. As far as he was concerned, he had gone as far as he could to include Molly in his new venture, but she wanted none of it. With that in mind, he could see there was really no way forward.

His only option was to make a new life without her.

Sometimes, though, it was hard – almost impossible – to close the door on someone you loved.

CHAPTER ELEVEN

THERE WAS A real buzz in the showrooms, and Jan was more excited than anyone. 'Ooh! It's been a long time since we had a party here. The last one was four years ago, when Archie Taylor got promoted to Head Office. I'd only been here six months and I was asked to organise the food and everything – just like now.'

'I hope you didn't cook this food yourself?' Charlie said cheekily. He glanced along the reception desk, where a generous finger buffet had been laid out – more than enough to satisfy the dozen or so staff who had stayed behind for the event.

'No, I did not cook it,' Jan replied huffily. 'Not that I couldn't have if I'd been asked, but I got all the stuff from the supermarket, like I was told to do, and if I say so myself, I think I've done right by everyone.' She gestured to the many trays. 'We've got sausage rolls, assorted sandwiches and cold potato salad; there's all kinds of meat and enough bread rolls to build a house.

183

We've got various pastries and all manner of desserts, and—'

'All right, all right!' Charlie's stomach was already rumbling. 'We've got eyes. We can see it all, thank you very much.'

'Right! And have you seen the balloons – forty of them, all colours and shapes? And the banners that took me a good hour to put up all round the walls. Oh, and what about the toy car on top of the cake? I bought that out of my own money,' She gave a cheeky wink, 'which I fully intend to claim back.'

Charlie looked at the little red sports-car which had been plonked atop the small round cake. 'It's a bit naff, if you ask me.'

'Damned cheek!' She clapped him round the head. 'I wasn't asking you! Now clear off and find something to do, while I sort out the plates and stuff. The party doesn't start for another half hour.'

Charlie slunk away, while Bill arrived to take up residence in the same spot. 'I hope they give *me* a party when I take up my promotion,' he said longingly.

'If *they* don't, *I* will,' Jan grinned. 'But it won't be like this. It'll be crisps and Twiglets and a can of Coke – if you're lucky.'

Bill ignored her teasing. 'I hear one of the top brass is making an appearance here tonight. Why's that, then?'

'Three reasons,' said Jan importantly. She counted them off on her fingers: 'One, Jack's leaving here after ten years' service. Two, on Tuesday, he takes up the managership of a state-of-the-art showroom. And three, it will also be his birthday. So, don't you think that's reason enough for them to send at least one representative from Head Office?'

'Well, I think it smacks of favouritism,' said Charlie, who had rejoined them. He grabbed a sandwich and wolfed it down before Jan could stop him.

'Give over, Charlie,' said Bill. 'I reckon you want to party, and make a fool of yourself with the ladies. The thing is, you're worried that the man from Head Office might not approve. He gave a knowing wink. 'That's the truth, isn't it?' Charlie was not best pleased. 'I'd say you're stepping out of line, young man. You'd be wise to keep your opinions to yourself!' With that he stormed off to his office.

~

An hour or so later, everyone was in happy mood. The party was in full swing, with the food and wine flowing, and everything as it should be. As might be expected, little groups formed to chat together, while others jiggled to the loud music played by a local DJ.

From outside, Molly saw it all.

Having heard about the leaving party from her gossiping ex-colleague Tina, she thought it might be her last chance to persuade Jack, that it wasn't too late for them to get back together. After a few playful sessions with puppy-dog Mal, she realised more than ever that she did not want to lose Jack, that she still wanted him in her life. Even at this late date, she was conceited enough to believe that she could still change his mind.

When someone suddenly came outside to light up a cigarette, she quickly stepped back into the shadows. Before she ventured inside, she needed to plan what she would say to Jack, and this time she must not get angry. Last time she had gone about it the wrong way, so now, having thought it through, she knew she must change her tactics. With Jack, honesty and calm debate got the best results.

Oh, but what if he told her to leave? What if he threw her out? She had to convince him that she was not here to make trouble. She was here to mend things between them, to make him understand that he was her man and she was his woman, and she didn't want him going hundreds of miles away.

The thought of Jack in some other woman's arms made Molly even more determined to keep her temper under wraps. That way, he would soon realise that she was still the same old Molly he had loved for so long.

Unaware that he was being spied on, Jack made time to do the rounds, chatting to everyone in turn, and making sure they were well taken care of.

'You're definitely the man for the job, we have no doubts about that.' Oliver Mason, Curtis Warren's second-in-command, had risen in the ranks from salesman to manager, and was now one of the most important men in the business. 'I don't mind telling you, Redmond, we gave a lot of time and thought to who we really needed up there, and at every turn your name kept coming up.' Reaching out, he gave Jack a pat on the back. 'It's no more than you deserve,' he told him. 'I know you'll do us proud.'

Jan overheard, and was quick to agree. 'You couldn't have chosen a better man, Mr Mason,' she said, smiling at the big man. 'But you're taking him away from us, and that's not fair, is it?'

Ignoring the fact that she seemed a little too merry, and definitely livelier than usual, he gave her his friendliest smile. 'Hello, Jan. Sounds to me like you're here to give me a ticking off?'

Jan giggled, 'No, 'course not. Why would I do that?'

'Well, because I've stolen your best boy, of course. But that's the way it is. We needed the best and we found him in Jack.'

For a time, the three of them chatted amiably, before Mason excused himself. 'I've got less than an hour to do the rounds before the presentation. After that, I'd best be away – long journey back to London and all that.'

He looked up, as though searching for someone. 'That reminds me. I'd best find out if the driver's had anything to eat. I hope he's not been helping himself to the booze. I don't want to end up in some ditch this side of London, do I?' Concerned, he hurried away.

When he'd gone, Jan held out her hand. 'Hey, Jack. Let's you and me dance, eh? Celebrate.'

'I'm not sure I feel like celebrating, really,' he said. 'I've got other things on my mind right now. Like selling my house, and moving from one end of the country to another. Then there's the scary business of being responsible for the success of a brand-new showroom – or, as Oliver put it, "the company's show-piece". It's a lot to live up to, don't you think?'

Jan had no doubts whatsoever. 'You'll make a *huge* success of it,' she said tipsily. Flinging her arms round his neck, she whispered in his ear, 'I love you to bits, Jack Redmond!'

Jack gently eased her off. He had avoided the booze, and thought it best to humour her. 'And I love you too,' he said kindly.

He had not expected her to take his comment liter-ally, so when she got him in a headlock and kissed him passionately on the mouth, he was taken completely by surprise – as were their fellow workers, who began shouting and clapping, 'Woa! Looks like the party's started.'

Outside, hidden from sight, Molly saw them through the window, and misconstrued the whole thing.

Turning away in anger, she did not see Jack desper-ately separating himself from Jan. When she looked up again, she saw how Jack had his hands on the other woman's shoulders, and his head bent to her, as though in tenderness, when in truth Jack was telling Jan she'd had too much to drink and he thought it might be a good idea if he got a taxi to take her home.

'Dance with me, Jack . . . please?' Jan was not ready to leave.

With a great deal of care, Jack got her to the other

side of the room, where he sat her down, while he went away to phone for a taxi-cab. 'Don't you move!' he said. 'I'll be back in a minute.'

'Promise?' Reaching up, she caught hold of his hand and pressed it to her face. 'Sorry, Jack. I've been a naughty girl. I expect the big boss will give me the sack now, won't he?'

'No, he won't. This is a party, after all. But you've definitely had one too many, so just you wait there. I won't be long, I promise.'

Once he was out of sight, Jan waddled to the bar and got herself another gin and tonic, which she knocked back in one choking gulp. 'I am *not* drunk!' she announced to the bartender. 'And I am *not* going home yet, because I want a dance with Jack!'

The young bartender had been hired in order to leave everyone else free to enjoy themselves. He acknowledged Jan's comments with a smile and a nod.

'What's your name?' Hoisting her generous boobs onto the bar, she leaned towards him.

'David.'

'Well then, David – I don't suppose you'd like to dance with me, would you?'

Blushing a fiery shade of red, the young man wasn't really sure how to deal with her. 'No. I mean – I *would* like to dance, only I can't, because I'm on duty.'

In truth, the last thing he wanted was to be dragged round the floor by a drunken woman, especially as he wasn't been being paid for tonight, was only doing this job as a favour for a friend, who was just starting up

189

in the party-bar business. This was his first contract, but yesterday he took ill and couldn't do it.

'You little liar!' Steadying herself against the receptionist desk, Jan shamelessly teased the young man. 'You're really nervous, aren't you? Is that because I've got big boobs, or because you think I'm about to drag you away and ravage you?'

Laughing, she slithered down the bar out of sight, then popped up again. 'Don't be such a party-pooper! Let yourself go!' Catching hold of him by the collar, she yanked him across the counter, her face mingling with his. 'Listen to me, David, my lovely. Like Jack Redmond said, this is a party, and everyone should be on the floor dancing.'

'I *can't*. I'm on duty.' He had to stop himself from smiling at her comical antics, Please, can't you find somebody else to dance with?'

'Oh, I will!' Casting him aside, she confided with pride, 'D'you want to know my secret, David?'

'If you like.' Anything to just get rid of her, he thought.

'I've made a decision. There might be some misery-guts who won't like it, but that's tough titty, mate! 'Cause when they do the announcement, I'm gonna stand up there and tell everyone what a wonderful man Jack is.' She paused. 'Except he won't dance with me! And I don't think that's nice, do you?'

'No. That's a terrible thing.'

'What would you call a man who refuses to dance with a woman?'

'I'd call him a rotter.'

At which she collapsed in fits of laughter. 'You know what, David!' she screeched. 'You just called *yourself* a rotter. What are you like?'

She didn't even notice as he made his getaway. Tomorrow, he fully intended to tell his friend that he would *never* do another staff party! Though when he glanced back to see Jan fawning over every man as she passed him, he actually laughed out loud, 'Women!'

Still giggling, Jan tottered towards the glass doors. She even did a little jig as she wound her wobbly way through the dancing couples. 'Don't mind me!' she said, knocking them about like skittles. 'A bit of fresh air, that's what I need. Then I'll be right as rain.'

In the middle of the dance-floor, while the couples swirled about her, she paused a moment to rummage in her bag, looking for cigarettes and lighter. 'Damn and bugger it, can't find nothing in this bloody Tardis. Come out, you little sods!'

Having located the said items, she continued on her unsteady course towards the glass doors, which led to the large area of decking and the garden below.

The company had created this extravagant recreation area to impress the customers, and it had proved to be money well spent. Salesman–customer consultations could take place here, and it was a pleasant spot for the staff to have a sandwich and drink at lunchtime, on the rare occasions when the sun shone. Or even to have a crafty cigarette if there was no one using the facility for business purposes. And when there were

191

organised functions such as a new car launch or business promotions, the decking area had proved to be invaluable.

From her hiding-place behind the fencing, Molly watched as Jan threw open the doors, then positioned herself against the wooden railings as she shakily lit a cigarette. She took a long, lazy drag, held the smoke in her mouth for a moment, then blew it out in a perfect circle of smoke. 'Hey . . . *Wow!* Look at that!' Thrilled when the halo hovered before her face, she blew another, then another. Like a delighted child, she poked her finger into the centre of each and every smoke-ring. Laughing aloud, she blew more, faster and faster, until she was surrounded by a haze of smoke-rings. And as they shrunk into varying shapes, she was beside herself, falling about, breathless with laughter.

A moment later, her laughter was cut short when Molly took hold of her by the shoulders and spun her round. 'Think you're really clever, don't you?'

Assuming the stranger had seen her wonderful smoke-rings. Jan bosted, 'Yea! I bet you couldn't make more than me.'

Molly shook her by the shoulders. 'Don't you come the innocent with me! I saw you kissing Jack. You'd better keep your hands off him. Do you understand what I'm saying?'

With the daylight fading and the booze having a delayed effect on her, Jan found it hard to focus. 'Who the hell are you? What makes you think you can tell *me* what to do?' She struggled to get loose, but Molly had her in a tight grip.

'Did you hear what I said, you silly bitch? Leave my man alone!'

'If you mean Jack, he's not *your* man . . .' She stared Molly up and down. 'Ah, yes! I know who you are now. You're the big-mouth troublemaker who embarrassed him in front of everybody.' In the face of trouble, she was beginning to sober up, though she still felt sick. 'You'd best face it, lady. You and Jack are finished . . . for good!'

'Shut your stupid mouth! You're wrong – there's no way we're finished.'

'What?' Jan could give as good as she got. 'After what you did the other day, I shouldn't think he ever wants to set eyes on you again. Jack is done with you. And if I fancy my chances with him, it's none of your damned business.'

Molly gave her a shove. 'I'm telling you for the last time. Back off!'

'Says who? I don't take kindly to warnings, and besides, this is a private party. You've got no right to be here. Bugger off, before I call security!' With a stomach full of booze and a head that felt three times its size, Jan had an overwhelming need to be sick.

When Molly slapped her hard across the face, it came as a shock. Furious, Jan hit out with everything she'd got – fists, feet and knees. Soon the two of them were writhing on the floor – until Jan brought up the contents of her stomach, the sight and stench of which sent Molly diving for cover. *'You filthy animal!'* she screeched, disgusted.

Suddenly, Jack was there calling for someone to help Jan inside. Taking Molly by the arm, he demanded, 'what the devil are you doing here?'

'I'm here to make up with you, Jack,' Molly whined. 'I know I've been an absolute cow. I should never have burst into the showroom like that, and I'm truly sorry. I want us to get back together, Jack. At least, let's talk about it properly. Away from here.'

'As you may have realised,' said Jack curtly, 'this party is to celebrate my promotion. In a short time, there'll be a presentation, and I can't just go swanning off with you, Molly. Especially when I know, from past experience, it would be a waste of time anyway.'

Molly was desperate, 'It won't be. Honestly. I've given this a lot of thought, and I miss you so much, I'll do anything to have it all as it was before. Please, Jack.'

Jack was sorry that she was genuinely upset, but he knew Molly, and he knew the score. However, because he still had feelings for her, he listened to what she had to say. 'So, what happened to Mal?' he asked. 'I thought you had a thing going with him. Weren't you getting married?'

'It was just me being angry with you, Jack. It didn't mean anything.'

'Does Mal know that?'

'Yes,' she lied.

'And you're ready to come up north with me?'

Her hesitation gave him his answer, but he asked again. 'It's a straightforward question, Molly, and I would like a straightforward answer. Are you, or are you not, ready to move up to Lancashire with me?'

But still she wouldn't give him an answer. 'Well, it's obvious that nothing has changed,' he said. 'You have no intention of giving an inch. You want to keep your house, your job and your life here, which is your choice. But I have a choice too, and now that I've made it, I'm not about to change my mind. It seems that while you're prepared to give up nothing, you want me to give up my plans – hand back my promotion and turn my back on the only hope I've ever had of getting at the truth of these nightmares.' His voice was heavy with regret as he told her, 'I really thought you would be behind me all the way, Moll. If you truly love me, like you say you do, then you wouldn't be trying to put every obstacle in my way, instead of helping me.'

Realising every word he said was the truth, Molly began to panic. 'No, Jack! You need to hear what I'm saying, that's all.'

'Oh, I am, Molly. I'm hearing you loud and clear. I still love you – I can't deny that. But I'm not prepared to dance to your tune for the rest of my life. Can you understand what I'm saying, Molly? Do you even *want* to understand?'

'Please, Jack.' The tears began to flow. 'Don't do this to me.'

It hurt Jack to see her this way, but he knew he was right to leave, to do what he had set out to do. 'I'm sorry it's come to this, but at least let's part on good terms, eh?'

Molly looked up at him, at that familiar, handsome face, with those sincere, kindly eyes, and knew she would never find anyone like him again. 'I can't uproot myself, Jack,' she said. 'I've worked so hard for what I've got, and I can't let it go.'

Jack gave a sad little smile. 'But you can let *me* go, eh?'

'No, Jack. You're the one leaving. Not me.'

'Yes, Molly, that's very true, but I have my reasons, as well you know – better than anyone.' His voice softened, 'So, it looks like the end of the road for you and me. I'm sorry about that, Molly. Really, I am.'

Without a word, Molly reached into her handbag and gave him back his key. She turned away with a parting jibe: 'You could never have loved me, or you wouldn't be leaving me behind.'

He watched her go, and his heart was heavy. There was no denying that they had deep feelings for each other, but try as they might, they could not find a way to be together. And that was the hard truth of it.

Downhearted, he made his way back inside.

~

Outside, Molly lingered for a while, half-tempted to go after him, yet reluctant to do so. Instead, she found herself accepting that their relationship really was over.

She felt bitter and used, hoping that he would come to regret his decision to leave her behind.

So many questions flitted through her mind. Why was it that every time she found a man she truly cared for, he always left her sooner or later?

She asked herself, 'Is it me? Is there something about me that puts men off?' For the life of her, she could not understand it. 'I reckon I'm good-looking, and I keep myself smart. I've got a good job with prospects, and I'm nobody's fool. I stand up for myself and I make decisions. So, why do they always leave me?'

She felt sorry. Sorry for herself. Sorry for her predicament, and her failures. But it was not her fault. None of it was her fault. 'I'm coming up to thirty, and I need someone to be with me . . . to share my life and do the things I like to do.'

Being without Jack scared her.

Being on her own scared her even more.

After a time, when the night air made her shiver, she headed across the courtyard to her car. Once there, she unlocked the door and got in, but she didn't start the engine straight away. Instead, she sat in the driver's seat, wrapped her arms round the steering-wheel and, laying her head on her arms, she sobbed as though her heart would break.

What was left for her now? Where could she go from here? Eventually, looking in the driver's mirror, she wiped away her tears. Assuring herself that her misery was all Jack's fault, a terrible anger rose in her. 'I'll teach him a lesson he won't forget!' she vowed. 'Somewhere along the way he'll want me back – and then he'll find it won't be so easy. Oh yes! I still have cards to play. You're gonna be sorry, Jack Redmond. Sorry that you ever let me go.'

With a turn of the key, she started the engine, then accelerated away at speed, pleased that she had thought of a way to hit back at him. Congratulating herself on devising such a clever little plan, she could hardly wait to get back home. First though, she stopped off at the pub for a drink, and a chance to get her thoughts together. 'Just the one,' she told the barman. 'I'm driving.' Normally she might have a couple. But tonight, she had to keep her wits about her.

Some time later, when she pulled up in the drive, the house was in darkness. A quick glance at the dashboard clock told her it was almost 11 p.m. 'It's a bit early for the boys to be asleep,' she muttered, climbing out to lock the car. 'Maybe they're out, but they never told me they had plans.' Lately, Mal seemed to stay over more than she wanted, but when he and Brian were working on a project, they worked day and night, poring over plans and finance. It irritated her. In truth, just lately everything irritated her.

A moment later she entered the hallway to find the entire house in darkness. 'I thought I told Brian to always leave a light on when he goes out,' she muttered crossly. Switching on the light, she slammed her keys onto the hallway table and, throwing off her jacket, went into the kitchen. When she switched on the light there, she got a fright because Brian was sprawled across the table.

'*Hey!*' Brian had been fast asleep across the table. 'Who's that? What's going on? . . . Oh, it's you, Sis. I must have fallen asleep.' Littered across the table was a sea of paperwork, with an open notebook alongside, into which he'd scribbled copious notes. 'What's the time?' Rubbing his eyes, he looked up at the wall-clock.

'Time you got some proper sleep.' Molly had no sympathy for him. 'Look at you! What d'you think you'll achieve, staying up till all hours, dozing over your work?'

'Aw, don't start nagging me. Mal stayed and we got a lot of work done. He's such a lightweight – he went off to bed ages ago. Hope it's OK with you that he's stayed? I said it was OK.' Brian gave her one of his little-boy smiles. 'Are you making a drink?'

'No.'

'Aw, go on, Sis. I know you always have a hot chocolate before you go to bed.'

'Not tonight, I'm too tired.'

'Well, my throat's parched, so *I'm* having a drink. I'll make you one while I'm at it, if you like?'

Molly declined. 'I'm going to bed. Goodnight, then. And don't stay down here too long. Not if you want a clear head in the morning.' With that, she headed for the stairs.

On the landing, she thought of her plan, and for one minute it seemed so drastic, she wondered how

Mal might take it. Then she thought of Jack and how he had dumped her, and her hackles were up.

Once in her bedroom, she stripped off her clothes. Then she sauntered into the bathroom, where she freshened up, sprayed a little perfume over her nakedness and, running a little light mousse through her hair, fluffed it up about her face. The smallest suggestion of eye-shadow. A delicate dash of lipstick, and she was ready.

Across the landing, Mal was in the spare boxroom, fast asleep, when he sensed the duvet being lifted. Startled, he opened his eyes, and she was all over him, kissing his neck, his chest; her body writhing, warm and silky, against him.

In the half-light from the window, he realised it was Molly, and he could hardly believe it.

When he opened his mouth to speak, she placed her finger over his lips. 'Do you still want to marry me?' she purred.

Unable to speak, Mal nodded.

'Have you still got the diamond ring you bought,?'

'Yes.' He assumed he must be in heaven, that she was an angel and he would wake up any minute. 'Are you saying you've changed your mind about marrying me?' he asked drowsily.

She smiled sweetly. 'Why do you think I'm here . . . in your bed?'

Mal found it hard to believe. Having her here like this, hearing her say she wanted to be his wife, was like his every wish come true. When he took her in his arms, with her words of love ringing in his ears, he was the happiest man in the world.

If only he'd realised, that even in the throes of making love, Molly felt no affection or joy. Nor even the smallest sense of guilt for her betrayal of this kindly man who adored her unconditionally.

What she felt was deep regret – at losing Jack. At the same time, she felt a sense of triumph, that her plan of revenge would soon be accomplished. In fact, she was determined to become Mrs Malcolm Shawncross as quickly as possible. Poor Mal was simply a means to an end. It was Jack she wanted. But first, she needed to punish him.

And if Mal got hurt in the process? Well, that was too bad. At times like these, there were always casualties.

CHAPTER TWELVE

Thomas took his old jacket off the hall-stand and shrugged it on. He then put on his cap and wrapped his black-and-white chequered scarf round his neck. On this bright June morning it wasn't really cold outside, but he was taking the lovely Eileen out, and he wanted to look his best.

She was decent and trusting, and it truly hurt him to see her the way she was. In a way, though, it was a merciful thing, he thought, because it prevented her from remembering all the bad things in her past. All the bad things that other people like him were doomed to relive time and again, through memories that were etched on their souls for all time.

Thomas wanted to believe that Eileen had escaped that kind of torment. He himself would never have that measure of peace, because far too much had happened over the years for him to ever forget, or forgive.

From childhood to manhood, Thomas Farraday

could recall each and every regrettable thing that had been done by him and to him over the years. When, as a boy, he had been bullied at home by his father, and then at school by his own classmates, the only way he could protect himself and avoid being singled out was to turn the tables and become a bully himself.

He was haunted by one particular incident, when a crowd of boys waited for him outside school one day, and menacingly crowded round him, intent on doing him harm. Terrified, he had reacted by tearing into them before they could start attacking him – and in the chaos, one of the boys was sent reeling backwards into the road. The car that was passing had no chance of stopping, and the boy was run over; he suffered injuries that put him in hospital for weeks. Afterwards, no one knew who had actually hit him during the scuffle, but there was an investigation and severe reprimands for all. Suddenly, bullying was a thing of the past, and no one was more relieved than Thomas. Except he still had to go home to his violent father every night, and to this day, he looked on that terrible situation as his right and just punishment.

When he met Rose Willis, the lovely fair-haired girl who would later become his wife, it was as though everything in his life had come right at long last. The years fled by and their love grew stronger, but sadly, they were not blessed with children. That was something Thomas had longed for. To be a father who could rear his children with love and respect, to be a friend and confidante, someone who would show them the way. But it was not to be, and in time he came to accept that.

But then later, when Rose's mother took ill, for weeks on end he was left alone, while she travelled the considerable distance to Lancaster to be there for her ailing mother. Of course he understood, but when he suggested bringing her mother home so the two of them could take care of her together, his wife would have none of it. She claimed it was her duty to keep her mother in the home she knew and loved, and of course he had to accept that decision, but what really hurt him was that she chose to visit alone.

When he offered to take time off from work, to go with Rose, she always refused, saying her mother was growing increasingly nervous and difficult, and that him being there would only upset her. And so, her visits to her mother grew longer, and he grew increasingly lonely, every minute of the day and night that she was away from him.

After her mother died, his wife grew cold and distant. Not long after that, the wife he so adored was gone for ever. The cruel, empty years that followed had been crippling.

Then one Saturday, Libby had asked if he could keep an eye on her mother, while she popped to the corner shop. Eileen had gradually gone downhill over the years – everyone had noticed and pitied her decline. So Thomas had gone next door and stayed with Eileen. She made him laugh, and when she smiled at him in that adorable, childish way, his heart came alive again.

Libby came home to find them chuckling and having a good old chin-wag. When Thomas retired, he told Libby he would sit with her mother any time. Libby began to lean on him more and more, until one day, with his blessing and mainly to bring some much-needed extra cash into the household, she acquired a part-time job at the local supermarket.

The day Libby began to entrust her darling mother to his care was the day that life began again for Thomas. It was also the day when he began to fall in love again – and it was a wonderful thing. Almost like being born again.

Closing the front door behind him now, Thomas left the house to go next door to Number 20.

Libby let him in. 'Hello, Thomas,' she said. 'How are you today? I was just telling Mum that you're taking her out for a few hours, and that she must listen to what you tell her, and stay with you at all times.' In a lower voice she confided, 'Knowing how she wanders off at the drop of a hat, I do worry, especially when she so loves to be near the lake.'

'Don't worry. I'll keep a sharp eye out for her. I'll never be more than an arm's reach away at any given moment.'

'I know that. But you didn't mind me saying something, did you?'

Thomas shook his head, 'Not at all! Now, look, my dear – you'd best get off to work. And stop worrying. Your mother will be fine. We both will.' He smiled down at Eileen. 'Won't we, sweetheart?'

'I am, yes, thank you, Thomas.' Eileen had gone into a little world of her own.

As always, believing it to be the right thing to do, Thomas corrected her: 'Eileen?'

'Yes, Thomas?'

'I just asked you a question, and you weren't listening.'

'Oh, and what did you say, then?'

'I asked if you and me would be fine on our day out, just the two of us.'

'Yes, Thomas. We'll be fine.' She looked up at him. 'We will, won't we?'

'We certainly will, m'dear.' He held her hand fast. 'There won't be anyone finer.'

'So, where are we going?'

'To the park, of course. You must remember that we talked about it yesterday.' He prompted her to think back.

Eileen gave a frown, then she was smiling, 'Oh, we're going to see the ducks . . . and we've got a lovely picnic . . .' She frowned. '. . . I think?' She glanced at Libby.

'Hey! What's all this?' Pointing to the bag on Libby's arm, Thomas chided, 'Don't tell me you've packed us a meal?'

'I have, yes. Sandwiches and fruit, and orange juice and some plastic cups.'

'You're too thoughtful,' he tutted. 'I know we're two old 'uns, but we're capable of finding the tearooms. I'm not short of a bob or two, neither. I'm sure I can afford a sandwich and a pot of tea.'

'No, Thomas. Thank you all the same, but it's enough you taking Mum to the park, without you having to spend your money as well.'

A few minutes later, Thomas had secured Eileen into the front passenger seat of the car and they were ready to leave. 'Right then, Libby, let's have that picnic bag.'

When she passed it over, he groaned and made a big fuss over it, as though in agony. 'Oooh, it's too heavy for an old fella like me!' He gave her a wink as he said to Eileen, 'I reckon your daughter's trying her best to finish me off!'

Eileen laughed heartily, 'You're a comedian, that's what you are, Thomas.'

Satisfied that everything was in order, Libby gave Thomas a little peck on the cheek, then hugged her mother. 'I'm away to work now, Mum. You have a really lovely day, and I'll see you both later.'

'And you be a good girl, while we're gone!' Eileen told her. 'Else you'll have your father after you.'

Her comment did not surprise Libby, but she felt obliged to remind her gently, 'Daddy was a long time ago, Mum,' she said softly. 'It's just you and me now.'

Though Libby's own memories of her father were very limited, she knew that he was always strong in her mother's mind. Whenever Eileen talked of him, Libby felt her pain. It was such a sad thing.

Eileen and Thomas waved her off. 'That's it, my beauty.' He made sure Eileen's seatbelt was secure.

Eileen was still waving. 'Where's she gone?'

'She has to be at work,' he reminded her. 'And now, we'd best be on our way.'

'Where are *we* going, Thomas?'

'Where do you *want* to go?'

'I don't know.'

'Yes, you do.'

'Do I?'

'Think hard, my lovely. We've been there before, lots of times. It's a place you love to be. It's where you always ask me to take you.'

Eileen went quiet, almost sulky. Then, with a little shout and a clap of the hands, she cried out. '*The park!* We're going to the park!'

Thomas gave a whoop. 'That's right, my darling. We're going to the park. What a clever girl you are.'

'I know.' She gave a proud little giggle. 'I'm a clever girl.'

Her simple joy made Thomas smile. In her declining health, he had never known Eileen be angry or spiteful. Instead she was always thoughtful and caring. Yet, she was often afraid, and occasionally she would jump at either himself or Libby for the simplest things, like forgetting to put the sugar in her tea, or plumping the cushion too much in her favourite chair.

Somehow, over the years, almost without him realising, this wonderful lady had become the light of his life. He never told her, because in the circumstances, it was not the thing to do. But it was a joy to be with her. Considering how very much he had loved his wife, his deep feelings for Eileen in these later years had come as a great surprise to him.

Corporation Park was not far away – through the back streets then along King Street and up Montague Street, and there, high above the town itself, was the proud, impressive entrance, hiding a secret that would amaze and delight the unsuspecting visitor.

Built many years ago, amidst great pomp and celebration, this magnificent park was not only a haven of beauty and delight, it was also a treasured refuge from the busy lives and relentless duties of the townsfolk.

With an impressive stone lion at either side of the tall iron gates, and the first sighting of that wide lane meandering its way up through the heart of the park, the mere act of leaving the mayhem behind, to stroll through that man-made paradise, was a joy in itself. If the heart was heavy when the visitor walked inside, it became lighter after spending precious time within the tranquil beauty of that most exquisite place.

'Here we are!' Because vehicles were not allowed within the park, Thomas turned immediately left before its gates. It took him but a minute to find a suitable spot for parking. 'Right then, m'darling, let's get you out.'

Just a few moments later they were ready to go, with the picnic bag hanging on Thomas's arm.

Eileen was like a child let loose in a sweet-shop. 'Ooh, can we go to the lake? I want to feed the ducks. I know we have bread, because Libby told me.'

'We can go anywhere your heart desires,' Thomas promised; and Eileen was content in the knowledge that he would keep his word.

'We're fortunate to have such a lovely day,' he said as they made their way down the lane and into the park. 'June can be a funny month sometimes. Even so, I'd have still brought us here, even if it was raining cats and dogs.'

'I never said it was raining!'

'No, sweetheart, I know you didn't say it was raining.'

'So, what did I say, then? Tell me what I said!' She grew agitated.

Thomas stopped by a rosebed.

'No need for you to get upset,' he said gently. 'You've done nothing wrong.'

Unsure, Eileen looked him in the eye. 'Who said I was upset?'

'No one.'

Eileen tutted. 'Oh, so that's all right then, isn't it?'

Thomas was very careful in his approach. 'Well, yes, everything seems all right to me.'

'So why have we stopped, especially when it's about to rain?'

He gave her a peck on the cheek. 'It's not going to rain, love. I think we got a bit lost in our conversation just then – about the rain and such.'

'*You* said it was raining, not me! You're all mixed up, Thomas.' She wagged a finger. 'I don't know what's wrong with you.'

Thomas felt the laughter bubbling inside, and try as

he might, he could not hold it back. 'Do you have any idea how much I love you?'

'I love you too,' she said sternly. 'Now stop being silly.' Then, in a quieter voice, she said, 'Thomas?'

'Yes?'

'You do love me, don't you, Thomas?'

'I certainly do, yes.'

'Do you want to know something?'

'If you like, yes.'

'I love you too.'

And because she had uttered those sincere words when her mind appeared to be fully alert, Thomas found he was too choked up to make an immediate reply. Then he cleared his throat and told her, 'That is such a wonderful thing for you to say.'

'Would you do something for me, Thomas?'

'Of course – if I can.'

The confident little glance she gave him was that of a woman at peace with herself. 'May I please have a proper kiss?'

Thomas was pleasantly surprised. He had already kissed her, but he thought maybe she'd forgotten.

Growing impatient, she raised her small hands to place them either side of his face, and when she smiled at him in a special way, with her brown eyes sparkling, he felt his heart turn over. 'I'm waiting for my kiss, Thomas,' she said. 'A proper one, mind.'

Gingerly placing his hands over hers, then easing them into his large fists, he leaned forward and kissed her softly on the cheek.

When he moved away, she caught hold of his arm and kept him there. 'Naughty Thomas!' She suddenly closed her eyes, lifted her face up to him, and in a small, trembling voice she whispered, 'Please, I need a *proper* kiss.'

In the whole of his life, Thomas Farraday had never experienced emotions such as now, when his heart turned inside out, and he was lost as to what he should do. There was nothing he would like more, than to give her a 'proper' kiss, providing he could remember what a proper kiss was! He had been without a woman for so long, he could hardly remember.

He must not take advantage of Eileen, in her fragile state of mind – that would be a shocking betrayal of trust. So he smiled and brushed away her request for a 'proper kiss'. 'We'd best get a move on, m'dear,' he said casually. 'We don't want to miss the ducks, now do we, eh?'

When he tried to make a move, she held him there. 'Thomas!'

'Yes?'

'I'm waiting.'

Emotionally torn, he leaned forward, like a shy boy on his first date. Tenderly placing his lips over hers, he was shocked by the warm softness of her skin against his mouth, and the way her lips opened to his.

When she raised her arms to wrap them about his neck and draw him ever closer, the long, sorry years fled away. He was a vibrant young man again, with a young man's heart and soul.

For what seemed the longest and most wonderful

moment of his life, Eileen held him close. She was his sweetheart, and he was her man. And the stirring of emotion, so deep and amazing, took his breath away.

It was a long kiss. The kiss of true lovers. And when it was over, he knew he would never forget that very special moment. He would cherish the memory. It would go with him to the grave.

When she released him and looked up into his astonished face, her tender expression revealed the true strength of the love she felt for him. It was there, too, in the light of her shining eyes. She was a woman in love. A woman who trusted him enough to allow him into her heart. In that lingering moment, her eyes told him more than a thousand words ever could.

Then, without warning, her smile was gone; the light in her eyes grew dim, and the cruel cloak of twilight passed over her mind. The magic had flown, and now she was fiddling with her hair, twirling it round and round in her fingers, until it seemed she might pull it out by the roots. 'Don't do that, sweetheart.' He softly laid his hand over hers.

'Thomas?'

'Yes, what is it?'

Her face lit up. 'I'm glad you're here.'

Thomas nodded. 'I'm glad as well.' Today was turning out to be a very emotional journey.

'I'm *really* glad you're here.' She was so pleased, she repeated it: 'I'm glad you're here.' Her voice faltered. 'Did I say that right, Thomas?'

'Yes, you said it right – twice, in fact.' The whisper of a smile crossed his face. 'Well done.'

When he now clapped his hands, she clapped hers too. 'See!' She wagged a finger at him. 'I know what I said, and it's not raining yet. So get a move on, Thomas, before the skies open!'

Because it had confused her, Thomas was beginning to wish he'd never even mentioned the damned rain!

It was as well she couldn't see him quietly smiling as he walked with her down the path beside the pretty flower-beds. With every passing second he loved her that little bit more, until his heart was fit to burst. 'I do love you, Eileen,' he muttered softly under his breath.

'That's 'cause you belong to me,' she said matter-of-factly.

The tears quickening in his eyes, Thomas pretended not to have heard her. Instead, he said in a firm voice, 'Watch out, you ducks, here we come!'

As they made their way up the hill, he warned himself that just now, when she claimed that he 'belonged' to her, Eileen was probably thinking about her late husband, Ian. She did that often, talking to him as though he was the husband she had loved and lost. Many times she addressed Libby, poor girl, as though her father was still with them.

Both he and Libby had come to accept the situation, but whenever Eileen addressed him as though speaking to her husband, the pain of it all was like a clenched fist inside Thomas.

The first stop was the lake. It was a long, hard walk, though as they followed the path up into the spinney, the birdsong and the pleasant scents wafting from the myriad blooms of every colour, shape and size, made the way less arduous and more of a journey for the soul. *'Look, Thomas – look there!'*

Eileen had spotted two doves. So close you could reach out and touch them, they were settled on a tree-branch, face to face, making loving noises while they inched closer together.

Thomas came to a halt a short distance away. 'Ssh!' Putting his finger to his lips, he whispered, 'We mustn't frighten them away,' and she gave a little nod of understanding.

For what seemed an age, Eileen remained mesmerised, her face tilted upwards and her eyes wide with amazement. She kept smiling at Thomas, who was congratulating himself because he'd chosen to go the longest route to the lake. He could so easily have gone straight up the main walkway, but they would have missed all the glorious sights that now surrounded them.

When they arrived at the man-made lake, Thomas slung the picnic bag over his shoulder and, giving Eileen his other arm to hang on to, they walked arm in arm to the bench at the edge of the lake, where he sat her down, before dropping the bag on the grass.

'Are you hungry?' he asked.

'Not yet.'

'Thirsty?'

'No, thank you, Thomas.'

Leaning back against the bench, she sat very still, watching the water as the gentle breeze moved it along in gentle ripples. And while she watched the water, Thomas watched her, thinking that he was more content than any man deserved to be.

After a while, Eileen grew restless. 'Where are the ducks, Thomas?'

'Oh, I'm sure they'll be along in a while. I expect they're hiding under the bushes, having a little kip.'

'Promise?'

'I don't know if I should.'

'Are you fibbing, then?'

'I hope not.'

'So, promise me, then.'

'What exactly do you want me to promise?'

She looked at him in puzzlement. 'How should I know?'

'Well, if *you* don't know, I'm sure I don't.'

'There you go again, Thomas! You've no idea what you're talking about. You've got it all mixed up again.'

Thomas pointed to the reeds. 'OK, then. D'you see them reeds there?'

'Where?'

He pointed again. 'There – see?'

'Yes.'

'Any minute now them ducks will pop their little heads out, to have a look at you and me.'

And sure enough, when Eileen stretched her neck to see, the mother and her babies swam out, as if to say hello. Eileen laughed and clapped her hands and if Thomas had not stopped her, she would have gone right to the edge of the lake to see them.

'Not so fast!' Carefully, Thomas took her by the hand and led her down the path, where the two of them stood on the grass to watch as the little family swam to the far edge and waddled ashore.

Eventually, Thomas laid out the picnic rug and the two of them sat and enjoyed a lunch of ham-and-cress sandwiches, followed by home-made apple pie, all washed down with a measure of orange juice from the little plastic tumblers packed by Libby.

When the meal was over and everything was put away, Thomas took out his pipe and puffed away contentedly, while beside him, Eileen was happy just to sit and throw bread to the ducks and other birds scavenging for crumbs of food.

Now and then, Thomas would steal a private glance at Eileen. He saw how she had her face upturned to the sun, and he thought this was how it should be: him and his darling, side by side, so very much in love as they watched the world go by. Then he thought of her late husband and he was filled with remorse. Ian Harrow should be here, sharing the day with Eileen. He should be here, to hold her and give her a 'proper' kiss. But he wasn't, and that was the shame of it.

When later, all his baccy was burned up, Thomas tapped out his pipe and put it away. 'Do you fancy a walk along the lakeside and up to the conservatory?' he asked Eileen.

'Oh, yes please, Thomas!' Eileen was excited. 'I would like that very much.'

He was thrilled that this time Eileen had not mistaken him for her husband, as she often did. This time, she had actually asked for 'Thomas' to take her.

Hoisting the empty bag over one shoulder, he linked arms with Eileen, taking great care to keep her away from the water's edge. 'You must let me know if you get tired,' he warned. 'I don't want you exhausting yourself.'

To which Eileen promptly replied, 'I'm stronger than you – that's what Libby said.'

Amused, he asked, 'Oh, she did, did she?'

'Yes.' Eileen tried to recall what her daughter had said. 'A man does not . . . have the same . . . he does not . . .' She stopped, then she blew out her cheeks in frustration. 'Oh dear! I know she said something. All I know is that I am a woman, and I'm stronger than you, 'cause you're a man.'

Quietly amused, Thomas gave her no argument, except to suggest, 'If it gets too hot, we'll go and sit under the trees, shall we?'

Eileen had a great passion for trees. 'Oh yes, I'd like that.'

Seeing that she looked tired, he slowed the pace as they headed off towards the tropical plant-houses. When they got within sight of the towering glass buildings, Eileen grew nervous. 'I don't want to go inside there. I don't like them big plant-things. They might gobble you up if you're not careful.'

219

Because of her fears and the fact that she was tiring now, Thomas took a different, much slower, route. Soon, they had passed the flower-beds, and now they had the old trees in their sights. It was rumoured that these ancient fields, and the timeless woods held many secrets. During the day the park was a bright, open space filled with families and echoing to the laughter of children, but when everyone had gone and darkness fell, it was a brooding, forbidding place. Maybe that was why, from midnight to sunrise, the park was deserted – even though the gates remained open.

Eileen was fascinated by the trees. 'They hide the sky and you can't see the sunshine.' Seated on a wooden bench beside the lion fountain, she pointed to the tallest of them. 'Look! I can't see the sun any more.'

'That's because the branches and leaves create a massive canopy, shutting out the daylight.' It saddened him to realize how Eileen's dementia would suddenly cut into her mind make her a small child again, even if only for a few moments.It was cruel thing.

'Thomas?'

'Yes?'

'Are the trees taller than the houses?'

'Much, much taller.'

'Look at that one.' She pointed to a particularly magnificent spruce. 'How did it get to be that big?'

'It's very old, sweetheart.'

'Yes, but how did it get so big?'

Not being an expert on trees, Thomas tried to explain in simple terms. 'Let me see. Well, first of all, they've got roots, y'see. The roots are deep under the ground. They're long and winding, a bit like arms. They can reach out, searching and feeling. Looking for any food or goodness in the soil. Then they suck it up, and it goes into the branches and the leaves, and that's how the tree grows so big.'

'Oh, now I see . . . I think.' When Eileen fell silent again, Thomas thought she might be getting tired. 'I reckon it's time we headed for home,' he said.

Eileen gave a little nod. She stared into the distance, her mind elsewhere.

'Is anything wrong?' he asked worriedly. She had grown unusually quiet.

In a soft, anxious voice, she asked, 'Can we go home, please, Thomas?'

'Course we can, my darling.'

'Thank you, Thomas.'

'It's my fault,' he chatted on. 'I ought never to have kept you out so long.' He had been enjoying himself so much, he'd simply lost track of time. 'I'm sorry I tired you out. But we'll be home soon. After you've had a little sleep, you'll feel right as rain.'

In the car, Eileen remained deep in thought. But when they approached Peter Street, she cried out, *'Stop the car, Thomas!'*

Alarmed, he did an emergency stop. 'Good grief, Eileen!' He felt shaken. 'Whatever made you scream out like that? Whatever's wrong?'

Leaning over, he checked her seat-belt and found it still fastened. 'You mustn't yell out like that when I'm driving along – unless there's an emergency.' A thought occurred to him. 'Do you want to spend a penny, is that it?'

'No.' She pointed down Peter Street, to the old church. 'I need to go in there.'

Thomas was puzzled, 'Why would you need to go into the church? We should be getting back, sweetheart. What if I bring you here on Sunday?'

'I need to go now.'

Thomas had little choice but to do as she asked. So he parked outside and walked her to the church doors. He was about to go in with her, when she told him emphatically, 'No. I need to go in on my own.' So he watched her go in, then returned to wait in the car.

A few moments later, unable to relax, he was out again, peering in through the big doors to see her kneeling up at the front, before the altar, head bent forward and hands together as though in prayer. Whatever was she thinking? He had never known her be like this before. A niggling thought came into his mind.

Braving her displeasure, he went softly to her side and knelt down, only to receive a scolding. 'You must go away from here!' she hissed. 'Please, Thomas, leave me be.'

Concerned, he returned to his car, from where he anxiously watched the door, waiting for her to emerge.

Inside the church, Eileen knelt before the altar, her head bowed and her heart heavy. She knew He was there, bleeding on the cross, punished for the sins of others. The tears trickled down her face. He was being punished for her sins too. He was suffering because of her, and the bad things she had done.

'I'm sorry,' she murmured over and over. 'I didn't mean for it to happen, and I'm truly sorry.'

She knew there was something terrible, but she couldn't remember what it was. Blinded by the tears, she looked up into that beautiful, loving face, and her heart was calmer.

There was so much she needed to tell Him. Secret things, that frightened her. A heavy burden which she was finding increasingly hard to carry. Time and again she had tried so hard to remember, but she couldn't. All she knew was that she had been bad, and that she needed to be punished.

She tried to remember but it was all muddled in her memory; it was midnight and the moon was low. Something bad was happening and the shocking things she had witnessed. 'Help me, Lord,' she murmured. 'Please help me.'

She began rocking back and forth, increasingly agitated. 'Oh dear! Oh, dearie me!' Her quiet sobs echoed through the emptiness. The darkness and the shocking images would never leave her. It was a terrifying burden.

Exhausted and unsure, she made the sign of the cross on herself, stood up, and out loud, she implored Him: 'Please, Lord, watch over me. Make me good. And please, I need You to love me.'

And then she stumbled down the aisle and out of the door, as though the devil himself was chasing her.

Shocked to see her hurrying towards him, sobbing and calling out his name, Thomas scrambled out of the car and brought her safely back. 'It's all right,' he soothed her. 'I've got you now.' He was unsettled. What could have happened inside the church to upset her like that? Yet, she had been unsettled since they left the park, 'Eileen?'

'I don't want to talk to you.' She was frantic. 'I don't want you to kiss me again!'

When she began sobbing, there was nothing he could do except start the car and drive her home. 'I'm sorry,' he said sincerely. 'You're right. I should never have kissed you like that.' Now he felt as though he'd betrayed her. He should have realised that when she asked him for a 'proper' kiss, she really had no idea of what she was asking. But it was not her fault. It was his! He should have been the responsible one.

~

They covered most of the journey home in absolute silence. But by the time they reached Bower Street, Eileen was chatting away as normal, as though nothing had transpired. Thomas was still in a state of anxiety, but Eileen was incredibly calm, even relaxed.

'Thank you for taking me to see the ducks, Thomas.' She patted his hand. 'When we go again, the little babies will be all grown up, won't they?' Her smile was wonderful.

Amazed and shaken by the complete change in her manner, Thomas answered softly, 'Yes, I believe they will.' The episode with the kiss, and then the need to visit the church, all appeared to have been forgotten. He was thankful for that much at least.

'Thomas?'

'Yes, m'dear?'

'I've been bad, haven't I?'

'How do you mean?'

'Tell me if I've been bad. I need to know.'

'Of course you haven't.' He was troubled by her question.

She gave a huge sigh. 'I love you, Thomas.'

In view of her upset today, he wisely decided not to respond to her declaration of love. Outside the house just as he was getting her out of the car, Libby walked along the street. 'Well, that was good timing,' said Thomas. 'Your Libby's here. Look!'

Libby ran to hug her mother. 'Did you have a good time today, Mum?'

Eileen nodded. 'We went everywhere. We saw the ducks and the big old trees, and it was sunny, then it was raining, and then it was sunny again.' She laughed out loud. 'Thomas got it all mixed up!'

Thomas explained, 'We did have a lovely time.' Handing Libby the picnic bag, he wisely made no mention of Eileen's disturbing mood, and how she had gone into the church, only to come out in a blind panic.

'She's tired,' he said. 'I really should have brought her back earlier.'

Eileen swiftly corrected him. 'My legs are tired, Thomas, but *I'm* not tired!' She gave a long yawn.

'Aw, she'll be fine.' Libby thanked Thomas. 'I'll get her a hot drink, then put her to bed for an hour. I imagine you're ready for a rest yourself. I can't thank you enough. You're a dear friend to both of us.'

'You get some rest,' he told Eileen. 'I'll see you later.'

Pursing her lips, she kissed him on the cheek. 'Thank you, Thomas.'

Feeling a little easier, Thomas said, 'It's me that should be thanking you. I've had a wonderful day.' Apart from the church episode, he thought worriedly. He was momentarily taken aback when Eileen said, 'You mustn't worry about me, Thomas.' He had an odd feeling, almost as though she was reading his mind.

Libby's voice cut the silence. 'You're very welcome to stay and have a drink with us, if you like?'

Thomas graciously refused, 'I'll no doubt see you tomorrow, eh?'

As Thomas said his goodbyes, he glanced back as Eileen turned her head to look at him. Her expression was one of gratitude, love and absolute trust.

He thought of the wonderful kiss they had shared and couldn't help feeling deeply guilty about it.

~

MIDNIGHT

It was almost midnight when Libby awoke. Something had disturbed her. She got out of bed and went to the window, to look out at the darkness. It was a strange night, she thought. Nothing moved. Everything was too still, too silent. The sky was magnificent – dark and ominous – a night you would not want to be out in. Through the branches of the trees, she could see the moon, hanging like a huge lantern, sending shivers of light across the darkness.

Entranced, Libby was loath to tear herself away, but then she heard the same sound that had awoke her before – a kind of muffled whimper, as though someone was crying. Immediately, she ran out of the room and along the landing. At her mother's door, she stopped to listen, and she heard the crying. 'Mum?' She tapped her knuckles against the wood. 'Mum, are you all right?'

There was another, different sound, like a chair being moved. 'Yes, thank you.'

Libby was not convinced. 'May I come in for a minute?'

'Why?'

'Just to see if you're OK.'

'All right.'

Libby went inside and found the room in total darkness but for the shaft of moonlight that filtered in through the window. 'Whatever are you doing there, Mother?'

Eileen was in her nightie, standing by the open window; the curtains, too, were wide open. The room was bitterly cold.

'Come away from there, Mother!'

Libby hurried across the room. 'It's freezing in here. You'll catch your death!'

As though she hadn't heard, Eileen remained where she was. 'Look at that.' Pointing to the trees, she told Libby, 'Did you know that trees have arms under the ground?'

Libby closed the window. 'Trees don't have arms,' she answered thoughtfully. 'They have roots – but I suppose you could say they might look a bit like arms, all long and skinny . . . alive and moving about.'

'That's right.' What Libby had said had reinforced the image in her mother's mind.

Libby sighed. She was tired after her stint at the super-market, and aching to get back to her warm bed. 'It's late, Mum. Why are we talking about trees, especially at this hour?' She was so tired she could hardly think straight.

Eileen was gazing out of the window. 'I like the trees,' she murmured, as though talking to herself. 'We need them, don't we? We'll have to get some and put them in the garden. Get Thomas some as well, and then we'll be all right, won't we?'

'Mum, can we talk about all this tomorrow?'

Eileen went on, 'If we have trees, and they have arms that go out looking for food, they'll gobble up all the good things, and the bad things too. And then the bad things are gone forever, aren't they?'

Libby drew the curtains. 'If you say so, Mum.' She was used to her mother's strange ideas when her mind wandered.

'That would be good, because then all the bad things could never come back. Nothing could hurt us any more, so we wouldn't be afraid then, would we?'

Libby led her back to bed. 'There is nothing to be afraid of,' she said comfortingly. 'At least not in here' – she glanced at the window – 'and not out there either.'

'Are you sure?'

'I'm positive. Now then, it's obvious you've had some kind of bad dream, but you should not be out of bed, especially with the window and the curtains wide open.'

She needed to know her mother was safe. 'Look, Mum, it might be best if you come and sleep with me tonight.'

Eileen was adamant. 'Certainly not! I have my own bed. I'm not a baby.'

'All right, but if you need me, just call and I'll be here straight away. OK?' Libby kissed her goodnight for the second time. 'I'm glad you enjoyed yourselves today.'

'Thomas kissed me.'

Libby smiled at that, 'He thinks a lot of you.'

'And I think a lot of him.'

'Good. Now, please – can we both get some sleep?'

Back in her own bed, Libby lay awake for an age, listening and wondering, and smiling at the thought of Thomas giving her Mum a kiss, 'Thomas kisses everybody,' she told George, her teddy bear. 'I bet he was a real ladies' man in his time.'

After a few minutes of blessed silence, with no sounds

emanating from her mother's room, she fell into a deep sleep.

Next door though, Eileen could not sleep. She got quietly out of bed again and, tiptoeing over to the window, she opened the curtains and looked out.

It was past midnight, but the scene had not changed. The skies were pitch-black, save for hazy shafts of moon-light. The emptiness beneath was interspersed with all manner of eerie things: crooked tree-branches and other, ominous shapes. Each one different, and so incredibly still.

Eileen's curious gaze fixed on them one after the other, looking, imagining, until the fear took hold again.

It was the same. Always the same.

Quickly now, she closed the curtains and climbed back into bed. She remembered what Libby had said, that they would talk about it tomorrow, but she didn't want to talk about it. Not any more. Not ever! Because if she didn't talk about it, maybe it would all go away, and she wouldn't be afraid ever again.

She searched her mind for the pictures, but she couldn't find them. They'd gone away. But they would be back.

They always came back.

CHAPTER THIRTEEN

Six weeks had passed since he and Molly had split up for good. And now, midway through August, Jack was ready to leave Bedfordshire for ever. Tess at Johnson & Everett had found a buyer for his house. Everything had gone smoothly and there was nothing to keep Jack there. It was time to take one last look around.

With bittersweet feelings, he wandered from room to room. It was strange that everything looked the same: the chairs stood where they had always stood, the red patterned rug lay in front of the fireplace, and even the walls were still adorned with framed pictures of vintage cars – though these were about to be taken to storage in Lytham, along with the furniture, until he found a place to buy. For the time being, he was renting a furnished house in Lytham.

He cast his gaze across the sitting-room, content that all of his precious books and photographs were now carefully packed into the large boxes which stood in the centre of the floor. His clothes, his laptop and most of his personal possessions had already been ferried up to Lytham.

He had spent four good years in this house, and there was no denying that he would miss it, just as he would miss his work colleagues in Bletchley. He had no doubt, however, that they would still meet up at various conferences and the like. For now, he had already said his goodbyes to them, and as far as he was concerned, that particular door was shut. It was now time to look forward.

Shrugging off the creeping sense of regret, he went into the hallway and ran up the stairs two at a time. His first stop was the main bedroom – his retreat, overlooking the back garden. He had found much-needed solace here, particularly when his childhood heartache played heavily on his mind.

He had slept here, and when times were good with Molly, they had made love in this very room.

Thinking back on it now, he knew he must shoulder some of the blame for the way things had turned out. He had given in to her until she became selfish and demanding – and he hoped she would not take advantage of Mal, as he was a good and generous man who doted on her. For that very reason, Mal might have to pay a hard price.

Jack had loved Molly, but he was not sorry to have left her behind. They each had a new life, a new beginning. And yet his was not really a beginning; it was more like a going back. After all these years, he was headed home, back to his roots.

Without him consciously trying to recall her, Libby came into his mind. Her name sat well on his lips: 'My dear friend, Libby.' He could see her now in his mind's eye – her small, pretty face and those lovely, honest eyes. And the way her nose wrinkled when she giggled, as she so often did. The thought of Libby was like a ray of sunshine to brighten this lonely day.

Libby had been someone he could talk to. She was thoughtful and generous. A loyal and caring friend, come rain or shine. Even now, with other matters on his mind, Libby was paramount in his thoughts. 'I expect, after all this time, she's forgotten all about me,' he murmured. 'I expect Libby's married now with a husband and children.' He found himself envying that man, whoever he might be.

Molly too had once been caring and loving. Recently though, he had seen a different side to her. When he had stopped dancing to her tune, she had revealed her true nature, and it was not pleasant.

Molly had proven to be a fair-weather friend. Like a child, she stamped her foot if she didn't get her own way, and that did not bode well for a life together; especially when she knew, more than anyone, how badly the nightmares affected him. Thankfully, for some reason he had not suffered a really bad one of late. Perhaps because there was too much to think about, too much to plan for.

When the loud rat-a-tat came at the front door, it startled him. *Hold on!* Springing up, he ran down the stairs at the double. *'I'm on my way!'*

Flinging open the door, Jack was pleased to see the small removal van at the kerbside. 'Are you Mr Redmond?' The man who spoke was of burly build, with a tuft of grey hair sticking out each side of his cap.

'I am, yes,' Jack confirmed. He led the man and his skinny mate along the passageway to the front room. 'A lot of the big stuff has been sold off or given away,' he explained. 'I thought I'd make a clean sweep. Everything is packed, apart from half a dozen small boxes.

Taking down the paintngs, the burly fellow carefully began bundling them up in bubble-wrap. 'Hey, look at that!' He pointed to the painting of a vintage car. 'My dad had one o' them! It was his very first car.'

When the packing and loading were done, and the form duly signed, the two men stopped on the path to light a cigarette. Jack overheard the big fellow going into raptures about the paintings. 'I can't believe he's got a painting of a Hillman Minx! I should've asked if he wanted to sell it.'

'Shouldn't think he'd sell it,' came the gruff reply. 'Class bit of engineering, that car was.'

'It's not the some these days though, is it? No quality. Same as today's music. Oh, but we used to have some great bands.'

The skinny man took a long drag on his roll-up. 'I always used to like the Beatles as a band,' he said, picking a shred of tobacco off his top lip. 'But I never could stand that Paul McCartney. He allus looked like a cocky little bugger to me.'

'Well, maybe that's because he's talented an' you never will be.'

'Huh! I'd like to see 'im shift a six-foot bed with iron legs on his own.'

The big man's laughter echoed down the street. 'Never mind *'im!* I'd like to see *you* do that on yer own. Even *I'd* 'ave to struggle. I might be built like a tank, but I'm only human. Yer daft sod! What are yer like? You'd be lost without me!'

As always, the foreman had the last word.

~

Jack took one last look around, then he left the house and went to sit on the front doorstep.

'You're leaving then, young man?' It was Miss Parrot from two doors down. Nobody knew her real name, but they nicknamed her Miss Parrot, because she had a habit of repeating everything anyone said to her.

'Yes.' Jack came to the gate. 'I'm off to pastures new.'

'Oh, "Off to pastures new," eh?'

'That's right. And I'd best be on my way.' He stood up. 'Bye, then. Take care of yourself.'

She gave a nod of her silvery head. 'Goodbye, then, and good luck.'

Somehow, the sight of her ambling off down the street made him feel sad. Now, with his worldly possessions gone and the house empty, he thought it best to get away, as fast and as far as he could. Putting his suitcase into the boot, he drove to the estate agency, where he handed in his keys.

'I'm sorry, but Tess has just left for an early lunch. Can I help? I'm up to speed with your case.' This was Tina Argent, the young woman who had tittle-tattled about him selling his house through this agency, instead of taking it to Molly's. Jack knew she had leaked the information. He gave her a searching look. 'I've sent everything else to the solicitor. Here are the keys.' He singled out each one. 'They all have a label. Back door. Front door. Then these others are for the little green shed out back, and the side gate.' He signed the necessary form, then turned to leave. At the door he was stopped by her quiet remark: 'Did you know that Molly and Mal got engaged?'

He nodded. 'Yes, I'm aware of that.'

'Ah! But did you know after they got engaged, they had a shocking bust-up and Mal threatened to call off the wedding?'

Jack was saddened by that, but not altogether surprised, knowing Molly. He was also angry that the information should be bandied about like this. 'I don't believe that's any of my business – or yours.' he told her coolly. 'And no, I would not have known if you hadn't told me.'

Leaning over the desk, he gave her a warning. 'But did *you* know that spreading idle gossip concerning other people's private lives, can get you into a whole heap of trouble?' He paused to let that snippet of information sink in. 'You could even lose your job. Is that what you want?'

Blushing bright pink with embarrassment, she said, 'I didn't mean anything by it – only I thought you should know, as you and Molly had planned to get married.' She saw his expression and stuttered, 'Sorry.'

'So you should be. So now let that be an end to it, eh?'

Her attitude became instantly sharp and professional. 'Er, thank you, Mr Redmond. I'll make sure these keys get to the new owner.' Swinging about in her swivel-chair, she pretended to be busy.

When she looked up, Jack was gone, and the door firmly closed behind him. Feeling humiliated, and grabbing up the bunch of keys, she threw them over to Tess's desk with such force that they caught the pen-jar, which flew off the desk and sent the pens flying in all directions. Scrabbling about on her knees to collect them before the boss returned, Tina made the air turn blue with her cursing.

～

Jack was not looking forward to the long drive, though he had already travelled the same journey several times these past weeks to keep an eye on his house and gradually take more stuff up. He had been very busy in his new job, sitting in on staff interviews and over-seeing the first delivery of new vehicles, and most importantly, keeping abreast of and also approving the security precautions at the new showrooms.

It was only now that he realised the true extent of

the responsibility he had taken on. But he would shoulder it with pride, and would repay the company with the same trust and loyalty they had shown him. The sad thing was, he had no one to share his new life with. No one to come home to of an evening and tell them how his day had gone. No one to ask about their day, or their achievements. No one to spoil, or to laugh with. And most of all, no one to fill the huge void that had arisen in his life.

Now, as he passed through the pretty village of Aspley Guise in central Bedfordshire, he planned to keep going northward on the motorway to the Keele turn-off. There was a café there, where he'd stop for a coffee and a bite to eat. From then on, it was only a matter of three-quarters of an hour and he would be off the motorway and on the main road into Blackburn.

The thought of one day actually buying a property in his hometown was both unsettling and a source of great excitement. Whoever would have thought when he was a boy, lonely and unloved, that one day he would be coming home, having done so well for himself?

Thinking back, he recalled his father's tragic end. Even now, after all these years, it didn't seem real. But then, tragedies rarely do. As for his mother, Jack doubted if she would even have cared about his success one way or another. He wondered fleetingly where she might be at this given moment in time. Was she still Mrs John J. Towner, with three stepchildren? And how did she physically look, after all these years, at the age of fifty? Would he recognise her if he saw her in the street? And would she be all over him if she knew he was earning a tidy salary, and planning to buy a house back in the town she had deserted, along with her son? Unsettled, he thrust her from his mind.

Two hours later, after a good run through thin traffic, he came off the motorway at the Keele stop, as he had intended. Having filled his petrol tank, he went to pay at the desk.

'Come off the motorway, 'ave yer?' The man behind the desk was round as a barrel. 'I avoid that motorway whenever I can,' he grumbled. 'The buggers can't wait to kill themselves. Damned fools – driving like lunatics!'

He took an interest in Jack. 'Yer a southerner, aren't yer?' He didn't wait for Jack to reply. 'I can tell from yer accent. Looking for lodgings, are yer? I reckon I could help yer there.'

'No, but thanks anyway.'

With the transaction complete, the man returned Jack's credit card. 'There you go then, mate.'

Jack thanked him again, then headed for the café across the courtyard, where he had a bite to eat and the best cup of coffee he'd enjoyed for a long time. Forty minutes later, he arrived at his destination.

~

Looking up at the monstrous glass-and-steel building that was Curtis Warren Motors, for a moment Jack felt tiny and insignificant. Even now, he found it hard to believe that the company had put such trust and belief in him. Here he was, Manager, and him only just past thirty. Jack was well aware that there were many other men, older and more experienced, who would have jumped at the chance to take on this responsibility.

'Mr Redmond!' A small, wiry fellow came rushing out of the main door. 'I saw you pull up. I know you've only just arrived, but if you can spare a minute, there are a few things I need to go through with you.'

Jack had already met the caretaker-cum-maintenance-man, and found him to be well disciplined, proud of his work, and with a pleasant character into the bargain.

'Hello, Steve, how are you?' They shook hands and entered the building together. 'How's it all going?'

'Everything is just fine. Except we did have a problem with the alarms.'

Everything's sorted now. Only last night I had to camp in one of the offices, as I couldn't get hold of the security people until this morning. Fortunately they sent a man round first thing, and he had it all up and running in no time at all.'

Apparently, he found spiders in two of the sensors, but he cleaned and secured them.

Jack was surprised. 'I still don't understand why they wouldn't come out earlier. As far as I know, they are on a twenty-four-hour call-out.'

'I've no idea, guv. I tried several times to contact them – right through the night, in fact – but there was no one answering . . . except for some posh answerphone voice giving me the office hours.'

'That's odd. I understood they had issued an emergency number, should they be needed at any time of day or night. Did you *try* the other number I gave you?'

For a moment, the little man looked at him as though he had no idea what Jack was talking about. When light dawned, he began frantically scratching at his ear. 'Oh, I'm sorry, Mr Redmond – I forgot all about that other number! Oh, dearie me! Oh, I'm sorry. Of course, I have the all-hours emergency number in my drawer – I completely forgot about it.'

He was distraught. 'That's an unforgivable mistake.' His voice fell to little more than a whisper. 'That's me down the pan, isn't it? I've lost my job, haven't I?'

Jack felt for him, but his first loyalty was to the company. 'I can't believe you didn't use that emergency number,' he told him sternly. 'There must be well over a million pounds' worth of vehicles at risk here, let alone the value of office equipment, garage machinery and everything else. Not to mention the crucial fact that if intruders *had* entered the premises, your own safety was at risk!'

Steve was acutely aware of his serious lapse of duty. He had no doubt that it was a sacking offence. 'I'm sorry I let you down,' he told Jack solemnly. 'I've no excuse, except that there's been so much to do these past weeks, it's been manic. But I made a serious mistake, and I understand the consequences.' He gave a little nod. 'I'll collect my things.'

As he turned away, Jack called him back. For a long, tense moment, Jack battled with his conscience. His head told him he was right to consider letting Steve go, because he well deserved it. But his heart saw the look of despair in the other man's eyes and something struck home. He knew himself what it was like to make a mistake. He also knew what it was like to let someone down; to be turned away when all you wanted to do was prove yourself. He recalled the days when he was just starting out, when no one believed in him.

He also knew he would not be standing here, on the threshold of his greatest achievement, if someone had not taken a chance on him; if they had not trusted their instinct that he was a good and loyal employee, in spite of earlier mistakes.

'It was a bad mistake, Steve,' he said firmly, 'and yes, it *is* a sackable offence. You put yourself at great risk, and left the premises unsecured, because you did not fall back on a simple emergency procedure as instructed. Even calling the police for assistance would have been better than nothing.'

Feverishly scratching his ear, Steve looked up, expecting and deserving the worst.

'If I didn't sack you,' Jack went on, 'and it got out, or anything like this happened again because you did not follow proper procedure, then of course, I myself would be held responsible.' He sighed.

'Look, Steve, I believe you've learned a valuable lesson. You were hired as someone we could rely on to keep this place up and running, and safe at all times. You must always have back up on security. Never leave anything to chance.'

'Yes, I know that, Mr Redmond, and I'll make sure

I don't neglect my duties again.' The little man was visibly nervous, constantly shifting from one foot to the other.

'There'll be no sacking today,' Jack concluded decisively. 'You made a mistake, but I do believe you'll be on top of things from now on.'

Greatly relieved, Steve nodded. 'You don't need to worry about me,' he assured Jack, 'I won't let you down.'

Jack patted him on the back. 'Good! Now let's put it to the back of our minds, because we have an important event coming up, and it'll be all hands to the pump.'

Both men went away smiling.

CHAPTER FOURTEEN

FOR THE FIRST time in his working life, Jack's name stood proud on the door of the manager's office. The office itself was an amazingly spacious room with a smart, glass-topped desk, and on the walls, Jack planned to hang his set of vintage car pictures.

Accompanied by his assistant Susan Wilson, he did a thorough inspection of the premises, to check on progress for the big open-day event on Saturday. It had taken several weeks of planning to get the new building ready to welcome the public. Jack was satisfied that Sue was already proving her worth and was more than capable of supporting him in his newly acquired role as manager. Moreover, her attention to detail was second to none.

'I'm concerned about your last email,' said Jack as they discussed the all-important event. 'You said you'd been let down by the caterers. Now, did you manage to find a suitable replacement?'

'I did, yes, Mr Redmond – and not only did they

turn out to be a good deal cheaper on their quote, but according to my enquiries, their service and range of food are excellent.'

'Well done!' That particular problem had been playing on his mind. 'Now then . . . how about a nice cup of coffee in my office, and we'll go over the last items on our list . . .'

~

Two busy hours later, they had gone through the last crucial matters, finalising the orders for the banners, brochures and other in-house publicity materials that needed to be picked up on Friday in preparation for Saturday's grand opening.

There was a healthy banter, and even a friendly disagreement or two between Jack and his new assistant, but between them, the task was soon completed, to their mutual satisfaction. Susan then went away to a meeting with the press officer.

While she was gone, Jack had a number of calls to make, including one to Head Office, to fill them in on what was happening.

Come early afternoon, it was time to view the house which Susan had organised for Jack to rent, until he found a place to buy. She had placed two properties on standby and needed Jack to make a choice. They drove off, Susan leading the way, with Jack following. The journey was a strange experience for Jack, because he knew most of the streets and landmarks along the journey; the most familiar and poignant being The Sun, the pub where his father and his mates used to drink on a Friday night.

The first stop was a house on Preston New Road. It was a grand, stylish house, on three levels, with a rise of steps going up to the front door. Inside, it was cavernous, with rooms of generous size, and an amazing view over to Corporation Park.

'What do you think?' Susan was eager to know.

'Well, yes. It's certainly a fine old house.'

Having walked the length and breadth of the house, Jack appreciated her choice, but decided, 'It's too big, too impersonal. I just can't see myself in it. Not even short-term.'

When he caught a glimpse of Corporation Park, a deep nostalgia took hold of him, and he vowed to come back later. There had been many times during his boyhood in Bower Street when Jack had desperately needed a friend and confidant. After his father later died from the injuries he suffered in the factory fire, his mother worked longer and longer hours at the hotel. Most of the time she didn't even seem to know or care that she had a son. She didn't ask Jack if he was missing his father, or whether he needed to talk.

Wise beyond his years, Jack understood that she was unhappy, that she needed someone. But so did he. Yet, while his mother took solace in dates with hotel guests, he was left to deal with his grief and confusion alone – as well as trying to cope with his schoolwork.

He was lost, and the one who cared was his friend, Libby. Thomas too, had been there for him, but Libby was nearer his age and understood. She too had lost a father – albeit a long time ago.

For as long as he lived, he would never forget that caring, wonderful girl. But, like everything else, good or bad in these past years, she was lost to him now. Like Molly. Like the house he had bought with such high hopes once he had moved to Bedfordshire.

Wasn't it strange – and unsettling, he thought – how life just ticks on, like a great timeless clock, going ever forward. Never backwards.

He thought about his nightmares; the fear of which had brought him back to Lancashire. Twelve long years ago, life and circumstances had taken him away; now they carried him back.

Tick-tock. Tick-tock. Never-ending. Never knowing in which direction life might take you.

But what of the nightmares? Had they too, come full circle, like the psychiatrist said? Was he now meant to find out what had triggered them?

He shuddered. Night or day, the images were never far away. Sometimes, if he just closed his eyes for a moment, he was back there, in that dark place of midnight, with the full moon overhead shedding a ghostly light over everything below. He could feel the chilling cold. And see those eyes . . . staring at him, drawing him down and down.

Jack forced the images to the back of his mind.

As he got back into his car, he was thinking of Bower

Street, where he grew up. He could be there within twenty minutes, he thought. He knew he wasn't ready yet, but one day soon, he would make his way there. Above all else, that was inevitable.

He wondered if Libby and Eileen were still living in Bower Street. Then there was Thomas Farraday, who by now must be in his late sixties, possibly edging seventy. Would he still be living in that same house, or had he moved away? Or even worse, perhaps have passed on.

And what about Number 20, the house where he grew up? Another family might be living there, with children. Or was it now the home of some happy young couple, just starting out, and as yet without kids.

The idea of seeing the house again made him feel deeply uncomfortable. And yet, like a homing pigeon, Jack had a deep, natural urge to head back there.

~

Not a half-mile away from Jack were two of the very people who had been in his thoughts.

'I don't want to go home yet!' Eileen was adamant. 'Why can't we go to the cannons, like you promised?'

'Because it might start to rain again, and besides, Libby will be wondering where we are.' Also, Thomas was tired, and though he would accompany Eileen across the world and back if he had to, his arms were aching at the roots and his legs were beginning to buckle under him.

'We've already been out longer than we said,' he reminded her. 'Matter o' fact, I'd best give Libby a call right now, to let her know we're on our way home.'

'You can't give her a call! How can you give her a call, when there's no telephone box anywhere?' She looked around, searching for the familiar red box. 'See – nothing!'

'Ah, well now, my beauty,' Thomas explained for the umpteenth time, 'we don't need a telephone box nowadays.' Proudly he showed her his little black mobile phone. 'Not now we've got these wonderful inventions.'

Eileen was wide-eyed. 'What is it?'

'You know what it is, m'dear. It's the phone that Libby bought me, so's we could keep in touch if we had need to.'

'I want to see the cannons,' Eileen persisted. 'And why were there no ducks at the lake?'

'Because we didn't go to the lake today, my darling. Don't you remember? You didn't want to go to the lake today.'

'We did, 'cause you nearly fell in. Your trousers got all wet.'

He smiled at the memory. 'That's right,' he said with a chuckle. 'You remember that, eh? But that wasn't today, my dear. It were last week. The wind got up and blew your hat into the children's pond at the far end of the lake. My trousers got wet when I retrieved your hat.'

Eileen thought for a minute and then she burst

out laughing. 'That duck pecked your leg, and you screamed like a girl.'

'I did, and yer right – I nearly fell in, trying to frighten it off. Good job I managed to keep my balance.'

'Thomas?' Already Eileen's thoughts were straying.

'Yes, m'dear?'

'Where did we go just now?' She was frantically trying to remember.

'You wanted to watch the children playing in the sand-pit,' Thomas reminded her. 'So that's what we did. Then, when you got hungry, we went to the little café and had a cheese-and-tomato roll and a pot of tea.'

'Oh, did we?' she still wasn't altogether sure. All of a sudden, she became very upset. 'You promised to take me to the cannons!'

'Yes, and I'm sorry, but it's too late. Like I said, we're headed back to the car now.'

Eileen had a suggestion. 'Can you tell Libby what a lovely time we've had?' Growing increasingly agitated, she pointed to Thomas' pocket. 'Call her on that little phone.'

Just to appease her, Thomas took the mobile phone out of his pocket and, after tapping out Libby's number, he gave the phone to Eileen. 'There! The number is ringing for you. When Libby answers, just talk into it, and she'll be able to hear you.'

When Libby's voice answered, Eileen was thrilled. 'I can hear her!' She got so excited, she accidentally pressed a wrong button and turned the phone off.

Throwing the phone to the ground, she said tearfully, 'It's your fault she's gone!'

Patiently, Thomas collected the phone and got Libby back on the line. But Eileen wouldn't talk to her, so Thomas explained that they were on their way home and returned the mobile to his pocket – it was then that she got upset.

Surprised but not overly concerned by her sudden change of mood, Thomas quickly led her underneath the big, stone arch, away from prying eyes. Stooping to wrap his strong arms around her, he held her close while she continued to weep and rant; until finally she was quiet.

At that moment, Jack Redmond entered the park through the same big arch. From a distance he saw the man holding the distressed woman and was about to step up and ask if he could help, when the man noticed him approaching and put up a staying hand, as though asking him not to interfere.

Understanding their need for privacy, Jack turned away. But something about that old man and his companion troubled him. Yet he had never seen them before. And in all probability, he would never see them again.

The uncertainty that ran through Jack's mind was also bothering Thomas. 'I reckon I've seen that young man somewhere before,' he murmured. 'But can I recall where? No, damn and bugger it! What's wrong with me?'

Now subdued Eileen heard him muttering. 'What are you saying, Thomas? What's wrong?'

'Nothing, m'dear. I was just thinking out loud. Sorry.'

She glanced warily at the departing figure of Jack. 'Is that him?' she asked.

'What d'you mean?'

'Is he the one who wants to hurt me?' She began to whimper.

'No. He's just a young man who happened to pass by when you were upset. Just a young chap out for a walk, like us . . . that's all.'

Eileen's panic was beginning to have an effect on Thomas, causing him to remember the past. Making him fearful. He glanced back, but the young man had already gone from sight.

He forced himself to be calm. In his mind he could see the young man's face, partially shadowed by the hood of his anorak. For some reason, he felt as though he knew him. Yet, how could he? Fearful things played on his mind, coming back to haunt him, in the same way Eileen was haunted. A sense of disquiet took hold of him.

Who was that young man? What was his name? No doubt the answer would come to him eventually.

~

'So, do you like it?' asked Susan. She and Jack had just viewed the house in Buncer Lane.

'It's perfect,' he answered. 'I feel completely at home here.' In fact, there was nothing about the house that

253

he didn't like. With big windows, a double frontage, an original cast-iron fireplace, and a stained-glass arc over the front door, he guessed it was probably Edwardian in date. All the rooms, upstairs and down, were square and straight, and of a manageable, homely size. At the front was a pleasant small garden, all set with shrubs and trees – one or two of which needed a trim, but that was incidental. The back garden was bigger, of course.

'There's a good feeling in this house,' he told Susan. The minute he had walked through the door, he felt at ease there.

Buncer Lane was long and winding, sweeping down to the main road. Just a short distance away was Bower Street, where he was born and bred. Jack wondered if that was partly why he felt so comfortable here, being within walking distance of his old stamping-ground.

'I'm so glad you like it,' said Susan. 'The owner had it tidied up and redecorated, and decided to let it out. But I think he has rather changed his mind, and now would like to sell it. But no one else has seen it yet, so I thought it was worth you having a look round.'

Jack was intrigued. 'It seems as though this house was meant for me! I'll give the owner a call – he might let me rent it from him while I decide whether I'm ready to buy it.

Sue told him she had already asked the owner if that was a possibility, 'He's quite agreeable on the idea, but only for a period of no more than twelve months. After that, if you've chosen not to buy, he will expect you to vacate.

Jack was relieved, 'I'm happy with that arrangement. Thank you Sue.' As it was, he did not envisage that it would take him twelve months to consider buying this delightful house. Jack had already decided that the front bedroom would be his. The decor was to his taste. Moreover, the room took the sun for most of the day, which made it seem bright and welcoming.

Crossing to the window, he took a moment to survey the scene below. With the house being on a curve in the road, he could see right down to the main thoroughfare, and from there in his mind's eye, he could follow the route to Bower Street. And that made him think fondly of Libby. Being so near to everything he had known as a boy made the memories even stronger.

'It's the right house, in the right place, and it has a good feel about it,' he said. 'Thank you for finding it, Susan.'

Smiling, she gave a little shrug. 'It's what I'm paid to do . . . boss-man!'

Jack laughed. 'Well, since I'm the boss-man, I'm saying you can go home early.'

When she drove off, he did one more tour of inspection round the house, then jumped into his Lexus and returned to the office to make some calls.

CHAPTER FIFTEEN

D R REED WAS an expert in his field and with the old doctor having recently retired, Eileen was now his outpatient. Today was their first meeting.

After a lengthy examination of Eileen's mental capabilities, Libby and Eileen were now seated before him; with Libby attentive as ever, while Eileen appeared agitated and constantly toyed with her fingers.

What he had to say, appeared to have little impact on Eileen, but it brought hope to Libby, 'Fiirstly, let me assure you, that your mother appears to be in reasonable health for a woman of her age, and I am fairly confident that she does not suffer Dementia, or the onset of Alzheimers, as was first thought. Having said that, she does have certain symptons that might initially lead to that conclusion, such as the psychotic tendencies . . . the sudden unprovoked anger for instance. The identity lapses, and intermittent loss of reality.'

Pausing, he glanced at Eileen, who at that moment appeared to be paying attention, and was looking right at him, 'Do you understand what I'm saying?' he asked her now.

Eileen nodded.

'Good. And if you're not sure of what I'm saying, you must stop me, and I'll go through it again.'

With Eileen's reassurance, he continued.

For a time, Eileen appeared to listen, then she looked away, towards the open window, 'I want to go now.'

Libby took hold of her hand, 'In a minute, Mam,' she promised, 'Let the doctor finish.' Even though it was understood how her mother still suffered the same problems, Libby was overjoyed at the prospect that there appeared to be some hope, 'This is good news, isn't it mam?'

Eileen raised her sorry eyes to the doctor, 'I need to see Thomas now.' There was such an emptiness inside her. Such fear, and a crippling sense of desolation. When she was with Thomas, she felt calmer, as though he understood, where others could not.

'I'm not mad, am I?' she asked the doctor now.

With a gentle smile on his face, Dr Reed slowly shook his head, 'No, my dear. You are definitely not "mad".'

Eileen was grateful for his answer. But then he did not know what she knew.

Thomas did though. Oh, yes. He knew.

~

Later, when Eileen and Libby went round to see Thomas, he was thrilled with the news, 'That's wonderful!' he gave them each a hug, 'So, what exactly did he say?' he asked Libby. Although, unbeknown to Libby, he had a very strong idea of what was haunting Eileen. And he was plagued with guilt.

Libby explained, 'He was almost certain Mam was not suffering from Denentia, or Alzheimers; though he would have to undertake more tests. Instead he suspects it's a much less invasive condition, called psychosis. It's a kind of disturbance in the brain, where reality becomes distorted, and memories get fragmented, along with deep depression.

'Can it be cured?'

'Sometimes yes, and sometimes not altogether. It requires treatment and monitoring, but there is hope.'

With her next words, she dealt Thomas a hammer blow, 'Apparantly, psychosis is triggered by some shocking, traumatic event. The thing is, when we did eventually manage to trace back to when Mam started to change, it ties in with the time when she lost Dad. So it could be that . . . but we can't be sure just yet.'

Deeply shaken by Libby's revelation, Thomas and Eileen instinctively exchanged glances. There was no need for words.

Each knew what the other was thinking as the years rolled away, to a time when they were younger; a time that was etched in their tortured minds, for all the wrong reasons.

As was her way, Eileen was soon chatting about everything else, and Libby was somewhat relieved that the ordeal at the hospital appeared to have already been forgotten by her mother.

A short time later, Libby coaxed her mother away, and Thomas was left.

To reflect on his guilt.

~

The following evening, Thomas tapped on Libby's kitchen door. 'Who wants to come next door and hear some *proper* music?' he asked, with a sideways wink at Libby.

'Me!' Eileen clapped her hands, the events of the previous day having now retired to the back of her mind. Laughing merrily, she got to her feet and swirled her skirt about. 'Look at me, Thomas!' she cried. 'I'm dancing!'

'I can see that!' he said, laughing. He took her in his arms and gently danced her round the room. Then he began to sing softly in her ear. It was her favourite artist, Nat King Cole, and her favourite song of all, 'When I Fall in Love'.

When Libby began to sing along, Eileen suddenly broke away and ran into the kitchen. Libby ran after her.

'Hey! What's wrong, Mum?' Cradling her close, she tried to make light of it. 'I didn't think my singing was bad enough to frighten you away like that.'

Eileen gave a shaky little laugh. 'I'm sorry for running off.'

'So, what's upset you then?'

Eileen replied with such clarity that Libby was taken aback.

'It's your father,' she said tearfully. 'Why did he have to leave us like that?' She shook her head as though in disbelief. 'I know he liked other women, but I never thought he would leave us . . . not with you being such a tiny little thing an' all.'

'Ssh, Mum. That was such a long time ago. After all these years, he's not about to come home, and it's no use you upsetting yourself. Keep the good memories, Mum. Try not to fret about what's gone, because it will only make you unhappy. And I don't want you to be unhappy.'

Libby could understand how hard it must have been for her mother to come to terms with what happened. In truth, Libby had always believed it was the trauma of losing her husband that had caused her mother's health to deteriorate.

From the other room, Thomas heard their chatter – about Eileen's husband being a womaniser, and how she had never really got over the shock of him deserting them. It made him think about what Ian Harrow had missed – seeing his daughter grow up, and having the joy of a wife like Eileen. He couldn't help but wonder whether Libby's father might have changed. If he'd been there for them just that bit longer, would he have learned to cherish these two wonderful people? And who knows, there might even have been other children over the years – a brother or sister or both for Libby.

It was a sobering thought. But he reminded himself

of the old saying: 'Once a bad 'un, always a bad 'un.' Maybe that was true, and this particular 'bad 'un' would never have changed his ways. In which case, Libby and the lovely Eileen were well rid of him.

It cut him deep, though, to think of Eileen, made to raise a child on her own, with no man to support her, eking out the days with her savings and doing other folk's ironing and mending. And Libby, never really knowing her father.

It was a sorry situation; one which he had tried hard to soften over these long years, by starting to love Libby as a daughter, and looking out for Eileen. He never dreamed that he would come to love her so dearly. At first it was just him being a good neighbour – cutting the grass, trimming the hedges and generally helping out. With the passage of time, though, he had learned to truly love Eileen.

When Libby looked up and saw Thomas at the kitchen door, she told him softly, 'She's all right, Thomas, really. She just got a bit emotional, that's all. She'll be fine.'

Eileen's mood swiftly changed. 'When we've heard the songs, can we have fish and chips, Thomas? You promised that we could have fish and chips.'

Thomas grinned. 'If I told you we'd have fish and chips, then we shall *have* fish and chips!'

Libby played her part, 'You two get along and enjoy yourselves. When I've tidied up, I'll go down to the fish-shop. If it's all right with you, Thomas, can I have my tea with you two?'

'Absolutely! Me and Eileen would have it no other way!'

Delighted, Eileen clapped her hands together. 'We can have the music playing, and eat our fish and chips as well. It'll be like a party, won't it?'

A short time later, after finishing a small pile of ironing, Libby called round next door, to find her mother sitting in the armchair, tapping her feet and singing along to the old tunes.

Thomas was in the kitchen, putting plates in the over to warm. 'I'm off to the fish-shop now, Thomas. Would you both like your usual – medium cod with chips?' They confirmed that they did.

'Ask if he's got any crackling,' Eileen called out. 'I do like a bit o' crackling!'

Thomas walked Libby to the door. 'I'm sorry about earlier,' he said. 'The odd thing is, Eileen's never asked me to dance with her before. Oh, she'll dance on her own till the cows come home, but that was the first time she's ever asked me to join in.'

He looked across at Eileen, who was softly singing. 'It's good to dance. Me and my wife had a passion for it. A man loves to feel a woman in his arms.' He sighed. 'I miss that.'

When the music came to an end, Eileen began yelling, 'It's gone! The music's all gone!'

Thomas hurried across the room. 'It's all right, sweet-heart,' he said. 'I'll soon have it back on again, don't you worry.'

On leaving, Libby called to her mother, 'I won't be

long, Mum. You just enjoy the music, and I'll be back with your fish and chips before you know it.'

Outside, the rain was falling fast. She stopped to pull up the hood of her anorak. It was a typical English summer!

CHAPTER SIXTEEN

O UTSIDE, ON THE opposite side of the street, Jack stood under a dripping tree, sheltering from the rain beneath an umbrella. After much soul-searching, he had finally plucked up the courage to come down to Bower Street. It was only a mile or so from Buncer Lane, but that short walk had seemed like the longest journey of his life. At one point, his courage failed him, so he dodged into the nearest pub for a pint and a quiet moment to think about what he was doing.

After a while, he reminded himself of his reasons for coming back to the North – not for the glory of managing the new showrooms, because that was an opportunity and a bonus. He had come back because of the nightmares, and because he needed to find out if the psychiatrist was right. But how was he going to do that? As yet he hadn't quite worked out the details. But he would – and soon – because it was constantly playing on his mind.

All these years, so many unanswered questions . . . If, as he truly believed, the psychiatrist was indeed right, then where else should he look, if not the very place where his dreams had started?

More than anything, he had come back because he knew instinctively that if he was to go forward, then he must first go back, to the place where it all began.

After leaving the pub, he had quickened his steps towards Bower Street. Within minutes, he was actually standing across the street from his old house. He found himself travelling back through the bad memories. He felt like a young lad again. He had felt vulnerable back then; and he felt vulnerable now too.

'Go on, Jack!' he urged himself. 'Knock on the door – just tell them you used to live in that house; that you're back in the area and you were just curious.'

He smiled to himself. 'They'll probably think I'm mad, or call the police – and I wouldn't blame them.'

He thought of knocking on the door of Thomas' house. Now, that was a better idea. Thomas wouldn't think he was mad if he knocked on his door. But he might not live there any more, of course.

At that moment he was surprised to see what looked like a young man dressed against the elements, and going down Thomas's garden path, towards the door. So another family must now be living there. Jack was disappointed.

Not realizing the 'young man' was actually Jack, Libby decided to call it a day. 'Next time I'm here,' he said to himself, 'I'll knock on that young man's door. Maybe he or his parents will know where Thomas has gone. They might even have an idea as to where Eileen and Libby are.' It was a comforting thought, but for now, he just wanted to get out of the rain.

Jack had a lot to think about. The fact that Thomas appeared to have moved out of Bower Street was a bitter blow, as he'd been so looking forward to seeing him again. He had not forgotten the help and support Thomas had given him when he needed it most. He wanted to thank him for his help and advice.

Naively, he had even harboured the hope that Thomas might hold the key to his nightmares. Maybe just to sit and talk with Thomas might somehow open a door in his mind – a door that would reveal the truth and give him peace.

Jack was fast becoming obsessed with the idea that he was close. He could not imagine what he might find when he began to probe deeper, but he had to believe. Because he could not live the rest of his life wondering. Never knowing . . .

Jack suddenly decided that he wasn't ready to go back to his rented house. Fired by a need to revisit old haunts, he made his way towards King Street and Whalley Banks. And as he walked, a feeling of warmth and belonging took hold of him. But the further along he went, the more he began to realise how everything had changed. There used to be a row of houses to the right; he recalled a fun-loving girl at school who lived there with her parents and her many brothers. They were a strong family. But the houses were now gone, to make way for a garage.

The parade of shops was still there, however – although what used to be a tripe shop was now a florist's. He recalled how a large family called Brindle, had lived in that very tripe shop.

He felt sorry to see that the little bridge was no more. With its arched back and curved walls, affording a way over the Blakewater, it had been a pretty thing – a familiar landmark.

The alleyway by the flower-shop was still there. He recalled the slaughter-house at the back, where the Brindle kids were not allowed to go; nor were they allowed to climb the big stone wall that overlooked the deep water below. Somehow though, they always found a way in through the gates when no one was looking. It was rumoured that a neighbouring child was drowned there, but Jack didn't know if that was true; he only knew what he had heard.

It was sad to see that almost everything familiar was gone. He understood, though. It was right that things had to change, because if time stood still, there would be nothing new or exciting to look forward to. No challenges. No new horizons.

But Jack remembered everything, as if a map had been imprinted on his memory, including every street, every house, every landmark. Just like he remembered the bold, flowered wallpaper pattern on his bedroom walls in that house in Bower Street. And the creaking third step as you went down the stairs. It always puzzled him as a boy, why the step never creaked when you went *up* the stairs. He smiled wryly, thinking that was a strange thing to remember.

Now uncomfortably aware of his sodden trousers and squelching shoes, Jack caught the unmistakable aroma of a chip shop – and his stomach began to grumble. He hadn't eaten for some hours, and even if he had to sit in a bus shelter to eat them, wouldn't it be fun to have a bag of fish and chips? He could watch the world go by while eating his dinner off his lap. But he'd have to be careful of his suit.

The more he thought about it, the hungrier he got. Following his nose, he quickened his steps.

~

'There you go!' The red-faced man finished packing the last hot, damp paper package into the two plastic carrier bags before handing them over. 'That'll be fourteen pound, please, love. I've thrown a few cracklings in.' He gave Libby a cheeky wink. 'I know your Mam's fond of 'em.'

While Libby counted out the money, he asked, ''Ow is she, by the way? We've not seen hide nor hair of her for some time now. Keeping well, is she?'

Libby simply replied that her mother had not been

too well lately. 'But she's getting on all right now. Content one minute and demanding the next.'

He laughed – a loud, raucous laugh that startled the little man next to Libby and made him visibly jump. 'Aye, well, that's women for yer!' he chortled, 'Want this, want that, and when they get it . . . they want summat else instead!'

'Stop yattering, yer silly old bugger!' That was the fat woman on Libby's right. 'We're 'ere for fish an' chips, not a bloody lecture!'

Libby was still smiling when she came out – until she saw Jack approaching. She recognised his demeanour and the way he held himself. He was the same man she'd seen outside Thomas's house the other night; but she could not see him clearly then, or now. 'I'm almost sure it's that man again!' She crossed the road, her face averted and her hood up.

Jack didn't notice her until she crossed the street and turned to look at him a second time. The glance was fleeting, but there was something about the boyish person that niggled him.

Shrugging it off, he went into the chip shop, where the fat woman and the proprietor were having a row.

'Mushy peas? I never asked for mushy peas – that were the young lass that just went out! I asked for beans. That's plain enough, isn't it?' She spelled it out for him: 'B–e–a–n–s.' Exasperated, she rolled her eyes. 'Oh, now, you've made me forget me potato-dabs. I'll 'ave two o' them, and forget the beans.'

The man behind the counter did not take kindly to being nagged at, especially in front of the other customers. 'Yer in a sour mood tonight, aren't yer, Betty?'

'What d'yer mean, sour mood? I'm *never* in a sour mood!'

'Well, you're in a sour mood from where I stand, but you'd best not tek it out on me, 'cause I'll give as good as I get, an' no mistake!' He came back at her with humour: 'What's up, eh? Is the old man not looking after yer proper – if yer know what I mean?' He gave a knowing wink to his audience.

'I know exactly what yer mean!' She wagged a finger at him. 'And what me and my old man get up to is none of your damned business! Some folks should look at theirselves afore they start pointing the finger at others. At least my Les doesn't ogle after other women. Oh, don't deny it! We all saw yer eyeing that young lass up and down as she went out of 'ere. Yer tongue were 'anging out so far it could'a shined yer shoes! Shame on yer, that's what I say. Randy old bugger!' She snatched up her goodies, threw the money on the counter and marched out, muttering and tutting.

Jack tried hard not to smile, but he wasn't the only one.

'Touched a sore point there, didn't I, eh?' The red-faced proprietor was laughing heartily. 'She's that easy to wind up,' he confessed. 'I love to get 'er going. It's the highlight o' my day.'

Jack had to chuckle at the older man's antics. If he didn't know he was back in Lancashire, he knew it now. It was almost as though he'd never been away.

~

Instead of a bus shelter, Jack found a bench near the parade of shops and sat down to eat his fish and chips. There was a plastic knife and fork inside the bag, but he set them aside and tucked in with his fingers. It was a joyful feast.

'That's the way to eat fish and chips,' said an old man sitting down beside him. 'I ask yer, what right-minded person wants to eat fish and chips with a plastic knife and fork?' He promptly took out his bag of chips and, stuffing them two at a time into his whiskered face, made a sighing noise after each bite whilst chatting away with Jack.

When he got up to leave, he turned to Jack. 'Where are yer from?' As he spoke, the remains of his hurried meal sprayed the air. 'I can tell from the way yer talk – yer not from these parts.'

Having taken a shine to the old man, Jack explained. 'I do come from these parts, only I moved away when I was eighteen.'

'Eighteen, eh? An' what did yer parents think o' that?'

Jack took a moment; even now the memories were painful. 'My father was caught up in a bad fire at the factory where he worked. He was badly hurt and never recovered.'

The man shook his head soberly. 'Oh, yer mean the one out Cicely way? I remember that fire. It were a bad 'un – took out half the street, it did. As I recall, four people were lost in that fire . . . So what about yer mum?'

Jack recalled his mother. Claire Redmond was a smart, attractive woman, but she was never a natural-born mother. In fact, during a heated row between his parents, Jack had once overheard her say she had never wanted children. It was a crippling thing for him to hear.

The old man was waiting for an answer. 'Aw, don't tell me *she* were caught up in that fire as well?'

Jack shook his head, 'No. She didn't even work at the factory.'

'So, why did yer leave? I'd 'ave thought yer mum would want you at 'ome, with her. Especially with her man gone, and you coming up to the age when you could earn some money.'

Jack wasn't enjoying this questioning, but he reluctantly satisfied the old man's curiosity. 'A couple of years after we lost Dad, she found herself a rich man, and moved abroad.'

The older man was shocked. 'So, did you 'ave older brothers or sisters to keep an eye on yer?'

'No.' Jack recalled the loneliness he had felt. 'I was an only child.'

'I see. So yer dad died and yer mum buggered off with a rich fella, leaving you to fend for yourself.' He shook his head as he moved away. 'It don't bear

273

thinking about!' Screwing up his chip paper, he placed it in a nearby bin. 'Women, eh? Can't live with 'em, can't live without 'em. Well, good luck to yer, son, and mind how you go, eh?'

Jack watched him amble down the street, shifting from one side to the other to avoid the puddles. He couldn't help but wonder if the kindly old man had also suffered at the hands of some woman or other.

Jack finished the last of his chips, which by now had grown cool. But the flavour was not lost, and he thoroughly enjoyed them, right down to the last morsel. Afterwards, he sat a while, thinking and planning, and feeling curiously at ease with the world.

Inevitably, his thoughts drifted to Molly. He hoped she and Mal were getting on all right. Strange to think she might be married to someone else. There was a time when he could not have envisaged his life without Molly in it. When he needed her, she had been there for him, a thoughtful and loving partner. And yet, from the moment he told her of his plan to move up here, it as if she became a different person. He missed her, but he was not sorry it was over between them. Because of the way things had turned out, he realised that he and Molly never really had a future together.

~

Thomas was worried. 'You reckon this bloke followed you to the chippie, then?'

'Well, to be honest, I don't know if he actually followed me.' Molly was beginning to wish she hadn't said anything about the stranger. 'By the time I came out of the shop, he was only just going in, so it could just have been a coincidence.'

'What's he look like?'

Libby pictured him. 'Tallish, probably about my age, but I couldn't see his face because he had his umbrella up and his jacket collar turned up.' Having just left her trainers in the hall, she now took off her wet socks. She hoped Thomas would drop the subject.

Having finished dishing up the food, Thomas handed her a nice hot plate of saveloy, chips and mushy peas. 'Don't worry about it any more, lass,' Thomas said. 'Leave that to me. You just put him out of your mind.'

Eileen was proud of herself. 'I set the table,' she told Libby for the third time. 'Did you get my cod?'

'I certainly did.' Libby pulled out a chair for her mother. 'I got you chips too, and if you want them, some mushy peas into the bargain.'

'I never asked for no mushy peas!' Eileen looked agitated.

'No matter. I'm sure me and Thomas can finish them off.' She helped her mother into the chair. 'All right, Mum?'

Eileen nodded. 'But I don't want you and Thomas to eat my mushy peas.'

Libby and Thomas exchanged a knowing smile, with

275

Thomas teasing, 'Too late! You didn't want any, so now they're all mine.'

'You behave yourself!' Eileen said with a chuckle. 'Yer an old devil, that's what!'

Folding his arms, he pretended to shrink from her. 'I wouldn't dare eat your mushy peas!' he said in mock terror.

Eileen was highly amused. 'Naughty man,' she kept saying. 'You're a very naughty man!' Then, to Libby's delight, she got stuck into her food, as if she hadn't been fed for a month.

~

Jack woke in a panic.

It had taken him a while to drop off to sleep, and when he did, he was instantly back there, in that pitch-dark place – only this time, *there was someone standing beside him.*

He couldn't see who it was, but he knew there was someone there – a shadowy figure, stooping down . . . reaching out with both hands. '**No! Go away!**' His frantic cries shook him awake, but he couldn't escape, because the figure was closing in on him . . . and those eyes . . . stark and staring, were looking straight at him. He was trapped, but he was awake. *He was awake.* And this time, he was more afraid than he had ever been.

Scrambling out of bed, he sat for a moment, the sweat pouring down his face, his body trembling from head to foot. The dream was the same, but different, because now there was someone else in it. Someone else was there, reaching down, wanting to take him away. The dream had changed. Everything appeared sharper. Nearer. And he didn't know how to deal with it.

He got up and began restlessly pacing the floor. 'Someone was there . . . they were right there, next to me.' Now he remembered the words. He could still hear the voice, soft and kind: 'Come away, Jack . . . come away.'

But he didn't want to go. Not yet. The eyes held him in a weird kind of fascination. So still, and cold. Staring right at him. Where was he? *For pity's sake – where was he?*

Wide awake, he could still feel the cold. It was bitter and sharp, piercing, right through to the bones. Wrapping the duvet around himself, he shivered uncontrollably. He'd never heard the voice before, but now it stayed with him, whispering in his ear: 'Come away, Jack . . . come away.' And he could hardly breathe.

He relived the dream carefully in his mind, looking for answers. One thing was now clear to him, which he had never realised before: someone else knew that place. Someone else heard his cry for help.

For some strange reason, being back in his home town was helping him to think with clarity. Maybe in time new things would come to the surface, and he would find the answer to his nightmares.

Calmer now, Jack went to the kitchen and made himself a cup of cocoa. He was desperately tired. But half an hour later, he was dressed and in his car. He started the engine and headed towards Bower Street. At this time of night, the roads were deserted, and unnervingly shadowy.

Crossing over into Spring Lane, he drove past the trees on the right, then turning right again, he passed the pub, and was soon in Bower Street. The streetlights shed a yellow haze across the houses, highlighting the house where Thomas used to live. Slowly, anxious not to disturb anyone, Jack parked the car a short way up from Number 20, the house where he was born.

Switching off both engine and lights, he sat there, his mind in chaos. 'What in God's name am I doing here?' He glanced at the clock on the dashboard; it was almost 2 a.m. 'I must be crazy.'

He sat there for a few minutes, his attention straying from the house he knew, to the house where Thomas had lived. All was still.

He brought his gaze to the house where Libby had lived; his best friend – the one he trusted above all others. Sadness flowed through him. Libby Harrow had been the one true mainstay in his young life. Leaving her behind had been, and would always remain, his biggest regret.

That first month in London, he'd many times picked up a postcard, ready to write to her. But for some reason, he never did. Maybe she was too close to his past. Yet he needed her to know how he'd worked hard to build a new life for himself, and how he had gone to college and got the 'A' Levels he badly needed to forge a career.

Looking at the house where she'd lived, Jack imagined her running down the path in her school skirt and white blouse, her hair tamed into auburn pigtails hanging down her shoulders, and her voice, calling to him: 'Hurry up, Jack! Or we'll miss the school bus and have to walk again!'

The memory caught his heart. 'Dearest Libby,' he said. A wealth of love trembled in his voice.

~

Thomas could not sleep. He was concerned about what Libby told him earlier, about the stranger. Even now, it played on his mind.

Having just woken from a shallow sleep, he instinctively went to the window and looked out. At first he didn't see the big Lexus parked some distance away, out of reach of the street-lamps. Then, as he turned away, a figure got out of the car.

'Who the devil's that?' he muttered to himself. The man's build was much the same as the description Libby had given him, but it was dark, and the shadows hid his face. Whoever the man was, there could be no mistaking his interest in Eileen and Libby's house, because Thomas could see that he was staring right at it.

Thomas' first instinct was to go out there and confront the stranger. Grabbing his trousers and shirt from the back of the chair where he had left them earlier, he hastily dressed. 'I'll have you, yer bugger!' he grumbled, as he kept the figure in his sights. 'You'll tell me what yer after, or I'll have the coppers on yer, an' no mistake!'

Suddenly the man climbed back into the car and within moments it was on the move. 'Dammit!' Thomas blamed himself, 'I wonder if he saw me watching him.'

As the car passed underneath his window, its back end was illuminated by the nearby street-lamp. 'Got yer!' Pressing his face closer to the window, Thomas narrowed his old eyes to see all the better as he hurriedly scribbled the car's number onto the wallpaper with a biro. 'Damn and bugger it!' He'd missed that last number. Was it an eight? Or it could have been a six. Never mind – he had most of the number-plate. That should be enough for him to keep a wary eye out.

Grumbling and moaning, he went down to the kitchen, where he sat at the table, drumming his fingers on the table-top. 'I don't like this business . . . not one little bit!'

A short time later, Thomas went back to bed, but he was too unsettled to sleep. All manner of questions ran through his mind, along with other things. Things long gone, but not forgotten. Bad things that troubled the mind.

Thomas didn't see himself as a bad man. He was a

man of good character. An honourable man, who cared deeply for those around him. Especially the two lovely women next door. Apart from himself, they had no one. For their sake, he hoped the stranger's appearance in their lives was just a coincidence, instead of a sign that the past was beginning to rear its ugly head.

For reasons of his own, that was something Thomas had always feared. Yet a part of him knew it was inevitable that one day this secret would be out, sadly some secrets could not be hidden away for ever.

For a time, he stood by the window, murmuring to himself. 'You were wrong to think it would all be forgotten,' he bowed his head in shame. 'There's an old saying, Thomas, and you would do well to remember it.' He said it now, clear and strong: *'Be sure, yer sins will allus come back to haunt yer!'*

He was not a man who read the Bible. But he knew more than enough about sinners repenting.

CHAPTER SEVENTEEN

THE NEXT MORNING, Jack was dog-tired, having had less than four hours' sleep. The images of midnight still clung to him. Even now, when he was wide awake and getting ready for work, doing ordinary things – everyday, wide-awake things – like trying to fasten his tie, like brushing his teeth and combing his wayward hair. Even while he was planning the day ahead, praying that the event tomorrow would run like clockwork, he could not shut out the image of those eyes. The expression in them as they looked at him; the sadness . . . the way the moonlight made them sparkle. And the unholy smell.

Afraid that he was going mad, he turned the radio on full blast. The soft piano music pacified his shredded nerves. It smothered the rising panic inside him.

Calmer now, he looked in the mirror and managed to tie the perfect knot in his tie. He examined himself with a critical eye: smart, dark-blue suit; crisp, white shirt beneath. All in all, he now looked like a man about to do business.

He didn't want to be seen as less than smart in his new position. As Thomas had told him once, 'First impressions are most important.' In fact, Jack recalled the very day he'd said that.

He was on his way to school. It was a hot July Friday towards the end of term, and it was the turn of his class to take assembly. Jack had stuffed his tie in his pocket as usual, the minute he was out of the house.

As he walked past, Thomas was at the gate. He asked Jack what he was up to at school that day, and Jack told him they were having a special assembly. 'There's a council-man coming to talk to us,' he explained. 'He means to ask us why we need a new gymnasium.' He told Thomas, 'I can't stand assemblies.'

Thomas asked where his tie was, and Jack pulled it out of his pocket to show him. Thomas was persuasive but firm. 'Put it back on, lad. You might not like the idea of listening to some bloke spouting off, but there's no need to look like a scruff, now is there, eh? Think about it, lad. Have a bit of self-respect.'

That was when he told Jack, 'Remember: first impressions are the most important.' It was sound advice, which Jack had never forgotten.

Looking at himself in the mirror, he was satisfied that Thomas would approve. He felt ready to face the world. 'Right!' Willing himself not to think about other things, he trained his mind on the all-important test ahead of him.

∼

Jack's right-hand woman, Susan Wilson, had proved herself to be as reliable as ever. Six of the company's more experienced salesmen were all geared up and ready for instructions; the ultra-efficient Susan had supplied them each with an information pack and a pen and notepad, in case they needed to make notes during Jack's welcoming speech as manager.

Jack's speech was planned for 8 a.m., when everyone involved in the big day tomorrow should be gathered in the main showrooms. After the speech, there would be a question-and-answer session, when every little detail would be gone over for the Saturday event.

Later in the day, a top representative of the company and his aide were due to arrive from Head Office. On Jack's instructions, Susan had booked two rooms at the five-star Chadwick Hotel. The two men planned to stay overnight, in preparation for attending the Saturday event, at which Curtis Warren himself would oversee the launch of his company's latest venture.

Susan had been keeping a lookout for Jack's Lexus. When she saw him arrive she called out to him, 'Good morning!' In spite of feeling frazzled by the heavy duties that had fallen on her shoulders, and having been at the showrooms since six-thirty this morning, she greeted Jack with a bright smile, saying, 'How are you today?'

'Ready for the fray,' he replied breezily. 'Or as ready as I'll ever be.' His quick smile amply covered his anxieties.

Susan glanced at her watch. 'We've got about twenty

minutes or so, if you want to go over anything? Or, if you'd rather leave it until later, that's fine.'

'No, let's get on with it.' Although he was satisfied that she could handle the duties he had given her, Jack was keen to see that everything was as it should be. After all, the prime responsibility for the smooth running of this enterprise was his, and his alone.

The next fifteen minutes confirmed his faith in her. Jack went through the advertisements due to appear in all the local papers today. Next, he checked the allocation of radio airtime, with the guarantee that, provided there were no big, unexpected news-stories, tomorrow's event would be widely broadcast. He also checked the names of each newspaper that had agreed to send a reporter to the actual event.

'Well done!' Jack was suitably impressed. 'You've excelled yourself, Sue.'

His comments put a wide smile on her face. 'Would you like to see one of the banners?' She pointed to a large box that had been delivered earlier that morning, as arranged.

'Absolutely!' Jack slit open the box with his penknife and, taking out one of the large banners, he unfurled it and laid it across his desk. Colourful and eye-catching, the design was first class. In addition, there was also a special promotion offer and an opportunity to draw the winning ticket for a new car, a Nissan hatchback.

'I'm glad Head Office took up my idea of a draw,' Jack said. 'If anything brings in the crowds, it's the chance of a freebie.' He gave her a knowing wink. 'Oh, and the quality of the product, of course.'

'Of course.'

The two of them went over every last detail of the next day's event, and before they knew it, it was eight o'clock. The troops were fully gathered in the main showroom, and now it was time for Jack to go out and speak to everyone.

'I don't intend making a long speech,' he confided to Susan as they walked through. 'I'll just welcome everyone aboard, outline the schedule for tomorrow, then it's back to work for all of us.'

With so much still to be done before tomorrow, Susan was in full agreement.

~

Molly was not content.

Mal adored her so much that she only had to say the word, and he would give her anything that was within his power to give. Yet still, she was not satisfied, and probably never would be.

Not without Jack.

He filled her mind, day and night. Despite the fact that she was now engaged to Malcolm Shawncross, she was still obsessed with Jack.

'Oh Jack, it was a mistake,' she murmured out loud. 'I should never have let you go.'

'What's that?' Mal returned from the kitchen. 'Sorry, love. I didn't hear what you said.'

'Oh, it was nothing. I was just thinking out loud, that's all.'

Handing her a cup of coffee, he sat on the sofa beside her. 'Just now when I came in, you seemed upset. Is there something worrying you? Whatever it is, we'll sort it together.'

'Like I said – it's nothing. Stop nagging.' Repulsed by his nearness, she inched away.

Mal sipped at his coffee. He felt unsettled. They had been engaged for three weeks now, but he still didn't feel as if Molly loved him like she should. He knew she was disappointed that they hadn't been away on that fortnight's holiday he promised her, but he and Brian were at a tricky stage with the barn project. He couldn't spare the time for a break just now.

Not certain what he should do, Mal decided to keep quiet. He had learned that when Molly was in one of her moods, it was best to leave her alone. She had a scary temper on her at times. So, he drank his coffee and waited. He hoped that if he waited long enough, she might tell him what was on her mind. Instead, the silence thickened.

Suddenly, she was on her feet and looking down on him. 'There's something you should know.' Her voice was intense. Too serious.

'What might that be, then?' His heartbeat quickened. And when she answered him, he was shocked to his roots.

'I made a mistake, getting engaged to you.' When he opened his mouth to speak, she went on, 'No! Don't say anything. I'm sorry, but I realise it now. I'm just not ready for a big commitment. It's over, Mal.'

There! It was said, and she felt all the better for it. Yet she had to be careful, because if she couldn't get Jack back again, she might well be left on the shelf.

Mal was devastated. 'Is it something I've done?' he asked. 'If I've upset you in any way, I'm sorry. I'll make it right. I love you, Molly – I always have, you know that.'

The smallest semblance of pity touched her cold heart, but she was not about to change her mind. She had been making plans, and today she'd managed to acquire the information she needed. So now, there was no turning back. 'I'm sorry, Mal. I really am.'

Heartbroken, he bowed his head. 'Don't let it be over, Molly,' he pleaded. 'Take as much time as you like to think it through, but don't finish it now, not like this. I can wait. I'll wait for ever if I have to.'

He felt like a coward. He knew he should be throwing her out, but she was in his blood. He could not imagine life without her.

Molly had a plan. 'I need to go out for a while,' she lied.

His heart lightened. 'That's a good idea. We can talk about it, away from here. Let's jump in the car and go to the Black Horse at Woburn. It's quiet there at this time of evening.'

'No! I'm going out on my own. Like you said, I need to think.' But not about him, she thought. Not about spending the rest of her life without him. It was Jack she needed to think about. She wanted him back, and to that end, she was prepared to do anything.

A few minutes later she was on her way out, leaving Mal standing at the window, feeling utterly wretched, watching her go. 'What's happening?' he kept asking himself. 'Where did I go wrong?'

~

In the pub down the road, Molly ordered her drink and took it to a corner seat.

'What's wrong with her?' The barmaid had never taken to Molly.

The landlord shrugged. 'Dunno.'

The barmaid gave a little snort. That bloke of hers – Mal, isn't it? – he needs his head examined, getting engaged to her. He can't have known what he was taking on, poor bugger.'

The landlord was surprised at her bitterness. 'Get over yourself, Sally. She's just having a bad day, like we all have sometimes.'

Sally swiped a cloth over the bar. 'You men! A woman only has to have a nice pair of legs and bouncy boobs, and you can't see beyond them. I've got her well and truly sussed, though.'

'Go on then, enlighten me,' the landlord topped up a pint of Guinness.

'She's one of those women who are all sweetness and light on the surface, when everything's going their way.

But once things begin to go wrong, you see their true colours.'

'I see.' He glanced at Molly, who was leaning on the table, arms folded and her thoughts seemingly miles away. 'If you ask me, she's had a bit of a barny with that bloke of hers.'

The barmaid tutted, then went to the other end of the bar, where an elderly man was waiting to be served. 'Yes, my darling – what can I get you?' Her smile was radiant, but when her attention slid over to Molly, she muttered a piece of advice: 'What you need, lady, is a man who can put you in your place. A good kick up the arse now and then wouldn't hurt you, either.'

'I beg your pardon?' The old gent didn't quite catch what she said.

Horrified, she spun round. 'Oh, sorry – what was it? Vodka and lemonade, and a gin and tonic?'

The old man smiled patiently. 'No. It was a pint of best, and a shandy for the missus.'

By now Molly had finished her wine and sat in the corner, growing increasingly morose and sorry for herself. 'Jack should never have left me,' she mumbled. 'He said he loved me, and yet he still went away. We should have talked about it more. He should have realised how much I needed him.'

The barmaid continued to keep a wary eye on her. 'Look at her now!' She nudged the landlord. 'She's talking to herself . . . losing the plot. Batty as a church steeple, she is!'

'Stop it, Sal.' The landlord had certain standards to maintain. 'She'll hear you.'

'So?' The girl gave a shrug. 'Good job 'n' all. Probably time she heard a few home truths.'

She spun round to deal with a customer. 'Hello, pint, is it? My, you're pushing the boat out tonight, and no mistake.' She gave his wife a knowing wink. 'Play your cards right an' you'll be in for a treat later,' she told her loudly.

The customer laughed out loud. 'Those treats are long gone,' he chuckled. 'It's a game of dominoes and a hot-water bottle now . . . more's the pity.' He gave a long, drawn-out sigh, as though he had lost something very precious.

'Give over!' the barmaid teased. 'It's never too old to enjoy yourself.' When he turned away, she called him back. 'Hey! Come in next Friday – we've booked a dancing stripper. That should start your engine, if you know what I mean?'

His eyes sparkling with anticipation, the man asked, 'Well built, is she?'

'Absolutely! Goes to the gym three times a week. Name of Jerry – tree-trunks for legs. You'll like him.'

The customer laughed so heartily, he had to put his pint down again. 'You're a one, aren't you, eh?' He went away to tell his wife, who judging by the sour look on her face, was not amused.

~

When, a short time later, Mal heard the front door opening, he ran to meet her. 'Where have you been?!' he demanded. 'When you rang earlier, you said you wouldn't be long.' He gave her a snippet of news she did not welcome, 'Mal's here. Have you two had a row?' Just then, Mal appeared in the doorway, 'I couldn't let you go like that, Moll we need to talk.' Ignoring him, Molly headed for the front door.

'Where are you going?' Mal was frantic. Let me come with you, please! We can go away . . . Thrash it out together. Please Moll?'

He followed her down the path. 'Don't do it, please!' he begged. 'I just need to understand what's happened. What's changed between us. There's no need to leave. Let's talk. We'll work it out . . .' His voice broke and he watched, helpless, as she climbed into her car.

'I need some space,' she tore the engagement ring off her finger and gave it to him. 'You said I could have as long as I want, and I'm due a week off work. So, now I'm doing what you said. I'm taking time out – by myself. I'm putting a distance between us, so I can think what to do next.'

Slamming the car door, she switched on the ignition, and before he could stop her, she was accelerating down the road.

'Don't forget to let me know where . . .' His voice tailed off. She couldn't hear him now, she was too far away. And he daren't even think about her not coming back.

Where would she go? Walking slowly back inside the house, he had no idea.

~

Molly though, had her destination all planned. And she couldn't get there quickly enough.

CHAPTER EIGHTEEN

'Susan?' Jack's voice echoed across the now empty showroom.

'Yes?' His assistant was texting her husband to come and pick her up.

Jack walked towards her. 'Here. This is for you.' He gave her a heavy, pink-wrapped parcel. 'Careful – don't drop it.'

'What's this for?'

'For all your hard work today, and in recent weeks. I think you've excelled yourself.'

'I don't know about that.' Susan flopped into a chair. 'I am worn out, though,' she admitted.

Jack sat beside her. 'Me too.' He hoped she liked the bottles of rosé champagne in a luxury silk-lined presentation box. It had not been cheap but she had more than earned it.

He could not believe how, with the help of every man Jack had available, they had dressed this place from top to toe, ready for the grand opening tomorrow.

He looked about, at the huge banners hanging from the ceiling, and four others around the walls. The sales brochures were placed at every strategic position, and each car was sparkling like a diamond, as was every surface, including the wide, wrap-around windows, and a floor that went on forever.

Even with two professional cleaners on hand, this was a huge and difficult building to clean. No one had been exempt from helping. Even with their own personal schedules to prepare, every last man and woman had rolled up their sleeves and got stuck in.

Crockery and cutlery were attractively laid out on long catering tables, ready for the food that would be delivered tomorrow. The Nissan hatchback that would be raffled took pride of place on a spin-around pedestal, its dark-blue body all polished and shiny, waiting for the lucky winner to claim it in December.

In two big boxes by the door were more banners of every shape and size to dress the building outside, and a pile of goodie-bags to be handed out as the throngs made their way through the doors. Every member of staff had been instructed to arrive by eight-thirty tomorrow to assist with the finishing touches before the doors opened at ten o'clock. Everyone was praying that the rain that had blighted this entire summer would let up, at least for tomorrow morning.

'I ache all over,' Susan groaned. 'Right – I'd better go to the car park. John will be here any minute.'

'I reckon we're a good team, you and me,' said Jack.

'We're not bad, are we?' she agreed. 'Thanks a lot

for the present – I can't wait to open it. Now, don't you hang about too long,' she advised. 'And don't lie awake all night thinking about tomorrow, or you'll be worse than useless.'

Jack smiled. 'I couldn't have put it better myself. See you tomorrow!'

~

Once he'd posted the completed and signed copy of the rental agreement in through the letterbox of his landlord's house, Jack went in search of a shop. He soon discovered a small supermarket not all that far from where he would be living. He vaguely recalled that it used to be a paint and wallpaper shop when he was a boy.

He glanced at his watch – eight-thirty already! Today had been fast and furious – and tomorrow would be the same. Jack couldn't wait to get started. He was convinced that, if they matched the client to the car, kept their prices as competitive as they could . . . then Curtis Warren Motors would get through the creeping recession with flying colours.

A short time later, having done his shopping, he was strolling through the car park, ready to open his car boot and dump his shopping, when he saw a woman standing by her car looking very distraught.

Quickly packing his shopping into the boot of his car, he offered assistance, 'Can I help?'

'Are you any good with cars?' The woman had also

just done her shopping and was growing frustrated. 'The trouble is, I can't get my old car to start. And I don't belong to any car-rescue scheme, so I'm in a bit of a mess.'

'I'll see if can find out what the problem is,' Jack promised. 'I run a showroom out at Lytham, and I've been around cars now for a few years . . . so let's see if I can figure out what's wrong, eh? Look, here's my card, so you know who I am.'

Jack soon had the bonnet up and quickly identified the problem. He could tell that the car was on its way out. He noted that it had 128,000 miles on the clock. However, he soon had the engine running, and all the woman had to do was to get behind the wheel and drive away.

'How can I thank you?' she asked. She thought instinctively Jack might be offended if she offered him money.

'Come to our special event tomorrow morning, if you can,' he suggested. 'Curtis Warren Motors, over in Lytham – the address is on the card. I'll look out for you. And who knows – maybe we can fix you up with a reliable new car.'

Bidding her cheerio, he returned to his own car. He had no idea that the whole incident had been observed by Libby, who had just emerged from the staff entrance at the back of the supermarket.

Having put her own shopping down for a moment so she could turn to close the door, she had paused, intrigued by the sight of a tall young man going to the other driver's assistance. He looked just like the stranger who had loitered under the trees opposite their house the other night . . . and who had been hanging around near the chip shop later on. She recognised his light-blue rain-jacket with its distinctive white panels. Thomas had spoken of him having a big black car and had spelled out its number, all but the last digit. Libby wondered if this man's car would be the same one.

It was something about his stance that she recognised – something about the way he held himself as he walked along, so sure of himself, sort of easy and confident. It *was* him – she would have bet her day's wages on it. But there was something else . . . something that made her breathing quicken, something that her heart knew even before her conscious mind had caught up.

Quickly concealing herself beside the paper recycling skip, Libby studied him more closely. Now that she was seeing him in daylight, and he was not completely hidden from sight by his brolly, she could see him for who he was. She could hear his familiar voice, and her heart did a somersault.

It was Jack Redmond!

For what seemed an age, Libby remained concealed but within hearing distance, until Jack had picked up his bags, got into his own car and driven off. Libby was amazed to see that yes, the car was black and the registration number was similar to the one Thomas had mentioned. Only then did she emerge into the open, stunned by the discovery that Jack was back in his home-town, Blackburn.

Suddenly she was fearful. What if she never saw him again? What if she'd found her dear friend, only to lose him again?

Sighing with relief, she then remembered he had told the woman something about Curtis Warren Motors in Lytham. Quickly finding pen and paper, Libby wrote it down. Later she would think what to do about it. She could look it up on her laptop.

For now, she'd better get home. Her mother and Thomas would have been expecting her at least half an hour ago, and she didn't want to worry them. Excited and reeling with the discovery, she located her car and drove away.

CHAPTER NINETEEN

Back in Bower Street, Thomas was worried. It wasn't like Libby to be late. He paced up and down, pausing only to look out of his window. 'She'll be here soon,' he told himself. 'Yes . . . she'll have been called to do summat an' nowt, and now she'll be on 'er way home.'

He toyed with the idea of calling her mobile phone. He even picked up the receiver and began to dial.

'No. Best not,' he decided. 'She'll think I'm checkin' up on her, poor lass.'

No sooner had he replaced the receiver than he heard her tapping on his front door. Crossing the room to let her in, he then gently woke Eileen, who had enjoyed a nice nap. 'Libby's here, m'darling. Time to go home.' He would have loved her to stay here with him, but sadly, that was not possible, for many reasons. Some of which were best left alone.

Libby was apologetic. 'I'm sorry I'm late, Thomas. I'll explain later on, if that's OK.' She went over to Eileen.

'Fell asleep, did you, Mum? I'm really sorry to be late.' She bent to kiss her. 'I'm here now though, and I'm ready for bed.' She saw her mother yawning. 'Much like you, by the look of it. The next time they ask me to do a late shift, I won't be so obliging.' She was positively bursting to tell Thomas about her sighting of Jack Redmond, but she remained calm in front of her mother.

Eileen had an impish sense of humour, which seemed to just pop out when no one expected it. 'Libby?'

'Yes, Mum?' Libby was easing her mother's shoes back on her feet. 'What is it?'

'Me and Thomas could get married,' she informed Libby. 'Then I can sleep here with him, and you won't need to worry about me so much.'

While Libby was taken aback, Thomas roared with laughter. 'I don't know as I could handle a tiger like you,' he teased.

When Eileen suddenly got up and was taking it upon herself to fetch her coat, Libby quickly went to help.

'Leave me be, now,' Eileen edged away. 'I'm not a baby. I can get my own coat.' Sometimes, however hard she tried, Eileen could not think straight, so when her head *was* clear, she cherished being able to do every little thing for herself, such as now. 'I'm all right, love. Stop fussing.'

Wisely, Libby left her to it.

In his usual gentlemanly way, Thomas walked them home.

'Are you coming in for a nightcap?' Libby knew she

should have phoned him about being late. It was obvious he'd been worried about her.

'Oh, go on then.' Thomas loved spending time under this roof. It was like home from home, especially when the two people he loved most in all the world were right here.

Libby was grateful for the company. There was a lot she needed to get off her chest. 'Mum?' She helped Eileen take off her coat. 'Thomas is staying for a nightcap. Do you fancy one?'

Eileen shook her head. 'No, thank you, dear. I'm very tired.' She glanced across at Thomas. 'I'll see you tomorrow, won't I, Thomas?' For some reason, she felt threatened.

'Yes, m'dear. You get a good night's sleep, eh?'

Eileen grew anxious. 'You're not going away, are you?'

Thomas ambled over to her. 'Will yer please stop getting yersel' into a pickle. I'm just having a nightcap with Libby, then I'm away to my bed, just next door. And that's as far as I'm going.'

Eileen needed convincing. 'Promise me you won't go away?' Her voice began to shake. 'Promise you won't leave me?'

Thomas took her into his embrace. 'You listen to me, my darling.' Holding her tight, he spoke softly in her ear: 'You and Libby are my family now. And I love you both, like my own flesh and blood.'

He held her at arm's length. 'I promise I will never leave you. Not as long as I live.' He then made her smile. 'You'll not get rid o' me that easy!'

Eileen looked into his eyes, so kind, so familiar. All these years she had trusted him. Good times. Bad times. Times when shocking things happen and you can never shut them from your mind, however hard you try.

Reaching up, she touched his face. 'Goodnight, old friend. God bless.'

'Night night. God bless.' He gave her a peck on the cheek. 'It's Saturday tomorrow. I'll think o' somewhere nice to tek yer, after I've spent a couple of hours on the allotment. No doubt there'll be blackberries down the lane.'

As she climbed the stairs he watched her every step. 'Sleep tight. Mind the bed bugs don't bite.'

'We don't have bed bugs,' Eileen called back indignantly.

'No, 'course yer don't. I'm just being silly, that's all.'

'Well, stop being silly then.'

He stood watching until she was out of sight, then he remained there quietly for a minute or two, his hands on the balustrade. His mind wandered back to a certain day many years ago. The sadness showed on his homely face. 'G'night, lass,' he whispered. 'I'm so sorry. I can't turn the clock back, but I can help you along the way.'

His old heart was sore. Where did the years go? Both he and Eileen were now of an age when looking forward was not a good idea. But, when all was said and done, it had to be better than looking back. Looking back was sheer torture – both for him and for that darling woman up there.

Eileen was a good woman. She did not deserve such heartache. The doctors told Libby that her mother's condition was not as bad as first thought, though it was bad enough, and could not be cured. They even gave her condition a name – psychosis. But Thomas knew different.

He alone knew the real reason for Eileen's illness. He knew why she sometimes lived in fear. He knew exactly when her condition had started. *And he knew why.*

All these years, he had blamed himself. And he would go on blaming himself, until the day he was called before the Good Lord to confess his sins. Maybe then, and only then, would he find peace.

It was Eileen that concerned him; because somewhere deep in her tortured mind, she knew it all. And she had no choice but to keep it hidden, for the sake of others. Meanwhile, the weight of it all continued to ravage her mind.

'Your cocoa is ready,' Libby called softly. 'Let's pinch a few of Mum's gingernuts and dunk them, shall we?'

Thomas sat down at the table and wrapped his big hands around his mug of cocoa.

'I've been thinking about taking your Mum for a trip into Blackpool on the bus, but I reckon it might be too much for her,' he said. 'What d'you think?'

Libby got her cocoa and sat opposite him, taking the lid off the biscuit tin. 'I'm not sure,' she said. 'Just now, she looked really done in, but that could be because she was late getting to bed. She does love

Blackpool, though. One of her favourite things is strolling down the promenade. She says it reminds her of when she and Dad used to take me to Blackpool as a small child.'

Her innocent comments struck deep with Thomas. 'I remember one time, you must'a been, what . . . eight or nine months old. You'd been to Blackpool with yer Mum and Dad, and as they brought you out the car, you were holding four big, coloured balloons. Laughing out loud, you were, and waving them balloons so high in the air, I thought they'd carry you off and we'd never see you again.'

He smiled at the memory, but then the darkness crept into his mind again, and wiped the smile away. 'Aye, that were a long time ago,' he finished lamely.

Just now, while her Mum was in bed and she had Thomas to himself, she had a question for him. 'Thomas, can I ask you something?'

'O' course! Ask away.'

'What was my father like . . . really?'

For a moment, the old man was taken aback. It seemed an age before he answered. 'I don't rightly know what yer mean, lass.'

'I just wonder, that's all, because I can't remember much about him, as I was only three when he left us. I do remember Mum crying a lot, I think – and Dad yelling at her. Beyond that . . . nothing at all.'

Thomas put her mind at rest. 'As far as I know, yer Dad were no different from many another bloke on the street. He worked hard, and I dare say he had a bet on the football pools, and a few bevies of a Friday night, but other than that, he and yer Mum got on all right . . . as much as any married couple get on.'

'Thank you.' She was grateful for that. 'I suppose what you remember as a small child can get a bit twisted. I mean, it would be a strange couple that never argues, wouldn't it? And Mum obviously loved him. Otherwise she wouldn't be sneaking out in the middle of the night trying to find him, would she?'

Libby pondered for a moment. 'Thomas, can I ask you something else?'

''Course yer can.' Uncomfortable at her questions, he prepared himself.

'If my Dad loved my Mum, why would he go off with some other woman?'

Thomas explained as best he could. 'Unfortunately, it happens, lass. Sometimes a man begins to get bored with life – especially if he works long hours, like your Dad did. So, he starts to wander, looking for a bit o' fun to spice up his life. It doesn't mean he's fallen out of love with his wife. But then one day, he meets a woman who's different from the others. She worms her way into his life. She's never going to be happy with a two-night fling. She's looking for someone to set up with, and once she sets her sights on a particular man, she usually gets him in the end – even if he's married with children. Women like that are home-wreckers wi' no conscience.'

When she was growing up, Libby had heard the gossip about her father and other women. 'That must have been so hard for Mum,' she said now. 'I don't know how she put up with it.'

Thomas gave a knowing smile. 'Ah well, she put up with it because she loved him and she didn't want to lose him. But in the end, she did lose him, and she's never really got over it.'

'Do you think she expected him to come back?'

'Oh, I'm sure she did. But when someone goes like that, there's not an awful lot can be done about it.'

Libby's anger bubbled over. 'Why would he do such a terrible thing, when he had a woman at home who idolised him?'

Thomas had no answers. 'Aw, now, lass, yer can't ask me that kind of a question. What can I tell yer? I just don't know.'

'Sorry. It was wrong of me to draw you in like that.' She sipped her cocoa, and changed the subject. 'Just now, when I went up to her, Mum was talking clear as a bell.'

'I know, and it's wonderful when she's like that, like her old self. But as the doctor told you, there will be days when she behaves normal enough, and other times she'll be lost . . . her mind wandering here and there.'

'We'll keep her safe though, won't we, Thomas?'

'Yer absolutely right there, lass.' Reaching out, he put his hand over hers. 'You have me, and I'm here to keep you *both* safe. Never you forget that.' He considered it to be his duty.

~

Unbeknownst to the pair chatting down below, Eileen had got out of bed and had made her way to the top of the stairs, where the stair-gate was fastened. She was still there now, listening to them, to Thomas' loud voice and her daughter's softer tones, growing more anxious with their every word.

Deeply disturbed, she carefully climbed over the gate, tiptoed down the stairs, and listened outside the door.

~

Libby finished her ginger biscuit and looked Thomas in the eye. 'Something very strange and also very wonderful happened this evening,' she said. 'I think I've solved the mystery of the man who seemed to be watching us, and I'm hopeful there's nothing to worry about.'

Trying not to show too much excitement, she related the whole story of what she had seen and heard in the supermarket car park. 'If it really is Jack, he looked so prosperous and successful,' she said. 'He's obviously done well for himself. I wonder how long he's been working at Cutis Warren Motors.'

She would never understand why Jack had cut off all contact with them. Perhaps she would get a chance, now, to ask him. It had felt so hurtful over the years.

Having put his glasses on, Thomas produced a copy of the local newspaper. 'Curtis Warren Motors, eh . . . ? That's the new garage in Lytham. It's meant to be a big, posh place. They've got adverts everywhere – they

309

even mentioned it on the radio. If I remember rightly, there's a big event there tomorrow.

'Are you really sure it's our Jack?' Thomas asked kindly. 'That poor lad went from these parts years ago. After what happened to his parents, I shouldn't think he'd ever want to show his face round 'ere again. Poor Gordon, copping it in the fire, then that stuck-up piece Claire Redmond pushing off with a Yank an' leaving her lad all on his own . . .'

But Libby wasn't listening. 'I'm *sure* it's him.' Her voice broke with emotion. 'Right from the first, I knew there was something familiar about him, but I couldn't put my finger on it. Jack Redmond . . . Oh, Thomas, I know in my heart that it's him! He's back. Jack's come home!'

~

Eileen recognised the name straight away. It was strange, how some names had stayed with her over the years. And now, hearing that he was back, she began to panic, because Jack knew. **He knew about the bad thing.** And now they would all know. That must not happen! That must never happen.

Her heart was racing; her mind was running ahead of her thoughts. She could hardly breathe. *He knew! Jack knew! He had always known, and now he would tell.* Confused and panic-stricken, she didn't know what to do.

She could hear Libby laughing, and Thomas, almost

310

ready to believe that Jack had really come back, saying how wonderful it would be to see him again. Eileen wanted to shout, to tell Thomas that it was *not* wonderful. It was the worst thing that could happen. The most frightening thing of all. And now, *it* would never go away. Not ever!

~

Thomas gave an involuntary shiver. 'Brr! It's draughty in 'ere all of a sudden, don't yer think?'

Far too excited to feel the cold, Libby was thinking about Jack. 'I'm sure I won't sleep a wink tonight!' She was so incredibly happy. Yet she tried not to get her hopes up too high. Just in case.

Thomas was wondering where the sudden chill was coming from. 'Is there a door open somewhere?' he asked.

The thought struck them at the same time. With Thomas on her heels, Libby ran into the kitchen. The back door was open, and they dashed outside. It was dark, and for a moment they couldn't see anything.

'Mum!' Libby called out. *'Where are you?'*

'Have yer a torch anywhere, lass?' Thomas asked. Then suddenly he said, 'There! Did yer hear that?'

Libby listened. What she heard was an odd, rhythmic sound, like sand shifting up and down a beach.

'There's a torch under the stairs.' She switched on the kitchen light and went to get it.

'Is there any way she can get out of the yard?'

'No, not since I had the back gate fitted with locks.' While Libby ran inside to get the torch, she could hear Thomas continuously calling out.

'Eileen, m'dear . . . it's me, Thomas. I can't see where you are. Call my name, lass, so I can come and get you.' Guided by the light coming through the kitchen window, he took another few steps forward, but beyond the narrow shaft of illumination, there was only impenetrable blackness.

A moment later, Libby came rushing back. 'I was worried the battery might have gone,' she said, handing him the torch, 'but it's working. *Mum! It's all right. We're not angry. Please . . . Just come inside, in the warm.*'

They found Eileen at the farthest corner of the garden, between the fence and the silver birch tree. Down on her knees, she was madly scrabbling at the damp ground with her bare hands and scooping earth into a pile.

When he realised what she was doing, Thomas was shocked. 'Oh, dear Lord!' He knew what was in her mind. *He had to stop her.*

'Eileen, love, please don't do this.' When he tenderly laid his hands on her shoulders, she flinched from him.

'*No!* Leave me be. I have to do it. You know that!'

She spoke again, this time in the softest whisper, and he knew it was for his ears alone. 'Please, it's time to tell the truth.' Her voice and her thinking were so clear, it shook him deeply.

Not having heard what her mother was whispering, Libby stepped forward. Speaking to her in that quiet, firm voice that usually got through to Eileen, she said, 'We're going back inside now. Come on, Mum. We'll help you.'

Eileen's bottom lip trembled. 'I need to stay here,' she confided in a whisper. 'Thomas knows.' She smiled up at Thomas, who was torn with guilt. 'It wasn't my fault, was it, Thomas?'

'No, my darling . . .' Desperately concerned he played along. 'It wasn't your fault. We all know that. But you should not have come out here. You must come with us now. You're getting cold, and Libby and I are so worried about you.'

'Come inside, Mum.' Cradling her tight, with Thomas guiding them in the light from the torch, Libby gently walked her mother back down the path. Libby was deeply distressed at the sight of her – clad only in her nightdress, now covered with dirt-stains. What had possessed her to sneak outside and dig a hole like that? And with such frenzy it was almost as though some unseen force was driving her to do it. Where would it all end? she wondered.

Once he had got them safely to the house, Thomas returned to where Eileen had been digging. What was she thinking? Even as he asked himself the question, he knew how her poor, sick mind was working. He knew the torment she was going through. And he could hardly bear it.

He kicked the soil back until the hole was full again.

'I'll come round and do that properly,' he murmured, 'sooner rather than later.'

Picking his way carefully back down the garden, he let the kitchen light guide him. What to do? How many times, when he had seen how the past was affecting Eileen's well-being, had he asked himself that same question, *What to do?*

There was only one solution, but he dared not take it. There were too many reasons why he couldn't go down that road. But how long could things go on as they were? Especially when, just lately, Eileen was beginning to relive the past. After tonight, he realised now that, instead of maintaining her peace of mind, his very silence was slowly destroying her.

Stopping in his tracks, he looked up at the night sky and, fixing his sorry gaze on the brightest star, he prayed, 'Help her, Lord. Please help her. I don't care what happens to me, but I'm asking you . . . please, for pity's sake, guide me to do the right thing for her. She's a good, kind woman, Lord.'

~

Inside the kitchen, Libby had washed and dried her mother, rubbed cream on her sore hands, and now she was putting a clean nightgown on her.

'Where's the boy?' Eileen demanded.

Libby was confused. 'What boy? There is no boy.'

Eileen got angry. 'Where is he? Where did you hide him?'

Just then, Thomas came into the kitchen. 'You mean Jack, don't you?' he said. 'Jack Redmond.' Only now did he realise that Eileen must have been listening to their conversation earlier.

Eileen began to cry. 'He knows,' she wept. 'He knows the secret place.'

Libby was out of her depth. 'What d'you mean, Mum?'

Afraid that too much had been said already, Thomas wisely suggested, 'I think we should just concentrate on getting you back to bed, Eileen.' Reaching out, he took hold of her sore hands and tenderly kissed them.

'Thomas?' Eileen responded sleepily.

'Yes, m'dear?'

'I love you.' Her voice trembled.

'Thank you,' he said humbly.

'Do you love me?'

'You don't need to ask that,' he told her. 'You know I do.'

~

Having got her upstairs, while Libby cleared up below, Thomas waited until Eileen had climbed into her bed. Then he drew the covers over her and kissed her good night. 'This time, stay in yer bed,' he ordered her kindly. 'I'm too old and knackered to be chasing after women these days.'

Eileen grabbed him by the collar and drew him down. '*Tell him!*' she hissed. She held him there, so close he could feel her breath on his face. 'Tell him to stay away, because they're watching. I don't want them to hurt him, Thomas. Please, don't let them hurt him.'

Thomas realised he could not leave it. He had to put her mind at rest. 'Who wants to hurt him?' he asked.

'Them!' You know who,

'Why would they want to hurt him?'

She looked nervously about, before answering, 'He saw it. The boy – Jack – he found them!'

'That can't be, m'dear. Jack was just a baby,' Thomas said. 'You're imagining things, Eileen. You must not think like that.'

'Listen to me.' She grew angry. 'The baby – the boy. *He saw them.*' She took a deep, invigorating breath, 'He was there. I took him away . . . I didn't want him to see, but it was too late! I ran, Thomas. I ran and I got the little lad, but it was too late.' She began to sob, clinging to him, looking for comfort. Looking for him to make everything all right. 'Thomas . . . I'm so very sad,' she sobbed bitterly.

For a long moment, the old man could not bring himself to speak. He loved Eileen so much, and it hurt him to see her tortured like this. Tenderly stroking her hand, he whispered in her ear, 'You need to get some sleep now.'

'Sing to me, Thomas. Please?' She loved to hear him sing. It made her quiet inside. It made her feel secure. And it helped her forget the bad things.

Very softly, he began to sing Frank Sinatra's 'My Way', one of her favourite songs. As he sang, the tears flowed down his face. The song said it all, word for word.

When he looked down on her, she was fast asleep. 'That's it, my love.' He leaned down to kiss her on the forehead. 'You sleep now. Tomorrow will be a better day, God willing.'

~

Downstairs, Libby heard him singing, and she smiled a bittersweet smile. Two lovely people, in their golden years, so much in love, yet so far apart. What future could there be for them?

She shook her head. 'Hmph! Some might say the same could be said of me.'

In the back of her mind, she was thinking of Jack. She could hardly believe that the man who had helped the woman in the car park could actually be the boy she walked to school with, all those years ago. Oh, but wouldn't it be wonderful to see him again?

She and Jack had been almost inseparable. A real little tomboy, in her torn shorts and with her curly cap of red hair, Libby had built dens with him, swapped stamps with him, gone on bike rides with him, had all sorts of adventures and scrapes with him . . . and often she felt she knew Jack Redmond inside out. In fact, Libby felt sure that she still had some of their school-books and treasures put away in a box somewhere . . .

While they'd been doing their GCSEs and then their 'A' Levels, Jack had grown moody and apart, and his studies began to suffer. Libby realised then that things going on at home – his father's injury and death, his mother's gradual abandonment of him, and the nightmares that plagued him – had all taken away his enthusiasm for learning.

The feelings she had for Jack made her shy, self-conscious and distant, and so she never told him how she really felt. She regretted that now.

But it seemed that fate might have given them a second chance. Libby promised herself that *this time*, if Jack really was the man she'd seen, and if he was a free man, she would never lose him again.

CHAPTER TWENTY

EVERYTHING WAS READY. There was a real atmosphere of excitement, with each member of staff eager to do their part to make the event a great success.

'Well, today's the day.' Jack mustered the troops. 'In half an hour, Curtis Warren himself is due to walk through those doors. He'll have his beady eyes on each and every one of us. Even when you're not aware of it, he won't be far away. He'll be in the background, watching you. He'll be listening to conversations and taking notes. So, remember, we're here not only to sell cars, but to build the reputation of this company. We need to establish a network of customers who will trust us and who will carry the word far and wide.'

He finished his short rallying speech by reminding them of the golden rules. 'There are three things to remember. One, listen to what the customer wants. Two, don't come down heavy for the hard sell. The customers don't like it, and it's proven to be counterproductive. I think you all know the third golden rule?'

He put his hand to his ear, waiting for the response, which came loud and clear, as they answered in unison: 'The customer is always right!' Laughter ensued as they released the pent-up energy.

Twenty minutes later, Curtis Warren walked through the doors, accompanied by his assistant from Head Office, who was taking lots of photographs. The big man moved amongst them, talking to each man and woman individually.

A short time later, the people started arriving. First it was a trickle, then a stream – until the entire place was flooded with people.

'You've done a good job,' Curtis Warren told Jack, and his delight was evident as he moved amongst the would-be customers.

The morning went well. There were numerous test drives and one-to-one consultations, and by midday a considerable number of deals had been clinched, much to everyone's satisfaction. The festive atmosphere, the free food and the raffle made it a day to remember. The raffle was to benefit the local children's hospital, a worthy and popular cause. People were more than willing to put their hands in their pockets and find £5 for a ticket.

~

Not many miles away, Molly, who had spent the night in a soulless hotel in Birmingham, was on the M6 heading towards Lytham St Anne's. Her company car, a bright-yellow VW Golf with *Banbury's Estate Agents* logos on its sides, was powering along in the fast lane.

When the driver behind started beeping his horn, indicating that she should move over to allow his huge four-by-four to overtake, she made a rude gesture but swerved left into the middle lane, and narrowly avoiding a lorry.

'Dopey cow!' bawled the driver of the Chelsea tractor as he roared past, but she was oblivious.

'I hope the cameras are switched on,' a woman said to her husband, who was driving her and their twin little boys up to visit her mother in Preston. 'She's weaving all over the place and not signalling at all! For God's sake keep away from her – she's putting us all in danger.'

Just then, a coach zoomed past, its horn sounding a loud alarm as Molly once more overtook without signalling their impatience to get to Jack, had overridden her common sense.

Behind the wheel of the Golf, Molly noticed none of this. Dressed in a smart grey suit from Wallis, and wearing a new pair of sexy high-heeled shoes, she hoped to wow Jack this morning – and then to win him back. She knew how important the grand opening was for him. Jan, the receptionist at Jack's old job, had told all the gossip to her friend Izzy, who went to the same gym as Molly. It was easy to overhear things when you were getting changed or using the same equipment.

Molly gave a happy little gasp at the misplaced thought of her future with Jack. There was still time, she thought; with Jackstill time to put things right, to make up for the past. Mal would soon find someone else, she told herself. All he needed to do was join one of those online dating agencies, and he'd soon be fighting women off. And then she and Jack could be together for ever.

For a moment, her features tightened and the old rage took over. Jack Redmond *owed her* – and now she was ready to call in the debt.

Doing a steady 70 miles per hour, Molly hummed along to her CD of *Abba's Golden Hits.*

A crack of thunder rent the sky as black clouds drew together above the busy motorway. Not another bloody shower! She consoled herself with the thought that once she and Jack were back together, they'd go on a little holiday. Somewhere far away from the so-called English summer.

As if on cue, the heavens opened and the rain sluiced down, flooding the windscreen.

Disorientated, Molly flicked the wipers to maximum speed. Then, as she reached to pump up the volume on 'Dancing Queen', her happy expression turned to one of panic as the spiky heel of her shoe caught in the carpet beneath the accelerator pedal. Trying to free her foot just added to the pressure on the pedal, which made the car go even faster and caused her to panic. Frantically grabbing at the steering wheel, she lost control altogether and the car veered at full speed straight into the side of a massive removal truck.

Molly's car was dragged along for half a mile before

the traumatised truck driver was able to stop safely on the hard shoulder and phone for the police and the ambulance service.

Molly's thoughts were not of her parents or her brother – and not of Jack, either. They were constant declarations of love for her.

CHAPTER TWENTY-ONE

Libby was lost.

Twice she'd taken a wrong turn in Thomas' old Austin, and now she was asking at the next garage, 'Can you please tell me where the new car showrooms are? Curtis Warren Motors, I think they're called.'

'Oh yes.' The big man at the till wiped a dewdrop from the end of his bulbous nose. 'Turn right at the next junction, and the new showrooms should be straight ahead. All glass and metal, they are. Like a flippin' palace, it is.' Libby thanked him and left.

When she had told Thomas of her plan to go to the opening, he had offered her the car, and wished her luck.

'Best you don't go on about young Jack too much,' he cautioned. 'We don't want yer Mum getting all agitated again like she was last night.'

Libby had promised to be discreet. Maybe Jack wouldn't even recognise her. She was no longer the teenager he had once known.

Getting back in the car, she took a look at herself in the mirror. She had taken extra care with her looks that afternoon. Her freshly washed hair was tied up in a silver band and she was wearing her prettiest outfit – a calf-length dress in softest blue.

Pulling into the car park at Curtis Warren's, Libby felt extremely nervous. What if Jack didn't want to see her?

People were getting in and out of cars, and there was a steady stream of people on foot, entering the wide glass doors. Taking a deep breath, she headed towards the entrance.

Inside, there was a smart reception desk and long tables covered with the ruins of what must have been a very nice buffet.

'Would you like a drink, madam?' asked a friendly young man, holding out a tray. 'We have orange or cranberry juice.'

'No, thank you,' she replied. 'I've actually come to see Mr Redmond.' She hoped she wasn't making a fool of herself, 'I don't have an appointment, though.'

'Mr Redmond is over there, but he's with a client at the moment,' he gave her a covert once-over. Nice figure, he thought.

Anxious in case Mr Warren had left some spies behind, who might be watching his every move, he decided to get rid of this visitor as quickly as possible and crack on with earning himself a commission.

'I'll see what I can do,' he said. 'Who shall I say is here?'

'Elizabeth Harrow,' she answered nervously.

'Very well.' He hurried away.

Libby watched as the young man spoke with Jack. When Jack glanced briefly in her direction, her heart turned over.

When he was told there was 'a young lady' waiting to see him, Jack's heart froze. Surely Molly hadn't followed him up here to create another scene? But no, he reassured himself, she was with Mal now.

'Her name is Elizabeth Harrow,' the young man told Jack.

'Thanks, Martin.' Jack was intrigued, but as yet the name had not sunk in. As he walked across the room towards her, Jack was impressed by the shapely young woman in the blue dress who was studying a catalogue. But when she turned to face him, he was visibly stunned.

'Libby? *Libby?* I can't believe it!' he exclaimed. 'What – how – oh, Libby, it's really you!'

And then he was hugging her as though he would never let her go. 'My Libby!' he gasped. 'I can't believe it!'

Aware of some curious glances, Libby stepped back. 'It's so wonderful to see you again, Jack!' she said simply. 'I found out by accident that you were back, and I just had to see you. Oh, Jack, it's been such a long, long time!'

'Twelve years,' he murmured, a million different feelings running through him. 'Libby, please, you must stay – say you will! I've got to be here until three-thirty, but I'd so much like to spend some time with you after that. If you're free, that is?' He held his breath.

'Of course!' she answered. 'I'd really like that.'

'Right, then.' Taking his car keys from his pocket, Jack placed them in her hands. 'Just follow me.' He took her out to the car park and showed her where his car was. 'First, have a look around the showrooms, and tell me what you think later. When you've had enough, go and sit in the car, if you like, and I'll join you as soon as I can after three-thirty. How's that?'

'God, she's beautiful,' he thought. Libby, his childhood friend; the girl he had left behind. He hoped to remedy that mistake, if he got the chance.

~

Libby wandered around the showrooms, but she was unable to take it all in, or even to concentrate. Finally, when she'd had enough, she went walkabout outside, occasionally glancing in through the big windows, where Jack was chatting with the customers, and occasionally returning her smile.

At three-thirty on the dot, he joined her in the car and, without any warning, leaned towards her and kissed her long and lovingly. 'My lovely Libby,' he whispered. 'You're so beautiful!'

Nervous at first, Libby slid her arms round his neck and kissed him full on the mouth. 'I've missed you, Jack.'

'And I've missed you too,' he admitted.

'So now, Jack Redmond, I want to know what you've been up to all these years.'

327

'All right, then!' Jack felt like a teenager, all excited and nervous on his first date. 'Let's get away from here,' he suggested. 'I know the perfect place where we can talk.'

Starting the car, he drove out of the car park and headed out into the countryside. Twenty minutes later, they arrived at a beautiful spot where he used to fish. Barges were berthed on the canal and there was a duck pond near by, and a cafe with a terrace overhanging the water. Libby loved it. 'Oh, Jack, it's heavenly!' she said. 'I never even knew it was here.'

Jack led her to a decking area overlooking the canal, where they could watch the swans and barges pass by. He couldn't take his eyes off her, and his heart was full. Libby was like a breath of fresh air. His mind harked back to the distant past, and he remembered how Libby always saw the good in everyone. Many times she had patiently listened to his troubles and calmed him, especially on the frequent occasions when he'd considered running away from home.

Now, when she ran ahead to stoop by the water's edge and talk to the swans, he had a strange, deep-down feeling that he was fated to be with her for a long time, maybe for ever, now that they had been reunited. 'Slow down, Jack, lad,' he cautioned himself. 'You've only just come out of one relationship – are you ready to take the plunge again? And with all your problems, would it be fair to land them on someone else?' He couldn't answer either of those questions. He needed to take it one cautious step at a time, because there was one thing he did know for certain, and that was that he wanted Libby back in his life.

And yet, apart from the fact that she wore neither engagement ring nor wedding band, he knew next to nothing about the grown-up Elizabeth Harrow.

~

A little later, they climbed the narrow wooden steps to the upstairs decking area, where they found an empty table. Situated near the edge, it gave a perfect view: they could see along the canal right down to where it curved away, out of sight. Moored alongside the towpath, the many barges made a picturesque sight, with their pretty lanterns and flower-buckets on their roofs.

'So, what do you fancy?' Jack felt the need to celebrate. It had been a red-letter day for him. Firstly, the grand opening of the showrooms had gone even better than he'd hoped. And now he was sitting opposite Libby, who had blossomed from a tomboy schoolgirl into this beautiful, graceful woman.

'Let's order something really special,' he suggested. 'I can't have a glass of champagne, because I'm driving, but *you* can.'

'No, not for me, thanks.' Libby had never been a drinker.

'Let's have something to eat instead,' he said. 'My treat!' He pointed to the blackboard with its chalked list of the specials of the day. 'I'm going for the blackberry pie and custard. How about you?' He always did have a sweet tooth.

Libby's mouth watered. 'I'll have the blackberry pie with custard.' She beamed at Jack for a second. The old camaraderie was back.

During the meal, they talked endlessly. 'Do you remember all those picnics we used to go on during the school holidays?' he said. 'You and your Marmite-and-cheese sandwiches! I never knew how you could bear the taste.'

'I wasn't too keen on your peanut-butter and jam ones either,' Libby laughed. 'And your Mum would never give you any chocolate biscuits, would she? I always had to sneak a Kit-Kat into your bag.'

'Didn't take much to please us, did it? We were dead lucky growing up in Blackburn, only a few miles from lovely countryside. I missed it when I was in London.'

'What – you went off to London, did you?!' Libby had no idea he had lived in the capital. From this point their conversation became more serious.

Jack told her the whole story of what had happened to him over the past twelve years, up to and including his relationship with Molly. Then he listened intently to everything that Libby told him – about her Mum's illness, her part-time job at the supermarket, and the way she had seen him in the car park . . .

By the time they had finished the meal, each of them knew a great deal more about the other, and almost all questions were answered. This time together had newly forged their strong friendship, and their hearts were warmer.

There was just one thing that Jack had kept hidden: the nightmares. Just as he thought it, Libby asked tentatively, 'Do you still have those bad dreams, Jack? I hope it's all right to mention them. I know they gave you a very hard time when you were growing up.'

Jack rubbed a hand over his face, aware that the dark circles beneath his eyes told their own tale.

'To tell you the truth, I still have problems with them,' he admitted in a low voice. 'I got some treatment for them, and that was one of the reasons why I came back up north.' He paused, his gaze resting on her face and his voice breaking with emotion. 'I guess the other reason was you. You were never far from my thoughts, Libby.'

They talked a while longer. Finally Libby said, 'Sorry, Jack, but I'm going to have to leave soon. Mum and Thomas will be back from Blackpool, in a while and I need to be here to help.

Jack was reluctant to let this special time end. 'We could walk a little way up the riverside first, couldn't we?'

Longing to stay, but anxious to leave, she glanced at her watch. 'All right, yes . . . but in fifteen minutes I really have to go.'

Jack was grateful. 'Thank you. I really hope we can do this again.'

Libby felt the same way. Being with Jack had made her feel like a real woman. But now she was also thinking of her mother. She wondered whether Eileen should know about this meeting. Or would it just make her worry that she could lose her daughter? Her mother needed her, and come what may, Libby would never, ever let her down.

Libby and Jack left the café and walked together along the towpath. At first they were a step apart, and then, as natural as breathing, he took hold of her hand. It felt wonderful to have his strong, warm fingers curled about hers.

'I never forgot you,' Jack said suddenly. 'I never could. Please forgive me for going without even saying goodbye.'

He cupped her face in his hands and, drawing her to him, kissed her full and long on the mouth.

And then they were crying and laughing, and they were holding each other, and the years rolled away.

'If I live to be a hundred,' said Jack softly, 'today will always be the most wonderful day of my whole life. You and me . . . here, together again. And the strange thing is, it's as though we never parted.'

He made her a promise: 'Fate has given us a chance and brought us back together, and I'll do my best to keep it that way.'

Libby nestled into his embrace. 'You're really home, now, Jack – back where you belong.'

And Jack's heart was content.

CHAPTER TWENTY-TWO

THOMAS WAS WORRIED about Eileen. Several times in the past half-hour, he had spoken to her and she had not heard him – or pretended not to have heard.

Despite her mood swings, today's outing to Blackpool had been a pleasant experience. The sun had shone beautifully for once, allowing all the families on holiday to enjoy the sea and sand . . . and after a half-hour's rummage, Eileen had bought a small present for Libby from the gift shop – a fridge magnet in the shape of a lobster with black, beady eyes. They'd watched a Punch and Judy show with a bunch of noisy kids, and they'd both joined in with all the necessary noises, egged on by the puppeteer. Eileen had even laughed out loud at one point, when the dog puppet ran off with a long string of cardboard sausages.

Now, having settled her on a towel on the big steps bordering the beach, Thomas thought she seemed at her happiest so far today, although a little distant in her mind.

'Thank you, Thomas,' she told him now, right out of the blue.

'What for, m'dear?'

'For everything. You've been the best friend anyone could ever have, and I love you. So does my Libby. You've been more of a father to her than Ian ever was. Please never forget that.'

Thomas felt deeply sad, about all the wasted years; about the shocking secret the two of them had been forced to keep. And look at the awful toll it had taken on them both . . .

'Are you hungry?' he asked Eileen, feeling more than a bit peckish himself. It had been a fair walk along the promenade. 'We could wander up to the Tower and get ourselves a snack,' he suggested.

'No thanks, Thomas. My legs are tired,' Eileen watched a young mum trying to drag a pushchair containing a baby over the sand, while at the same time keeping an eye on her other child. A boisterous little chap of about three, he was even now heading straight towards the water, lured by the waves splashing onto the sand.

'Dylan, come back!' the woman shouted, but the lad naughtily ignored her and ran on, splashing in the shallows. He was laughing and jumping up and down in the water to show his mum what he could do – and then suddenly, a bigger wave knocked him over.

'Stay right here and don't move,' Thomas told Eileen. 'I'll go and get hold of that child.'

Eileen was aware of the danger. 'Hurry up!'

Puffing and panting somewhat, Thomas reached the sea and scooped up the bawling child, who had dropped his bright-red bucket in the water. The waves were now carrying it away, as they would have carried him away, a few seconds later.

Hurrying down the beach, the young mum took the crying child from Thomas' arms. 'I told him to stay by me, but the little devil's got a mind of his own,' she complained. 'He's asking for a smack on the backside, he is. Just wait till his dad gets to hear about this!'

They walked up the beach, back to where the baby slept in the pushchair, 'My husband's driven over to Lytham today to see some new car placc, and he's dumped me at the beach with these two. You need eyes in the back of your head with young children.' Putting the sopping-wet child down on the sand, she took a towel out of the pushchair and began to change him into his bathing trunks.

'My name's Marie, by the way,' she said. 'I really don't know how to thank you.'

Still out of breath, Thomas told her 'It was a pleasure, Marie. I'm Thomas. Enjoy the rest of your day, now. And you too, Dylan.' The youngster had got over his shock and was digging at the sand with a plastic rake.

Thomas then stumbled off back towards the steps,

his shoes full of sand and his socks wet, his eyes on the lookout for obstacles, careful not to fall over.

When he reached the flat area near the steps, he looked up – and saw to his dismay that Eileen had vanished. His heart sank.

∼

As Thomas had set off across the sand to rescue the young boy, Eileen had slipped into a world of her own.

It was midnight. A moon hung, huge and golden, in the sky. She had to find the child – and bring him away.

'You shouldn't be out here, my darling – it's so dark and cold,' she said, trying to stop his crying. 'Come with me, come away into the warm. Don't cry, my lovely.'

She remembered the weight of him in her arms, his tiny hands clinging to her as he sobbed pitifully.

The staring eyes followed them, accusing them . . .

Even now, while Thomas rescued that frightened child in the sea, the eyes were watching. Just as they had been when she too had rescued a child. The eyes were always watching, and her torment would never end. It was time to finish it.

∼

Marie saw her first. Eileen was walking into the sea. She shouted out, *'Hey, Thomas, it's your wife – she's in trouble!'*

Pausing only to tug off his shoes, Thomas ran down

the sand as fast as his old legs would take him. He knew what Eileen meant to do, but he couldn't let her do it.

His frantic cry echoed across the beach: *'Eileen! Stop!'*

Other people ran to help, but they were too late. Eileen's head had gone under the water.

With strength born of fear, Thomas launched himself into the sea and, spotting her dress floating on the surface, he swam out and grabbed her. Gasping and spluttering in the waves, he managed to hold her head above the water. Some bystanders helped them out of the water, and a young man immediately started on the emergency resuscitation procedure while someone else rang for an ambulance.

Shivering with shock, Thomas knelt on the sand, holding Eileen's hand and praying as he had never prayed before. Weeping, he whispered:

'Please, God, let her be all right. I know it's a judgement on us, but I swear to You now that if You spare this dear woman, I'll do what she's always wanted – I'll go to the police. Oh, Lord, please don't take her from me.'

Then there was the sound of sirens, and he knew help was on its way.

Shivering and desperate, Thomas sat in the back of the ambulance, wrapped in a blanket, holding Eileen's hand. 'Stay with me, sweetheart,' he pleaded. 'I need you to be with me. I'm nothing without you.'

He knew she had meant to end her life, and he knew why. Day after day, year after year, the strain of concealing the truth of that unforgettable night had been destroying her from within. The torment must have finally proved too much for her. When the waves lapped over her, he wondered, had she found a certain peace in letting go of the burden she carried?

He was the one who should have drowned. For he was the one who had persuaded Eileen to keep the secret. He was the weak one, while she was the stronger.

Eileen was right. They should have told; they should have been prepared to accept their punishment. And now, for her dear sake, it was time to confess.

Whatever the consequences.

Thomas felt an immense relief that, one way or another, it would soon be over. The truth would be out, and the world would have to judge them.

But first, he had to make a phone call to Libby.

~

Later that evening, while Eileen slept peacefully in her hospital bed, Libby remained by her side, while Thomas made his excuses and left the Victoria Hospital in Blackpool. He had told Libby, who planned to stay with Eileen all night, to take the car back to Blackburn with her mother the next day, as he had something important to do in Blackpool and would come home by public transport.

He thanked the heavens above that Libby had not blamed him for the accident, only blessed him for his quick thinking. Distracted though he was, Thomas had noticed the glow in Libby's cheeks. When there was an opportunity, he hoped he would be able to hear how her meeting with Jack had gone.

Dressed in clean, dry clothes brought by Libby, and feeling fortified by the cup of tea and sandwich she had fetched for him earlier, he took a taxi to the Central Police Station in Bonny Street.

Walking in, Thomas told the Sergeant behind the desk: 'I want to speak to someone in authority.'

'Well, I'm in authority,' the young man answered. 'You can speak to me, sir. What's the problem?' He thought it might be a traffic matter, or badly behaved children, or a complaint about dog mess – they were the top three topics of grievance. Nothing could have prepared him for what Thomas had to say:

'I am here to confess to a murder.'

The patronising smile fell from the Sergeant's face. 'A *murder?*'

'That's right. I need to see someone senior – someone who deals with serious crime. I need to tell them what I did. It's time, d'yer see? It's time to tell.' He felt so tired. He wanted to get the confession off his chest.

The shocked young officer nodded. 'I see. Please take a seat, sir, and I'll find someone to look after you.' He gestured at the bench against the wall. Thomas shuffled across the room and sat down.

The DCI appeared two minutes later and led Thomas down a corridor to an interview room, accompanied by a young WPC. Thomas put his shoulders back and held his head high. His story was waiting to be told. It was a story that would both shock and horrify.

~

Thomas told everything to DCI David Morgan. He told him how, on a late-December day nearly twenty years ago, he had committed murder. He could no longer live with the guilt, he said, and that was why he was here.

As Thomas went on, Morgan began to realise that this was no deranged person off the street, wasting police time. This was a man bent with grief and regret, and his halting confession sounded tragically authentic.

Thomas continued to describe the harrowing events that had caused him to commit murder, until every single detail had been confessed. Then, and only then, did he allow himself to break down. As much as anything at that point, he felt a great sense of relief.

At long last, he had unburdened himself and Eileen of the terrible thing they had done. And now, there would be a devastating price to be paid.

CHAPTER TWENTY-THREE

THE STORY OF what had happened all those years ago in Bower Street quickly spread far and wide, to be greeted with shock and disbelief by everyone who knew Eileen and her kindly next-door neighbour, Thomas Farraday.

When the two murder victims had first disappeared, many local gossips had secretly believed that Ian Harrow had run away with Rose Farraday. However, Eileen and Thomas had quenched these rumours by telling any nosy-parkers that Rose had decided to stay in Sheffield with her mother and make a new life there, and that Ian Harrow had left Blackburn to take up a position in London, where he'd fallen in love with a secretary and settled down with her, deserting his wife and daughter. These things happened – marriage break-ups were common enough. And it was obvious how upset both Thomas and Eileen were. Everyone knew that Eileen in particular had never been the same afterwards.

Now that the shocking truth behind the disappearances was out, newspapers, radio and TV competed to describe the gory details of what had taken place on this quiet street. The discovery of the two skeletons beneath the birch tree in the Harrows' garden was the most exciting news to have come out of Blackburn for a long, long time.

That Thomas Farraday – an ordinary and decent man, looked up to by many local people – could commit such a heinous crime, was beyond belief.

The finger was also pointed at Eileen Harrow – an equally inoffensive woman, but never a murderer? That was hard to believe.

Some said the pair should be put away for the rest of their lives. Others defended them. 'They must have been driven to it,' they claimed. 'These are good, ordinary people, just like us.'

Poor Libby was shocked to the core by recent events. It was too much to take in – she felt as if her entire life had been a lie. Eileen, always waiting and hoping for Ian to come home, even going out to seek him in recent years – had known all the time that her husband was dead. She had even helped Thomas to bury him, one dark and terrible night. Oh yes, she had known all along where her missing husband was – lying next to Rose Farraday beneath the birch tree in her own back garden!

Libby felt confused and shocked. For most of her life she too had secretly waited for her father to reappear one day and to love her, when she now knew that such a reunion had never been possible.

She thanked God that Jack was there for her, listening to her, helping her through. He gave her strength and comfort, but he couldn't take away the horror of it all.

It sickened Libby that, as a child, she had played in the very garden where the two bodies had lain, over the self-same spot where the police had erected their tents, cordoned off by scene-of-crime tape. And she still found it hard to believe that Thomas was a killer.

If only Thomas and her mother had gone to the police immediately, and confessed all . . . but then Libby realised that her mother would have gone to prison, and she, still so young, would have been put into care or placed with a foster family. She began to understand their actions. Maybe they had done the best they could, to keep mother and child together. But the horror of it all would never leave her – she knew that now.

~

From the other side of the room in his house in Buncer Lane, Jack looked at Libby curled up on the sofa. He too had been devastated by these shocking revelations, and to be honest, he could barely get his head around them. He still felt that the whole truth had yet to be revealed.

Going over to Libby, he sat down and gathered her in his arms. 'Something isn't right,' he said. 'I *know* it. How could two such caring people ever kill another human being?'

Libby's voice broke. 'Oh, Jack, what's happening? I can't take any of it in. Why did Mum tell the police that it wasn't Thomas who killed them, but *her*? Mum doesn't know what she's saying. They should understand how ill she is. She must feel so scared and alone.' Sobbing, she was comforted by Jack's strong embrace.

'They won't harass her,' he assured Libby. 'The doctors have said she mustn't be questioned any more.'

'But she keeps on claiming that *she's* the guilty one, over and over, and now I'm worried that they're going to believe her. Jack, why is she doing it?'

'She's trying to protect Thomas, that's why. I'm sure the police know that. DCI Morgan seems to be a decent bloke who has long experience in murder cases. When they allowed me to see Thomas, he kept insisting that your mother wasn't involved. We just have to hope that the real truth will come out at the trial.' He gave Libby a squeeze. 'Keep strong, sweetheart.'

Deep down, Jack had been wondering whether his nightmares were connected with the murders. Ever since the arrests, his dreams had become even more vivid. When asleep, he often felt that he was on the verge of understanding.

All cried out for now, Libby snuggled up to him. 'I'm so glad I've got you, Jack. If it hadn't been for you, I don't know which way I'd have turned.'

They sat there for a time, holding each other, consoled by the knowledge that their love, built on the deep foundations of the past, was strong enough to see them through anything.

~

On the day of the trial, in the Spring of the following year, Jack escorted Libby into the courtroom. 'Stay calm,' he whispered. 'We have an excellent defence team.' Then he sat beside her and held her hand as the proceedings opened.

For Thomas, standing in the dock, the sight of a frightened, pale-faced Libby was almost too much to bear. As for Eileen, he was grateful to know that she had been well looked after in a unit of the local hospital for patients with mental-health problems, and that she was doing very well. There had been an improvement in her memory and her general health, since she was at long last free from the fear of discovery. Nothing that anyone did to her now could compare with the horrors of the past.

The prosecuting team gave Thomas a hard time, and the jury looked on severely as he kept on denying that Eileen had had any hand in the killings.

The defence lawyer said kindly, 'Mr Farraday, I'd like you to go through the events of that fateful day. Just tell us in your own words, including every detail, no matter how trivial, exactly what happened.'

Thomas, who had told his tale many times, prepared to relive it one more time. He practically knew the words off by heart now, but he wanted the jury to know how it had been.

'It was late Saturday morning and I'd been fixing

the dripping tap in the kitchen. My wife, Rose, had been on at me about it for some time. She had gone over to Sheffield to stay with her mother, who she said was still poorly after her heart surgery and needed her there. Well, I was tidying up when I heard an argument next door. Lots of shouting and banging and screaming – which was strange, as I'd never heard Eileen and Ian row before. What's more, I'd seen Eileen go up the road with the pushchair earlier, when I'd gone to the front door to put out the milk bottles. We'd exchanged greetings – commented on the likelihood of snow, as far as I remember. She said she was off to town, to meet up for lunch wi' another mum from the toddlers' group, and then go round to her house for the children to play together wi' some of the new toys they'd got for Christmas. She said she wouldn't be back until teatime.'

Thomas cleared his throat. 'That's why I knew it couldn't be Eileen next door, so I got worried. Thinking I'd better do something, I went round and knocked. No one answered, so I opened it – there's none of us down Bower Street who bother wi' locks when we're at home – and that's when I saw them. They were at the top of the stairs – Eileen's husband Ian, and my wife Rose. They were neither of them dressed proper, just in their underwear. For a moment I couldn't take it in, like – my wife, being next door, when I'd driven her up to the station only a few hours since. It was only later that I worked out what had been going on between them two. Anyway, they didn't notice me at first. He was telling her he was going away to start a new job in London, that she couldn't stop him or follow him there, and that he was sick of her anyway – that he was sick of his life, an' come Sunday, he'd be away to start a new life.'

The jury listened intently.

Thomas took a deep breath. The only sound that could be heard in the courtroom at that moment was Libby's muffled sobbing, until Thomas went on:

'I saw them fighting like cat and dog. She hit him hard in the face, and then he went mad. I ran inside, just as he struck her and violently flung her away from him. She stumbled backwards and fell all the way down – and I could tell she'd broken her neck, from the way she were lying at the bottom of the stairs.'

Thomas mopped his eyes. 'If it's of any interest, I don't believe that Ian Harrow meant to kill my wife. He was in an evil temper, that's all. I think he panicked when he realised what he'd done. He saw me and realised that I'd witnessed it all. He tried to get away when I chased him upstairs. Then he came at me like a madman, and I' – Thomas stumbled over his words – 'I had to kill him. It were self-defence.'

'Describe how you killed him,' said the barrister.

'I picked up the heavy metal candlestick on the mantelpiece in the spare room. I only meant to knock him out, but it came down hard. He fell and didn't move no more. I were half out of me mind with shock. I didn't know what to do. My first thought were to hide the bodies. I couldn't have poor Eileen coming home

347

to that.' He looked at the jury. 'That's why I didn't call the police, as I should have done.'

'What did you do next, Mr Farraday?'

Thomas rubbed his head. 'First I put them in the cellar and then the next evening, when Eileen was out hunting for Ian and I was babysitting Libby, I set about moving them. I had a sheet of tarpaulin in my shed, so I ran down their garden, wrenched a couple of fence panels out, squeezed in through the space to my shed, and got the tarpaulin out. I carried it back to the house, put my wife on it and then dragged her down the garden and placed her in the shed. I thought she were going to wake up at any minute and ask me what the hell I was playing at.' His voice broke and he wiped his eyes again. 'I did not want to believe that she were gone.'

He paused, his gaze falling on the floor, then he gulped and went on: 'Her neck were all bent to one side. . . Getting Ian out of house, well, that were more difficult. He was a big man and he weighed a ton. I rolled him onto the tarpaulin, tied the ends with twine and then dragged him down the stairs.' Making the sign of the cross on himself, he muttered, 'May God forgive me!'

Thomas looked sadly at Libby before continuing: 'I laid them side by side in the shed and covered them over, deciding that when I got a chance, I'd bury them another night and no one would ever know that anything untoward had occurred. As it happened, it took me a few days to find the nerve to bury the bodies.'

The barrister leaned forward and said in serious tones: 'And Mrs Harrow had nothing whatsoever to do with this?'

'No, sir!' he was adamant. 'Nothing whatsoever, sir. It were just me. No one else was involved.'

'I see.' The lawyer asked for permission to bring in two witnesses. What followed sent a shockwave through the court and had reporters scribbling frantically.

Eileen was called first. Haltingly, with gentle persuasion from the barrister, she told her story. She was no longer afraid. With her mental health improved of late, she was able to go over the events, without fear of failing in her presentation. Clearly and willingly she simply told the truth. Her evidence had been deemed reliable after a doctor's report had sanctioned her appearance in court.

Addressing the jury, she gave her own version of the events of that day.

'I was due to meet my friend Hilary at the Health Centre, where she ran the toddlers' playgroup. I'd told Ian I wouldn't be back until teatime.' She took a moment to remember. 'He said I was to ring him when we needed picking up. I know now that he was only too pleased to be rid of me, so's he could be with Rose.' She gave a choked cry. 'He took her to our bed.' There followed a heavy silence, broken only by Eileen's sobbing.

'Mrs Harrow, would you like to take a moment? Maybe have some water?' enquired the solicitous defence counsel, hoping to calm her. But Eileen had already got herself under control. She was determined not to lose the thread of what she needed to say.

'When I got to the Health Centre, there was a message waiting for me. It turned out that my friend's little girl had spots, and they thought it was chicken-pox, so we all went our different ways. I put my baby Libby in the pushchair and got home as fast as I could.'

Now came the difficult part. Eileen knew that she would have to convince the jury that she, and not her beloved Thomas, was responsible for the death of her husband Ian.

'When I got home,' she began steadily, 'I saw that the front door was slightly open. I pushed it open, and saw Rose Farraday lying at the bottom of the stairs, with hardly any clothes on. I could tell immediately that she was dead. It was awful, and there was the sound of a fight going on upstairs.

'I quickly shut Libby in the front room and ran upstairs. Ian and Thomas were fighting. Thomas was trying to get away, but Ian was like a madman, with his hands round Thomas' neck, choking him. It was terrible!'

She covered her eyes and fell silent for a long moment, then described in halting tones what happened next.

'I shouted at Ian to stop, but he wouldn't. Thomas was going blue and I knew Ian was going to kill him, so I picked up the candlestick from the floor and clouted Ian on the back of the head. I just wanted to make him stop. But he wouldn't stop, and Thomas couldn't breathe. I was terrified, so I hit him again, and this time he fell in a heap on the floor.'

Facing the jury, she said in a clear voice, 'That is the truth, so help me God.' When she started sobbing, one of the courtroom clerks gave her a glass of water to sip from. Someone brought her a chair.

'What happened next?' asked the barrister.

Sitting on the chair, Eileen then explained how Thomas had removed the bodies in the dark of the following night, using the tarpaulin to wrap them in. 'I wanted to phone the police and tell them what had happened, but Thomas wouldn't let me. He said I would be sent to prison and that Libby would have to go into a home, and I didn't want that. And while I was trying to decide what to do, the days passed, and I knew it was too late to put things right.' Her composure cracked as she thought of it all now.

The barrister asked if she was able to go on. 'Yes, sir,' she replied. 'I have to tell it all now.' She continued:

'I was babysitting my neighbour's little boy in my own home.' She glanced at Jack. 'I had to keep things normal, pretend that everything was the same as usual. Looking back, I don't know how I did it. I told my husband's parents that he'd run off with another woman. They never came to visit any more, and now they're both gone, with their son . . .

'I looked after next door's little boy when his parents had to go out. Thomas hadn't buried the bodies yet . . .' She faltered. 'I was worried about that. I put young Jack to sleep on my sofa, and he went straight off. Then I popped upstairs to check on Libby. When I got back downstairs, only a few minutes later, the little lad had disappeared. I was frantic! Somehow he'd opened the back door, or I might have absent-mindedly left it open earlier. But little Jack had gone down the garden, looking for me – barefoot and in his pyjamas in the snow. I found him inside Thomas' shed . . . where *they* were. Thomas hadn't replaced the fence panels yet. Little Jack was icy cold and screaming, the poor little love! And where I found him, the corner of the tarpaulin was open and . . .' she faltered, '. . . the eyes. Oh, dear God!'

For a brief moment, she was back in the garden, picking him up and wrapping her cardigan round him to get him warm. Her soft sobs could be heard all round the courtroom.

'Thank you, Mrs Harrow. That will be all for now.' The barrister turned to the Judge. 'Your Honour, may I call my next witness, Major Gareth Smythson?'

A tall man in his mid-forties came down from the witness waiting area and took his place in the box. With his short hair and erect stance, he looked a real soldier.

'Major Smythson, thank you for attending,' said the barrister. 'I would like you to tell the court what you know about these events'

'Before I joined the Army,' began Smythson, 'I lived with my family at Number 12, Bower Street, just along from Mr and Mrs Harrow's house. I had turned eighteen the day before and had gone out with the lads to celebrate. The following day, I had a very bad hangover. When I heard the yelling and angry voices coming from Number 16, it riled me up. I went into the garden and stood on a box to see what the devil was going on. That's when I saw Mr Harrow and Mr Farraday fighting. They were right up against the upstairs window, and for a moment I thought they would come crashing through the glass. I could see Mrs Harrow in the background. She was screaming, "Ian, let go!" and trying to pull them apart. Then she raised her hand and I think she hit her husband, but just then I was called back inside.'

'Did you ever suspect that anything untoward had happened?' asked the barrister.

'No. I went into the Army the week after that . . . My papers had arrived at last.'

'And can you explain why no one else tried to intervene in this fighting? Surely, if you heard it, someone else in your street must have done so too?'

'Yes, sir, that would seem likely. However, the sales were on, so people might have been out shopping, or back at work, or possibly still on holiday, sitting at home watching all the special Christmas TV programmes. And in those days, people tended to let domestic arguments run their course.'

~

When the jury returned, their verdict was that Eileen was guilty of manslaughter. The Judge gave her a suspended sentence, since she had saved Thomas' life, and because of her precarious state of health.

Thomas was found guilty of perverting the course of justice. He was given a two-year sentence for this. With good behaviour, the Judge said, he might be released the following summer.

CHAPTER TWENTY-FOUR

WHEN EILEEN WAS released into Libby's welcoming arms, she refused to return to Bower Street. It was hardly surprising. The house had its dark and terrible secrets, and no one who had been involved in the tragic events there would want to go back.

Jack had arranged for Eileen to move in with him and Libby; Thomas had agreed to join them when he was released. There was plenty of room for all in the big house in Buncer Lane. Thomas intended to sell his house too, once he got out of prison; in the meantime, various sympathetic neighbours were keeping it aired and tidy inside and out, to deter vandals or burglars.

The improvement in Eileen's health and well-being was remarkable, now that the burden of secrets she had carried all these years, was finally lifted. It was not just her and Thomas who had paid a price. There were others. But it was over now, and she felt at peace with herself. The only source of her depression now was the thought of poor Thomas in jail, unable to walk freely wherever he wanted, to savour the changing seasons and enjoy being in the fresh air. On their visits to see him in prison, he had promised Libby and Eileen that he would work with them in the garden of the house in Buncer Lane, and they spent many happy times discussing the new layout, features and plantings they had planned.

Libby too had turned her back on the family home. She loved living with Jack, and now that her Mum was safe again, there was nothing to stop them from being married.

~

Nine months after their wedding, a son was born to Jack and Libby Redmond – a February baby.

'We'll call him Thomas, shall we?' Libby murmured to Jack as he sat beside her, holding their newborn son in the Royal Blackburn Hospital Maternity Unit.

Jack had been thrilled to actually see his son being born. Could life get any better than this? His work was going wonderfully, with a great team behind him. The house was feeling like a real home – the first one he'd ever had, he realised now. And he was married to his boyhood sweetheart and was the proud father of a son.

~

In April the next year, when Thomas was released and the family went to collect him, he sat in the back of the car next to little Thomas in his baby seat. It was a deeply moving moment for the old man.

On baby Tom's first birthday, Thomas and Eileen were married in the Registrar's Office in Blackpool, where they planned to have their honeymoon. Little Tom was dressed as a pageboy for the occasion, and although he could only stand for short periods, wobbling around on his fat little legs, he still looked the part.

'I'm so happy for you, Mum,' Libby whispered to Eileen.

'Love is strange, isn't it?' Eileen whispered back. 'All them years, Thomas was living next door – and now we're together, like it should have been from the beginning . . . Ah, well, this is a real happy ending for us both, isn't it, Libby?'

'Yes, Mum. It is. We're really blessed.'

Never having been informed of Molly's road accident, Jack remained unaware, as he cut all his ties with his previous life. He was back to where he belonged, and life was good.

Jack was content. He knew now what had happened on that terrible night when he was just three years of age. He would be forever grateful for the psychiatrist's advice and the path that Molly had set him on. But it was Mr Howard who unearthed the truth. He had led him out of his personal midnight, and towards the dawning of this glorious new day. He now had a family of his own, and wonderful hopes for the future.